Arcania: Beyond Where the Sidewalk Ends
Book Four: Somewhere From Some Far-off Place

All of the text and illustrations in this book, including cover art, are the work of R.S. Royall and are human generated. No A.I. has been used.
First edition published June 1, 2024.
© 2024 Royall, LLC. All rights reserved.
Published by Cabanga, an imprint of the Royall company.
128 Race St., Grass Valley, CA 95945   +1 (808) 301-0535

No part of this publication may be reproduced, stored in a retrieval system, or transmitted in any form or by any means without written permission of the publisher or author, except for brief quotations and excerpts for professionally published critical articles and reviews. For copyright permission contact Cabanga books or visit www.rsroyall.com for more contact information.

This is a work of fiction. The story and illustrations are products of the author's imagination. Names, characters, places, and events are products of the author's imagination or are used fictitiously. Consistent with any literary work, indeed any creative work in any medium, there are many sources of inspiration for the work herein: life experience, wondrous creations from other artists, ideas channeled from the chimes of spirits, notions conjured from the clouds, wonderings summoned from the swamps of the ether... Regardless, no part of this story — character, person, or place — is intended to represent any person, character, or place occurring or existing, past or present, outside of, or beyond this book and the story herein. Any resemblance to actual events, locales, characters, or persons living or dead, real or imaginary, is entirely coincidental. Any opinions, thoughts, or actions expressed or implied in this book are intended to be those of the characters alone and not necessarily of the author or anyone else.

ISBN 979-8-3225501-3-6 Paperback

Arcania: Beyond Where the Sidewalk Ends

Book Four

Somewhere From Some Far-off Place

Story and illustrations by

R.S. Royall

A Cabanga Publication
"Evolution through Imagination"

For Shel.

And for Matt.
Thank you for sharing your dad with us.

"The journey is the destination!"

Devoted

I heard that absence makes the heart grow fonder,

So away I go, away to wander,

Wander far from the ones I adore,

So that I may love them even more.

Contents

Introduction
    Me & Him, Always 1

Chapter One
    The Farmer & the Queen 7

Chapter Two
    Silver Fish 27

Chapter Three
    The Missing Piece 35

Chapter Four
    The Big Sleep 57

Chapter Five
    Runners 71

Chapter Six
    Storm 93

Chapter Seven
    The Search 111

Chapter Eight
  War & Peace.................................. 123

Chapter Nine
  The Whale-eater & the Dreams of Tomorrow
  153

Chapter Ten
  Namesake 171

Chapter Eleven
  The Ball Game 189

Chapter Twelve
  Tell Me 209

Chapter Thirteen
  No Happy Endings 223

Chapter Fourteen
  The Return 243

Chapter Fifteen
  A Dreamer 261

Somewhere From Some Far-off Place

Introduction

Me & Him, Always

Introduction

Me: Well, this is it.

Him: Yes it is! ...Um, what's it?

Me: This! The last book!

Him: Ohhh, that's riiight! I forgot. Huh. Wow. Bummer.

Me: Bummer?

Him: Well, yeah. The story's over. Means we're done. Finished. All washed up. Kaput. Old hat! Old shoes, old shirt, old news... Just plain old. A couple o' has-beens we be.

Me: Hmm. We might have to agree to disagree on that, Mr. Old Hat. I say we're just gettin' started.

Him: Just gettin'... just gettin'...? What do you mean, just gettin' started?! Gettin' started on gettin' finished maybe.

Me: What I mean is that the end of one story is often the beginning of another. And this story's no different. These books we've been narratin'? Well, they're all about how young Shelby got his start, aren't they?

Him: Ahhhh, I think I see what you mean.

Me: Yeah? You sayin' what I'm knowin'?

Introduction

Him: Yeah! I'm gobblin' up what you're throwin' down, my brother. ...Or is it gobblin' down what you're throwin'—

Me: NO, no! You got it right the first time. This right here is just the end of the beginning, not the beginning of the end.

Him: Yes! I love it!

Me: Well, then, now *that's* settled, what's say we get on with it?

Him: Absolutely, Me. Let's do it. Why don't you start, for old time's sake. You know, since you're the old hat and all.

Me: Well, I don't know about that... but okay. Here goes... Salutations my good people, and welcome back to the story of Arcania. Welcome back for the final chapter in our adventure!

Him: So exciting! Yes, yes, welcome back for the final... Um... Hey, Me?

Me: Yesss?

Him: Well, I was just wondering if we could call it something other than the *final* chapter? That just sounds so... final.

Me: Uh, okay. What did you have in mind?

Introduction

Him: Oh, I don't know. Somethin' softer maybe, like the *next* chapter or the—

Me: Are you feeling sentimental, Him?

Him: Of course! I don't want to say goodbye! It's been an incredible journey. Our little Sheldon has grown so much!

Me: True. He's certainly experienced a lot. Do you recall in the last book, his friendship with Joythea really developed?

Him: Yeah! And when Izzy, that silly elephant, finally came back! ...Or how about when he stood up to King Skippy?

Me: Yes, that was impressive. And making all those new friends, Sandovar and the Boogies.

Him: And the pirates!

Me: Right. And how all of them, at the end of the last book, decided they're going to rescue Ingonyama from the king's prison?

Him: Boy, do I! I can't wait to see what happens next!

Me: Well what's say we get to narratin', see how this thing turns out?

Him: Groovy.

Me: Groovy?

Him: Groooovy.

Introduction

Me: Oh, just one more thing, Him.

Him: Yeah, what's that?

Me: Heads up 'cause there's no prologue in this final... er, I mean, *next* book.

Him: What?! No prologue?!?

Me: Nope. We just dive right in, straight to the meat and potatoes.

Him: Huh. Well, okay then. I guess meat and potatoes are okay. But I like ice cream more. Can we just skip to dessert? Just get right to the good stuff?

Me: Hmm. I suppose. Why not? Let's just get right to the good stuff. Let's have our cake and eat it too!

Him: Mmm. Caaaake. But... I thought that was like a law of physics or something: you can't have your cake and eat it too. Are you sure we can do that? You sure that's... legal?

Me: Him, you and I can do whatever we want. We're telling the story! We can defy even the laws of physics! Heck, you think ol' Shelby obeyed the laws of physics in his writings?

Him: Huh. No, I s'pose not. Hey! You're right! Stories are more interesting and fun the more creative you get! I say let's go for it! Let's dive right into the dessert. Let's have the cake, eat it, and— Heyyy, I have an idea! How about we make our cake so that each time you slice into it, more

Introduction

cake shows up?! A cake that multiplies the more you divide!

    Me: Him, I've never been a big fan of math but that just might be the best idea I've ever heard! So what you're saying is, there's enough cake for everyone! I totally get it! In other words, there's enough creativity to go around, for the stories to never end! And everyone gets a slice! ...Or better yet, everyone can add their own ingredient!!

    Him: Yes! Exactly!

    Me: Him, you're a genius!

    Him: Gee, thanks, Me! So... you ready to get this story going so we can generate infinite channels of potential creativity for our audience? Spark inspiration? Inspire imagination?

    Me: Well, I think the answer to that is: what would Shel do?

    Him: He'd inspire!

    Me: Exactly. So let's do the same. For Shel.

    Him: For Shel.

    Me: Groovy... two times!

    Him: Groovy. Two. Times!

Chapter One

The Farmer & the Queen

Riding atop the intimidating, inimitable, idiosyncratic, Izzy the elephant, the infamous band of Boogies at her back, was none other than Joythea the brave... and giggly. With an intense stare fixed on destiny, she led the lion-freeing mission through the streets of Kantytown, right up the royal steps of the Peanut Butter Palace to the entrance of the great hall, and, throwing open the doors, ran right smack into... a mountain of goopy, droopy spaghetti!

I – The Farmer & the Queen

An avalanche of overcooked, day-old pasta poured from the castle like lava. A tsunami of sticky red sauce and icky noodles from the previous night's party washed over the Boogies, burying any and all who traveled in the caravan that day. All but one.

"Look out!" cried Joy as she leaped from her elephant-head platform onto a stone ledge supporting a small gargoyle that looked a bit like one of the flying shoe crew.

"We've been shanghaied!" Mortimer the pirate cried as he became entangled in the goop.

"I always knew I would go like this — death by spaghetti!" cried Tickletoes, dramatically slipping under the noodles and out of sight.

"Oh, cut it out, Tick!" Fickles yanked his partner out of the starchy tomb. "No one's dying today. Uh, except maybe little Sheldon. Shelby? Anyone seen Shel?"

A small arm popped up from under a mound of noodles. It appeared to be Shel's two fingers, pointing skyward in a peace sign, signaling that he was okay.

"There he is!" yelled Pickles. "And he's ordering two hamburgers! Somebody get that kid a pair of patties!"

Fickles slapped a hand over his face. "Is everything always about food with you?" Pickles nodded with pride.

"I don't think he's ordering anything except a helping hand," remarked Izzy, reaching down with his trunk to retrieve the kid. "If he wants food, he need but open his mouth and this ridiculous mush will flow right in."

I – The Farmer & the Queen

With his head covered in a mop of spaghetti and meatballs, and a bit of cheese on his nose, Shel looked like a real-life Aiken Drum. "Thanks!" he coughed, emptying his mouth and nose of noodles and sauce. Izzy chuckled and patted him on the back.

After clawing their way out of the slop, the caravan — covered head to toe in pungent marinara — reconvened in the courtyard at the base of the palace steps. Sandovar yanked his scimitar from his gullet and looked around to assess the chaos. "Just what in the blazes is going on here?!? There's no one around. Look!" He swung his sword in a wide arc, presenting an empty courtyard. "The place is deserted. What in the name of Hades' hairdo happened here?"

"Oh, why, haven't you heard?" A voice sprang out of nowhere. The spaghetti-covered Boogies turned to see a large polar bear dancing his way toward them. He was skipping and kicking his legs all over the place.

"Is that... the polka?" squinted Sandovar.

"I think it's the hokey pokey," guessed Pickles.

"That there jig be the ol' jitterbug," asserted Captain Jarbison.

"Actually," *tippity-tap, kick ball change,* "you're all correct." The bear sauntered up to the Boogies with a final spin and bow. "There's a bit of every dance in my walk. Can't help it. Been dancin' for years. Not *four* years. More like ten or twelve... Hard to keep track..."

I – The Farmer & the Queen

"Arrr! What be thy name, furry man?" Captain Jarbison interrupted with an outstretched sword, making no attempt to hide his crotchetiness. "And where be the crew of this here shanty town? Tell me quick b'fore I shave ye bald!"

"Pardon me?" reeled the bear, showing off a set of impressive teeth and even more impressive claws.

"Ah, you'll be needin' to excuse me mate." Mortimer put his hands up and stepped between the blade and the bear. "Captain Jarby here graduated from nasty school he did."

"That be a bloomin' lie! ...I never graduated. I was kicked out!" yelled Jarbison, "...on account uh bein' too ding dang down-n-dirty," he added quietly. "Anyway, this man here—" he pointed with his sword back at the bear.

"Let me stop you right there." The bear held up a paw about the size of Jarbison's head. "I'm not a man at all, pirate! And you'll do well to lower your weapon and take a lesson from your more civilized friend here, thank you very much. I'm a bear if there ever was one, with the teeth and claws to match, mind you. The name's—"

"Tooky?" Izzy blurted out as he rejoined the group, shaking noodle remnants from his limbs.

The bear's eyes lit up. "Izzy?! Is that you? Ho, ho! So the rumors *are* true! You've returned! ...After all this time!"

"Donachtuk, you old dog. Where in the world did *you* come from?"

I – The Farmer & the Queen

"Why, I've been here the whole time! Circus is all but disbanded, but some of us are still around. You know, doin' this and that." The bear did a little tap dance to illustrate 'this' and 'that'.

"Huh. I see." Izzy turned to face his Boogie friends. "Everyone, I'd like you to meet Donachtuk Nanook, the dancing bear from up north, in *cold* country."

"Hi everyone. Please, call me Don… or Tooky if you like." The group mumbled greetings. Sandovar, having known Donachtuk for some time, bowed his usual bow.

"Don," continued Izzy, "where is everyone? Right now I mean? This place looks like a deserted island."

"Everyone is with the king," replied Don, "saying prayers and last goodbyes, putting in final requests…"

"Requests?" Captain Fickleface balked, picking bits of noodles from his beard.

"Yeah, you know, for things like new shoes, ponies, and T.V. sets." Don shook his head. "It's as if people think he's Santa Claus."

Izzy nodded. "Because of the sandwich."

"Well, I imagine it's because of his big, jolly belly, and the beard," replied Don. "His red robes don't help any either…"

Izzy squinted.

I – The Farmer & the Queen

"Oh! You mean why are people saying last goodbyes?! Yesss, the sandwich... which *you* all made him eat."

"Hang on just a minute!" called a voice from the crowd. "We didn't force him—"

"Ah, you must be the infamous Sheldon," asserted the bear. "The one who's given the king so much grief."

"Grief?! Are you kidding?!" Shel snapped. "We just—"

"Cool down, kid. I'm just messin' with ya. I'm not your enemy. Nor do I judge your actions. I'm a friend. Isn't that right, Izzy?"

Izzy nodded. "For certain. Tooky is a good guy, don't worry, Shelby. He didn't mean anything by it. And because he's such a good guy," he turned back to Don, "he's going to take us to see the king. Isn't that right, Don?"

"Oh, I'm not sure that's such a good idea, you guys." Don fumbled his paws. "I mean, the king blames you for his demise, and he'll likely want your heads on a plate if he catches you."

Feeling the time was right, Joy approached and curtsied. "Mr. Nanook, you may not know me but I know you. I used to watch you dance in the circus when I was a kid. My name is Joythea."

Don's eyes widened. "My goodness, aren't you adorable." A grin spread across his face and his feet began to jiggle. His legs soon joined in, doing a kind of funky chicken boogaloo and he bowed to her. With a wink of his

I – The Farmer & the Queen

eye and a twitch of his brow, he invited, "Would you care to dance, my dear?"

Joy was caught by surprise but recovered gracefully. "Oh, Tooky, you're so sweet. I'd love to. But only for a minute, okay? We have an important errand with the king." Don didn't hesitate. He swept Joy off her feet and waltzed her through the courtyard. As the swaying couple moved, the caravan followed like a puppy, having become rather fond, and therefore protective, of their darling Joy. Don twisted and bopped and tangoed with his skilled dancing partner, out of the courtyard, down a rose-lined lane, along a pathway encircling a pond, and through an archway of vines weaving in and out of cascading branches from an old willow tree. There, in the middle of a large, colorful garden, the couple concluded their dancing soiree with a spin, a dip, a bow, and a curtsey.

"Thank you, Don," Joy smiled, catching her breath. "May I ask where you have taken me and my caravan?"

"*Her* caravan?!" grumbled Sandovar under his breath.

Don started, "My lady, this is—"

"The queen's garden!" concluded Izzy, glancing around in awe.

"That's right. Been here before, Izzy?" asked Don.

"No. I never knew where it was. Nor was I ever invited. I only heard tales of how amazing it was... and still is apparently!"

I – The Farmer & the Queen

"Indeed it is!" agreed Don. "This garden once belonged to a farmer named Simon. But that was long ago. The garden was much smaller back then."

"Oh, allow me!" Sandovar raised his sword, unable to resist a good storytelling. "When Simon was just a boy, he planted a jewel — a diamond — and from that diamond, he grew a whole garden of jewels."

Don nodded. "Right-o!"

Sando ran the dull edge of his sword over his beard as if brushing it. "...I always wondered where a peasant son of a farmer got hold of a diamond?"

"He found it," answered Izzy, "inside of a fish." Shel and the group turned their attention to the elephant, who was rummaging through the garden foliage as if looking for something. "As a boy, Simon spent his days playing and fishing in the Sonrisa River instead of working the fields with his dad. One day, he saw something shimmering in the water, like nothing he'd ever seen before."

"A diamond!" blurted Shel, eyes sparkling at the notion of treasure.

"Close," replied Izzy. "It was a fish; a fish that shined all sorts of brilliant colors: sapphire blue, emerald green, ruby red... gold... silver... Of course, Simon became obsessed right then and there with trying to catch the unique specimen. He fished every day, trying to catch that prize. Well, eventually he did, and to his great fortune, the fish turned out to be magical, for when he ate it—"

I – The Farmer & the Queen

"Hang on!" Shel interjected. "He found a magic fish and he *ate* it? That's terrible!"

Izzy nodded, his eyebrows remaining aloft as his head descended to level. "He had his reasons. You see, inside that fish, the boy discovered treasure! Not just one diamond, but a whole mess of jewels filling the belly of that magic guppy." Shel's eyes grew wider. He was hooked.

Seeing the youth's exuberance, Sandovar flung his sword around for dramatic effect. "Simon knew his father would have wanted him to trade the treasure for a plow or a horse. But, being a dreamer like you, Master Sheldon," Sandovar pointed his sword at Shel and winked, "...Simon kept the jewels a secret. Instead, he buried them right back in the ground where jewels are born." Sandovar punctuated his animated tale by stabbing his sword deep into the soil.

"That's right!" chimed Don with a wiggle and a shuffle. Simon's magical story was coming to life. "Who knows why Simon did what he did? Maybe the fish told him to do it or gave him instructions..."

"The fish *told* Simon to eat him?" Shel shook his head.

"No!" Don laughed and twirled in a pirouette (not unlike Joy, which made her laugh too). "I don't know how," the bear continued, "but somehow Simon knew there was magic in the soil, right here in this very spot. That, or those jewels were magic."

"Like Jack Spriggins' enchanted beans!" squawked Shel excitedly.

I – The Farmer & the Queen

Don smiled and nodded. "Exactly! And before long, that boy had sprouts of jewels popping up everywhere, sending colors in all directions: jade greens, garnet reds, purples and oranges of opals, flicks of gold speckled here and there…"

Shel was in wonderland, imagining the jeweled treasure, gemstone rainbows reflecting in his pupils. "Wow!" he said slowly, wiping a spot of drool from his mouth. "Then what happened?"

Izzy laughed in appreciation of Shel's exuberance. "Well, Simon spent all his time tending his garden and growing his wealth while his father tended to the family farm, wishing his boy was there to help him. When the boy's father eventually passed on and the farm fell into the hands of the commonwealth, the boy — by then a young man — realized he'd been so focused on growing his own *branch* of the family tree that he'd neglected his *roots*. Roots are very important you know. As any farmer will tell you, the roots need as much attention as the branches… perhaps more."

Don nodded. "Right! After his father's passing, Simon attempted to grow food here in this garden, his way of resurrecting the memory of his dad. He planted asparagus, tomatoes, rhubarb, potatoes… cherry and apple trees too. Didn't take long, however, for him to realize he didn't know the first thing about growing food. He had an unrivaled green thumb for growing pearls and platinum but couldn't grow a peach to save his life… literally. You see, as the years wore on, the once young man grew older and ever more desperate to produce food."

I – The Farmer & the Queen

Shel cocked his head. "But... if he was so desperate for food, why not just go to the market and *buy* some with his treasure? He must've had plenty of money!"

"Of course he had money," answered Izzy. "He was the wealthiest man in the land. But it wasn't desperation for *food* so much as *sustenance*, soul sustenance. He was desperate to reclaim the legacy of his ancestors, to revive the memory of his father and recover the years he'd given to his lifeless rock garden... instead of to living things, things that grow and give life in return. He wanted more than anything to get back the years he'd missed with his family. He was perhaps the richest man in all the world, but he would've traded all the garnets in his garden, all the stars that heaven yields, for just one more day with his dad in the fields."

Sandovar smiled at the poetic pachyderm. "Very nice, Izzy. That's true. But!" The chief yanked his sword from the ground. "He didn't *have* all the stars to give, did he? He only had his entire fortune. And one day, a wheelin', dealin' salesman happened upon the jewel farmer and the two struck a deal. In the end, Simon gave up his garden, jewels, land, and all. And in return, the salesman, who was very resourceful and well-connected, was able to reclaim a good portion of Simon's family farm from the commonwealth. The salesman got Simon his farm back, along with a team of horses, a herd of cattle, a trough of pigs, a gaggle of geese, a coop of chickens, a flock of sheep... goats, rabbits, dogs, cats, birds, bees, owls, bats... even an emu or two. You name it, Simon got it. He even got a barn-full of machinery and a host of farmhands needed to run it. ...He couldn't grow it, so he *bought* back his ancestral lineage. And wouldn't ya know it, after years of digging in the dirt, he even developed a green

I – The Farmer & the Queen

thumb for growin' delicious food, to the extent that he became — with the help of his farm hands — the most prodigious farmer in all the land, rivaling even the Gambrine! That man and his farm grew the tastiest food that ever did come out of the earth."

"But he lost his treasure!" complained Shel "He became a poor farmer in the end!" The twinkle in Shel's eyes grew dull.

"Quite the opposite!" rallied Izzy. "He became wealthier than ever! True wealth, Shelby, isn't measured in riches of jewels or money, but in family... good friends, good food, and good, rich soil if you're lucky to have that too, which Simon was. He even met a nice woman, and together they had a son, who eventually took over the farm. It's fair to say they didn't have a whole lot of money, but they had peace and love and everything they needed. And they were surrounded by beauty and the solace of a life rooted in nature."

"Indeed," added Don the bear. "Sadly, Simon was only able to enjoy so much of that life before his years caught up with him and he passed on."

"Oh, no! That's terrible," noted the tender-hearted Joythea.

"Yeah... terrible. ...Er, so, what happened to the salesman? The one who got the jewel garden?" asked Shel, the reflection of rubies and emeralds still glinting somewhere in his mind's eye. Joy frowned at him.

I – The Farmer & the Queen

"Ah, that man, my young friend, became the first king of the land," answered Don, stretching tall to look as royal as he could.

"What?! That was Skippy?" Shel asked.

Don laughed, "No, that was Skippy's dad. He enjoyed many years of growing his wealth, which helped secure his reign. Eventually, however, time caught up with him too and he too passed on, but not before marrying and having a son of his own, an heir to his throne. Solomon Skippingston they named the child."

"So what happened to all of the jewels? Where'd they all go? How come they're not still here," pressed Sheldon, his mind desperately clinging to treasure.

"Haha!" Laughed Taudello, nudging his mate, Mortimer. "That there be a true pirate in the makin'!"

"Well, if you must know, the jewel plants eventually all withered away," Don replied.

"What?!" Shel lamented. "Why?!"

"That's just what plants do sometimes, in the absence of a caretaker. You see, through the chaos of losing her husband and trying to raise her son on her own, the queen neglected her garden. And so the jewel plants eventually died off. What treasure remained was picked through over the years by... well you name it, whoever was lucky enough to stumble upon this place. Even your Boogie chief, Sandovar of Sandeen, found a few morsels here and there as I understand, before the place turned mostly to dust."

I – The Farmer & the Queen

Donachtuk's ascended brows begged a courtesy from Sandovar and the chief obliged.

"At your service!"

Don continued after the chuckles died down. "Though the jewels were all harvested, the magic in the soil remained, for those with the magic touch that is. When the Peanut Butter Prince became king, retiring the queen mother of her duties to the commonwealth, the queen rediscovered her love of plants, and eventually reclaimed this garden as her private sanctuary — though, sadly, she was not able to grow more jewels."

"But, if you can believe it, she ended up marrying the jewel farmer's son! ...In an odd twist," exclaimed Sandovar.

"Is that so?" asked Joy. "How romantic!"

"Yup!" replied Don, taking Joy by the hand and spinning her around while continuing the story. "She used to come here every day. And one day, the son of the jewel farmer — Simonson was his name — he came back to the secret garden to discover the legacy of his father, and that's when he met the widowed queen. They became instant friends, spending a lot of time together; and they ended up falling in love."

"Awwww," hummed Joy.

"Magic indeed," agreed Izzy. "And Shel, for a time the queen's cousin, who had studied language arts, used to hold classes in this garden, teaching children the Language of the Flowers. ...Or reminding them, I suppose... You recall the

I – The Farmer & the Queen

language I was telling you about?" Shel nodded. "This place was perfect for teaching Artilan, on account of the essence of life being so readily available and abundant in the soil."

Shel looked around at the magnificent scenery. "I can see why." He turned in circles, mesmerized by the rainbow cornucopia of flowers and plants.

"It is a lovely place, isn't it?" offered Don. "I come dancing here every Friday. It is Friday, is it not? Friendsday as you Westerners like to call it."

Shel was suddenly struck with the realization that he'd been in Arcania — that he'd been gone — for over a week! What must his parents be thinking?!? Would he be presumed dead??? Would they even welcome him home when he returned?? His return! He hadn't thought about that in a long time.

"Yes! I believe it is Friendsday," remarked Sandovar, jolting Shel out of his ruminations. "And I'm sorry to say, but speaking of, I feel compelled to remind everyone of our purpose. May I ask, Mr. Nanook, why is it that we are here in the queen's garden when we wish an audience with the king?"

"Right!" Don replied. "We are here, Chief Sandovar, because... Oh! here she comes now!"

oooooo

I – The Farmer & the Queen

The queen's garden was adorned with an abundance of lilies from around the world: yellow African Queen Trumpets as big as footballs, spotted purple Arabian Knights, Black Spiders, Manitoba Mornings... all adding an air of mystique to the courtyard. Fire Kings and Stargazers splashed deep orange here and there; and snow-white Casablancas, which were Don's favorite because they reminded him of the Arctic. If the visual array wasn't sufficient to overwhelm the senses, there were plenty of aromatics to do the job. Tucked between the lilies were every type of sage imaginable, from azure and scarlet salvia to the anise and horminum varieties which looked like blue and purple butterflies fluttering hither and thither. The scents dancing in the air (like Donachtuk the bear) were enough to lead visitors on imaginary trips to woodland forests, desert lowlands, and tropical paradises, all in one sitting.

oooooo

"May I present," Don began with an outstretched paw and a dancer's bow, "Her Royal Highness, the queen mother."

An elderly woman in casual yet elegant robes and a jeweled crown on her head acknowledged the bear's invitation with a gracious nod before addressing the group. "So, this is the company that is going to save my son." The 'company' remained quiet, wondering who would speak as their representative, but also distracted by the kangaroo, monkey, and zebra following the queen.

I – The Farmer & the Queen

"Queen Ruth," Don filled the silence, "may I present our esteemed guest, also from Falconovich's hometown, Mr. Sheldon Silvers." Shel's ears perked up and his eyebrows followed, the introduction catching him by surprise.

"Pleasure to meet you, Mr. Silvers. I trust your time in Arcania has been enjoyable?" Other than a nod and slight grin, Shel stood stoic like a garden statue, feeling rather speechless in the presence of the queen mother. No matter. Don moved on, relieving Shel of the spotlight.

"Speaking of Falconovich, look who's returned from his globe-trotting adventures! It's Izzy the— well, you know. It's Izzy. Everyone knows Izzy."

"It is wonderful to see you again, Mr. Tuskinsky. You look well," the queen passed a smile and a nod in the elephant's direction. Izzy nodded in awkward silence in return, following Shel's lead.

Don continued. "Okay then. You know Sandovar, chief of the Boogies."

"Indeed. The famous Sandeen sword swallower."

"*Infamous*, if you please," corrected Sandovar with a grin and a bow.

"Infamous indeed," replied Ruth with an acknowledging nod. She turned back to the bear. "Did I see you dancing with a pretty young lady, Mr. Nanook?"

"*Ahem*." Don cleared his throat. "Yes, Your Majesty. May I also present Lady Joythea… um—"

I – The Farmer & the Queen

Joy stepped forward and bowed. "Joythea Aquarius Costeros, at your service, Your Majesty."

"Ah! Costeros." The queen pondered something as she tapped her pointer fingers together. "Your mother and I were close friends, if I have the correct family. As children we used to play by the shore. Tell me, how is Queen Theia?"

"Queen?" Shel whisper-coughed in surprise. Joy pretended not to notice.

"She is well, milady, though her age restricts her, and so she too spends her days in her *own* garden under the sss—" Joy caught herself, "Under the... care of her... um, caretakers."

The queen looked at Joy curiously. "I see. If you're insinuating that I spend most of my days here in my garden, my dear, then you... are correct. It is the place I find most peaceful and relaxing in all the world." The queen noticed some commotion behind the crowd. "But do be careful, Mr. Sheldon, that plant there might have a bite out of your knee should you get any closer. It's quite attractive, I know, but it does especially like the taste of youth." Shel jumped backward, getting some distance from the kid-eating plant. The queen chuckled. "Please do come here, young man." Shel stumbled forward and knelt in front of the queen. "Hmmm," she murmured. "Proper... but unnecessary. Please stand up so that I may speak with you directly."

Shel stood and was immediately interrogated. Queen Ruth had all sorts of questions about who he was, where he was from, and why he'd come to the Land of Happy. While the queen was brought up-to-speed on Shel's adventures in

I – The Farmer & the Queen

Arcania and the mission to save the dentist, the rest of the caravan found comfortable places to sit, sip tea, and chit-chat with the queen's zebra, monkey, and kangaroo. Meanwhile, Izzy caught up with Don on the whereabouts of the other circus actors, while Joy slipped away for a much-needed dip in the nearby pond to refresh her... sea legs.

"Miles, you should not eat any more of those green bananas; you'll make yourself ill," said the queen to her monkey before turning to Shel. "So, Mr. Shelby, your plan is to convince my son to release the sharpshooting lion in your care so that you may rescue your dentist friend and bring him back here to save my son. Is that accurate?"

"Yes, Your Majesty. All of that is right. Except, it's not *my* plan. We all sort of put it together. Joy actually came up with the idea I think."

"Is that right? Well, it's a nice plan; logical, reasonable, and commendable. Good work everyone. I'm afraid, however, there is one flaw."

Shel's smile flipped upside down. "Oh. Um, what's the... flaw?"

"It won't work," the queen replied, nonchalantly snipping dead blooms off a climbing rose bush.

"Ah. I see." Shel dug his foot into the dirt, a little annoyed at being shot down.

But the queen wasn't finished. "It won't succeed as it stands anyway. You see, my son can be extremely stubborn, and he happens to blame *you* for his predicament. So, he's

I – The Farmer & the Queen

not going to be inclined to release the lion into your care. Nor is he going to trust that you will bring Ingo back once you've rescued your friend. Nor is he going to believe that you will bring the dentist back to save him. So, you see, that is three strikes against you. You do know about the game of baseball, being from Chicago, I presume?"

Shel nodded then dropped his head in frustration at not being trusted. "But we're telling the truth. We *will* bring Ingo and Manny back! The king *needs* Manny!"

"Indeed he does," agreed the queen. "But he may not be able to see that if he is blinded by spite. Or he may not wish to admit it even if he does see the truth of it. Regardless, your plan won't work, not without someone he trusts forcing him to listen. I think I may be able to convince him. Come, gather your party; we will go see my son together, and together we will get you the army you need to free your friend and save the king."

The queen then leaned over and picked a most unusual flower, one which looked very much like a human nose. As she sniffed it, reveling in its intoxicating aroma, the flower sniffed her right back as if to requite her affection. It was a tender moment, quickly dismantled by a disturbing commotion from the corner of the garden ensnaring the queen's attention.

"Donachtuk Nanook!" scolded the queen. "If I've told you once, I've told you a thousand times, that is *not* how we water the plants in my garden! Use the bathhouse by the pond, you wildebeest!"

Chapter Two

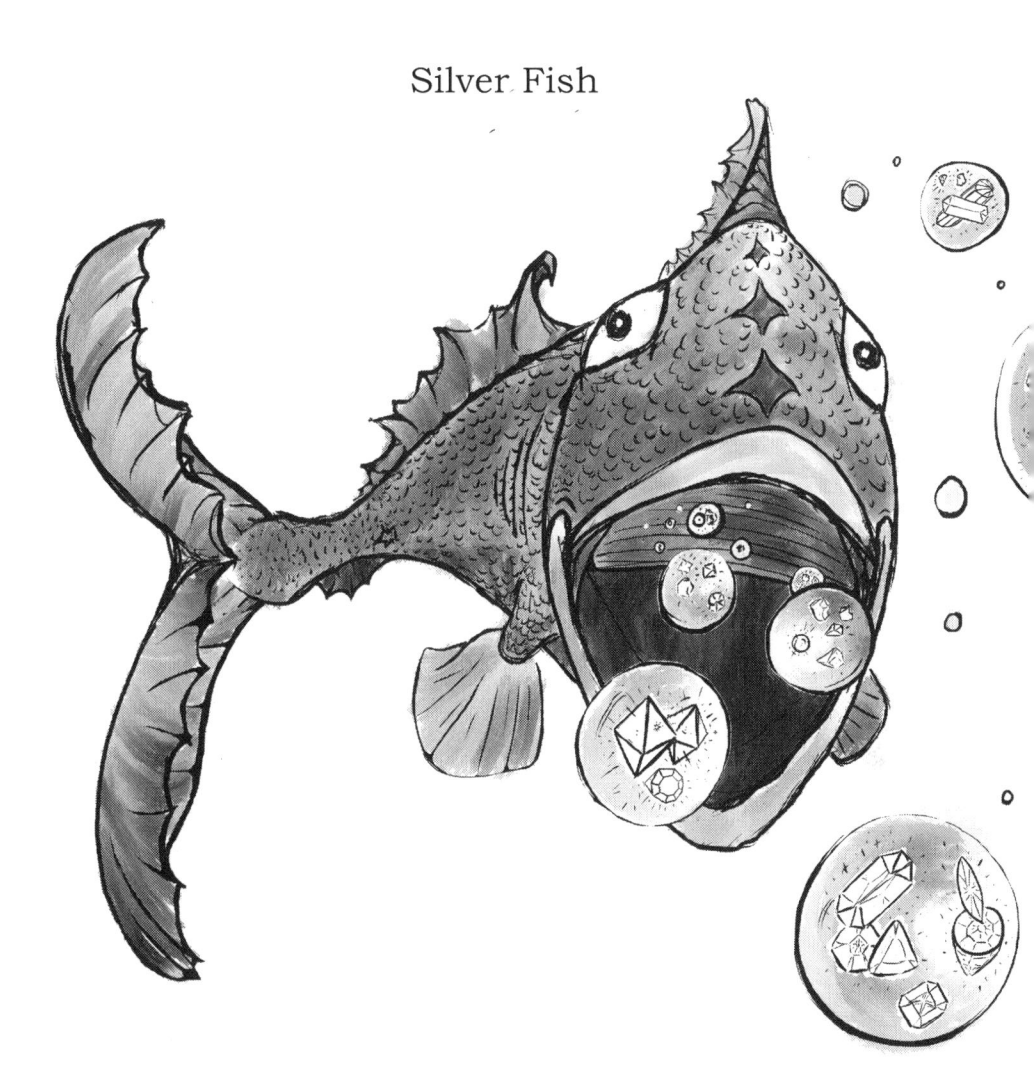

Silver Fish

As the caravan approached the infirmary where the king had taken up residence, the royal guards swarmed the Boogies, encircling them with shields raised and spears lowered...

II — Silver Fish

The caravan, however, did not respond. No swords were drawn (much to the dismay of the pirates) and no words were exchanged. Nothing needed to be said as the guards knew they were to escort the so-called 'traitors' directly to the king, while the traitors — er, the Boogies — needed an audience with His Majesty.

"Well, if it isn't the rotten convention!" blasted Katya the witch, with a sideways grin.

"Takes one to know one!" countered Izzy with a slanted smile of his own, eliciting a chuckle from the crowd.

Upon seeing the caravan approach, Longsmiles struggled, making all sorts of noises of castigation and reprimand, doing his best to scold and threaten. "Mmfrrlurghurklummm!" he murmured, but no actual words escaped his stuck jaws. He tried to stand and draw a sword (which incidentally would have been just for show since the king hadn't a violent bone in his body) but he was too weak. He had not eaten anything in more than a day and was depleted from trying to overcome the adhesion of the Peter Pan sauce. So, he simply sat back down and wept.

His audience waited.

When he'd calmed down, he signaled for his royal paper and royal crayon and began to write a royal message. Once finished, he held the paper up for all to see, pointing directly at Sheldon.

"*YOU* did this to me!" Shel read the message aloud. It was precisely as the queen had predicted.

II — Silver Fish

Longsmiles turned the paper back and wrote another message. Again, as the queen predicted, this one — which he directed toward Alice and the royal guard — read, "Seize the boy!" But just as Alice made her move, a commanding voice rang out from the crowd.

"If you please!" exclaimed the voice, with resolute authority. As the crowd turned toward the voice, a pathway opened between the king and the interrupter, who happened to be his mommy.

Shel was jolted by the recollection of his dream about the jungle chief and almost being dinner were it not for the girl calling out, "Me first!" He looked at the king, half expecting to see a cannibal sitting on a throne of bones. But no, Skippy was still there and he looked terrified. His eyes were wide in surprise at the queen mother approaching his makeshift gurney-throne. The medical trolley had been adorned with strings of pearls and necklaces of fine jewels as a way to simulate a 'throne away from throne' for His Majesty.

"Wellllll, I see you're putting to good use your father's spoils from my garden," scoffed the queen. Her son grumbled the best he could. "Bit of a sticky situation you've gotten yourself into, my son. I told you one day that habit of yours would be your undoing. I told you so, right along with every other person in this kingdom. You're the only one who refused to acknowledge the destructive habit."

Nobody nodded their head in agreement more than Katya the cook witch. And don't think the king didn't notice! Skippy was growing furious. He tossed his paper and crayons to the floor like a toddler. The queen mother's eyes

II – Silver Fish

rolled disapprovingly and she sighed before continuing. "You've already had the pleasure of meeting Mr. Silvers." She paused and stared at her son quietly. "And I believe you also already know his companion, Miss Joythea Costeros." Another dramatic pause. "Well, Miss Joy and Mr. Sheldon have a proposition for you. You will hear them out if you've any notion at all of what's good for you." The king tried to protest but the queen mother ignored him. "Splendid! Mr. Sheldon, Miss Joy, if you please."

Shel knew that out of the two of them, Joy was the natural leader and should be the one to do the talking. But when he looked at her she just smiled and nodded, encouraging him to proceed. So, Shel took a deep breath and mustered his courage. "Mr. King, Sir Highness, Your Royal... um, ness..."

The king closed his eyes and shook his head. He would have gritted his teeth had they not already been fully gritted. Shel looked at Joy and she gave him sweet eyes and an encouraging smile.

"Sir, I think it's plain to see, and I think everyone here, all of these good people who care so much about you, they all will agree, you need a dentist... badly. And not just any dentist. You need the best! Well, sir, my friends Fickleface, Picklepots, and Tickletoes—" Shel pointed toward the back of the crowd where the boot crew stood, "They've found Manny the dentist. You all know Manny. He's the best there is. Isn't that right?" Shel looked around and was greeted with nods and affirming mumbles. Shel nodded in return and looked back at King Skippy. "We're going to go get him and bring him back here, to help you." The king's expression

II — Silver Fish

softened as the words 'help you' came to him. Shel continued. "But, Your Highness, Manny is being held prisoner by the Gambrine." The crowd gasped. "Sir, there are just too many of them." Shel paused, knowing his next statement was going to be difficult. "We need your help in order to save him. We need your help in order to save *you*!" The king's eyes lifted and met with Shel's. "We need the lion."

Shel could see the fire instantly reignite in the king's eyes. Clearly, his answer was still no. Then, the crowd, expecting the boy to do something like plead or pray, was caught by surprise when Shel — for he had expected this response — calmly asked the king, "Sire, have you heard the story of Lester the Wish Collector?" The king's reply was little more than a squint. "Well, it's about a boy named Lester, obviously, who encounters a genie. The genie grants Lester three wishes. But, thinking he's clever, Lester just wishes for more and more wishes in an attempt to ensure that he will never run out, so that he will always have enough wishes to wish for things for the rest of his life. Each time he has a wish to spend, instead of wishing for things like a new bike or an ice cream sundae, he just wishes for more wishes. Eventually he grows old and dies, having never gotten to use any of his thousands of wishes for anything meaningful."

King Skippy was appalled. How could a stranger, from Chicago of all places, think he could come here, to the king's own Land of Happy, and presume to teach the king himself a lesson about life?! Yet here he was. And Longsmiles had to admit that he wasn't quite sure what this young man was getting at.

II – Silver Fish

"Don't you see? You're the king! Your wish is the command for thousands of people. You have everything at your very fingertips. But so long as you refuse our help, you're just sitting on your wishes as your own demise comes closer and closer." The king continued to stare and squint at Shel, contemplating the young man's argument, but remaining unconvinced. "Are you really willing to give up all of this?" The youth spread his arms wide. "Your friends, your family, your kingdom, just so you can cling to your obsession, hold fast to your ego?" The king pursed his stuck lips, displaying his impressive stubbornness. "You're going to deprive the kingdom of her king just so that you can keep someone in prison for defending an innocent family?"

The king's defenses were clearly still up but his eyes began to lower. Shel noticed that he was gaining the advantage. It was time to close out the inning. "Or," he added, "will you use your power as king to save a life, so *that* life may go on to save another, and then *that* life may go on to save a king? A king who is beloved by his people and who is needed by his country." With each breath (through his nose), Skippy considered the words of this young man who had apparently found his courage and his voice.

The crowd stood silent, admiring the speech. Those who were old enough to remember thought this young Sheldon reminded them of a once-young Skipingston. The king stared at Shel. Eventually, he signaled for paper and crayon and began scribbling. He turned the paper around to reveal the question, "Have YOU heard the story of the silver fish?"

II – Silver Fish

"Ummm," Shel hummed. "Is that the story of Simon and his sparkly diamond fish?" The king's eyebrows lifted. He was surprised that this stranger would know about the story of his father's jewel garden. Longsmiles looked at Alice and nodded for her to continue on his behalf.

"It is the same, Mr. Silvers, but few know the full account. You see, Simon, the fisherman who caught the magic fish, was promised by the fish all sorts of riches if only Simon would release him. So, of course Simon let him go, only to have the fish swim away and not fulfill his promise. Well, one day, Simon happened to catch that very same fish again. And just as before, the fish made many promises if only Simon would let him go. This time, Simon built a fire and cooked that fish for dinner. And it's a good thing he did, otherwise he would not have found the jewels inside of the fish and our king would not be king."

Shel turned to look at Izzy and Joy. Joy knew where this was going and stared fixedly at Longsmiles while Izzy shrugged. During Alice's recount of the story, the king had been scribbling on several paper boards. He handed the boards to Alice who turned them, one at a time, so that Shel could read the words for himself.

"If you do not come back," Shel read the words aloud slowly, "...my little silver fish full of promises..." Shel pointed at his own chest and looked at the king with an inquisitive expression. "Am I the silver fish?" The king nodded prophetically. Shel gulped and read the third board. "I will catch you again..." Shel looked up from his reading with alarm as the king scribbled on yet another piece of paper then spun it around. "...and I will fry you up and eat you...?

II — Silver Fish

What?!" Shel's eyes looked as wide as Izzy's and he took a half step backward, nearly falling over. Suddenly, a reservoir of memory hit him like a tidal wave as he recalled being chased on his horse by the cowboy outlaws from his dream, how one of them shot him, and how that felt awfully familiar to when he and Izzy were being chased by the Worst and he got scored by the monster's claw. He then recalled his first encounter with the pirates in the Sonrisa desert and how they gave him the same sensation as the pirates in his dream, the ones who tied him to a pole. Then there was Skippy, reminiscent of the jungle cannibal chief. And then... *Oh my!* He gasped, putting his hands over his mouth and spinning around in sudden realization. He glanced at Joy just as a loud screech jolted the crowd. Everyone looked up to see a magnificent eagle soaring overhead.

Could Joy be... the mermaid? Shel thought almost out loud. The answer to that question would have to wait, however, as Queen Ruth snatched Shel's arm and pulled him through the crowd. He kept his eyes locked on Joy the whole time. As he stared at her, she saw something telling in his expression and sensed that he'd figured out her secret.

"Come along, my boy," Ruth whispered. "Mustn't dawdle. The king has conditionally granted your request. Best take him up on it before he changes his mind." Izzy, Joy, Sando, and the rest of the caravan quickly followed Shel and the queen as they headed straight for the palace dungeon.

Chapter Three

The Missing Piece

III – The Missing Piece

A lonely lion sat in his cold, dark prison cell made of stone and cement and iron bars, playing a game of rummy with a small mouse. Over the years the cat had grown accustomed to the dark, and to being alone. The mouse, who had wandered in obviously by mistake, hardly counted as a proper companion on account of the rodents' modest size, her timidness, her flightiness... her inability to make a proper toasted marshmallow sandwich — which everyone knows is a favorite of lions. However, when one is lonely enough, a mouse can be the best friend in all the world, for a mouse will not yammer on and on about their own troubles. Instead, they just sit quietly, judgment suspended, twitching their little nose, staring with those beady, black eyes, patiently listening to your tales of woe, waiting for you to share a crumb of bread or cheese or strawberry, please.

So it was that when a horde of clamoring rabble came wandering into the dungeon, the lion quickly picked up his little friend, placed the rodent in his mouth for safekeeping, and withdrew into the corner of his cell to wait silently in the shadows for the ruckus to pass. But pass it did not.

Instead, the disturbing clamor paused in front of the lion's (and the mouse's, thank you very little) cell door and eventually quieted, waiting for the lion to emerge from his hiding place. The lion, however, stubborn as a splinter, refused to come out into the light.

Wasting no time, an ominous figure emerged from the crowd and advanced with purpose, identifying themselves as the leader of the intruders; in other words, the lion's first target! Clearly, these uninvited guests had come to take the big cat away and deal with him properly, once and for all.

III — The Missing Piece

Unbeknownst to them, however, this lion had plans other than dying that day. He would not be going quietly, without a fight!

As the advancing creature moved into the light cast by the mobster's torches, from his shadowy corner, the lion squinted through a distant fog of recognition. Could it be?? He stepped from the shadows, face screwed up in confusion and disbelief. "Do I know you?"

"Been a long time, old friend," said the visitor as he took another step forward, fully illuminating his face.

"Iz... Izzy? Is that you?"

"Yes, it's me, and Sandovar and Donachtuk the bear... and the queen mother herself. It's good to see you again, Ingonyama. Now, pack your things. We've come to get you out of here."

Upon Izzy's modest, and therefore unorthodox, introduction of Her Royall Highness, the queen mother stepped forward. "Hello, Ingonyama. I trust my son hasn't been mistreating you?"

"Your majesty!" Surprised, Ingo stood and approached the bars of his cell, throwing a nod in for good measure.

"My son has agreed to release you into the care of Izzy and the Boogies," the queen continued. "You are to accompany them on a quest to recover Manfred Pfaffen Jr., the renowned dentist from Champion Valley. He has been captured and enslaved by the Gambrine colony. Once he is

III – The Missing Piece

retrieved from captivity, you are to bring him back here. The king is in dire need of him."

Ingo stayed silent for a time, contemplating the queen's news. "Probably safe to assume I am to be re-imprisoned upon my return?" the lion asked astutely.

"That remains to be seen," answered Ruth. "Men have been known to find it in their heart to pardon those responsible for saving their life."

"His life? The king is in mortal danger?" asked Ingonyama, thoughts rushing through his mind, not least of which involved the possibility of refusing the offer and instead gaining his freedom by simply waiting for the king to die. He quickly realized, however, that by refusing to help, he could be charged with further crimes against the crown, securing his place in that cell for the remainder of his days.

"I'm afraid the king's days may soon come to an end if he does not soon receive medical attention," explained the queen. "Which is why we must insist on prompt action. So, let us not delay. Are you ready to accept the king's terms and get out of this wretched confinement?"

Ingo hesitated still. "May I ask how he has come to mortal danger? What happened?"

Izzy stepped forward and pushed his face against the cell bars at the height of the lion, looking the cat right in the eyes. "Ingo, we don't have time to explain all the details right now. We can fill you in on our way back to camp."

III – The Missing Piece

The lion looked into Izzy's eyes and could almost read his thoughts. "He is in need of a dentist, you say? Would it be too bold to assume it has something to do with a peanut butter sandwich?" A giggle was heard from behind the crowd, presumably from one of the flying shoe crew. The untimely disturbance ensnared Ingo's attention and he examined the rabble standing behind Izzy. "I'll take that as a yes." The lion looked back at the elephant. "I see you have a small army with you, my old friend. Why do you need me?"

Izzy nodded. "We sought you out because we needed an expert tracker to discover Manny's whereabouts. But, it turned out the Festoon Brigade was able to locate him on their own. You remember the Boot Brigade... and their dentist friend, Manny, right?"

The shoe crew popped their heads out from the crowd and smiled. The lion did not smile back. He simply looked at them, one eye in a scrutinizing squint, the other wide with skepticism. Satisfied enough, he looked back at Izzy.

"No," he said plainly.

Izzy was taken aback. "What? You don't remember—"

"Of course I know the Boot Brigade. Of course I know Manny, Israel. My answer is no. You've wasted your time coming to get me."

"But... Ingo, I don't..." Izzy looked back at the group then back at Ingo. "Don't you want to get out of here?!"

"If you don't need a tracker but you've come here anyway, I must assume it's because you need a warrior, that

III – The Missing Piece

you are planning some sort of rescue mission and you need fighters. Well, my fighting days are over, Izzy. You, most of all, ought to understand why."

The elephant lifted his head in astonishment. "You can't mean you'd rather stay in this cell than help rescue Manny and save the king!"

The lion took a deep breath and replied slowly. "When I was captured by the king, I made a vow never to harm another creature again so long as I live." He paused for another breath. "After witnessing the tragedy of what happened to your family, Israel, I just went blind with rage. The king's men shouldn't have been there, hunting innocent animals. There's no excuse for that. But they didn't deserve the fate I gave them. I deserve to be where I am, right here in this cell, alone." The mouse protested, squeakily reminding Ingo he wasn't alone, but no one took notice.

Everyone stood silent, feeling at a loss from this development. They needed Ingo and his battle expertise, his leadership. Beyond this, they didn't want to see the great Ingonyama waste away in solitude. Izzy's attempts to convince Ingo were as if the elephant were tightrope walking on an unraveling string, a string that Ingo was attempting to light on fire.

Just then, amidst the grave silence, Shel stepped forward, confidence fueled by his recent victory with the king. "Mr. Ingonyama, sir, my name is Sheldon. I came to Arcania from Chicago, like your dad." Ingo cocked his head and squinted. This was certainly unexpected. He watched with great curiosity as the youth pulled the blue puzzle piece from his pocket and held it out. "I found this on the sidewalk

III – The Missing Piece

in Chicago, after I ran away from home. It's... er, this *was* me." The lion looked utterly confused. "I just mean that I used to be one lonely puzzle piece, part of a big picture but left out... I was out of place in the world. But being here with Izzy and Joy, and Fickles and Pickles and Tickles, and Sandovar and Morty and Taud, and everyone... I feel I'm not a missing piece anymore." Shel took a breath, acknowledging the changes that had taken place within him. "I know right now you probably feel all alone down here in this dark jail cell, far away from everyone and everything..." Shel looked down and noticed the mouse looking up at him, nose twitching. "Not completely alone I see," he said with a smile and the mouse smiled back, finally someone acknowledged her. "But, maybe you could use this, like I did... to help you find your own picture, rediscover where you fit." He shrugged. "After all, the big picture is incomplete without each and every piece, no matter how small. Right?" He looked back at the mouse who smiled and nodded.

Ingo followed Shel's gaze to the mouse. He bent down and picked up his tiny friend and she blinked at him, encouraging her friend to consider the newcomer's insight.

"I know that you still have an important role to play, Ingo," Shel continued. "This picture..." he spread his arms to indicate the whole group, "just doesn't make sense without you." Nods and mumbles of agreement filled the dungeon. "Can you see the picture? The story of Manny and the king? It's the story of all of us. Your story. If you can't yet see it, all you have to do is... imagine." Shel handed the lion the puzzle piece.

III — The Missing Piece

Ingo held the piece in his paw, considering the gesture from this young stranger. He was struck rather speechless, as were Izzy and Joy and the rest of the group.

Queen Ruth, however, was not. "Here here. Well put, young man. Seems we'll make a prince of you yet."

Shel replied sheepishly, "Um, if it's all the same, Your Majesty, I've always preferred the idea of... of being a knight."

"I see. Well, if a knight you are to become, then under a knight you must apprentice. Isn't that right, Sir Ingonyama?"

The lion perked his droopy head up and looked at the queen sideways. "Sir?" he asked hesitantly.

The queen nodded to the jailer who swiftly sprang at the cell, fumbled with a ring of keys, then unlocked the door. Ruth stepped inside the cell then turned toward Sandovar. "Mr. Sandovar," she said.

"My lady?"

"Your sword, if you please."

Without hesitation, the chief unsheathed his scimitar (from his side, not his belly) and bowed his head as he held the sword out to the queen with both hands, one on the blade and one on the hilt. The queen took the sword with both hands wrapped around the thick handle. Though it was heavy for an old woman, especially a dainty queen, she handled the sword gracefully, for this queen had spent her twilight years turning soil, weeding and pruning and

III – The Missing Piece

harvesting, milking cows, shearing sheep, and so on. She was not as dainty as she appeared. She turned the tip of the sword toward Ingo. "Kneel, Ingonyama Nifumo."

The lion vacillated. After all, going from spending days on end in a cold, dark prison cell to suddenly having so much attention from old and new friends alike, especially royalty, and then to be surprised with such reverence and honor… well it was all a bit overwhelming to say the least. Still, the lion knew better than to refuse his queen and what was likely to be a once-in-a-lifetime offer. He dropped his head and bent down on one knee. The queen placed the sword atop his shoulders thrice, one shoulder then the other, and then a final light tap atop his head. "Rise, Sir Ingonyama, knight of the Land of Happy and protector of her people… and of her king," she added with lofty brows.

Before he stood, his head still lowered, Ingo opened his paw and considered the little blue bit of puzzle that Shel had given him. Though overwhelmed by the turn of events, the simple piece somehow made sense, made him feel like he might have some purpose left after all. Izzy and the queen and everyone who had come to collect him were there now because of an unfolding story. Whether the story was about Manny the dentist, King Longsmiles, or neither of them, it seemed these folks considered the story incomplete without the missing piece called Ingonyama. That much was clear. Just one question remained: who was this curious young man bringing life lessons all the way from Chicago?

oooooo

III — The Missing Piece

With Ingonyama freshly knighted and freed from prison, it was time to get on with the mission. The queen led the caravan out of the dungeon and back to her garden. As soon as they'd settled in, Ingo got down to the business of discussing strategy. He was a natural leader given his status as an elder and his years of experience in battle. Under different circumstances and no better option, leadership might have fallen to Sandovar or one of the pirates. But the truth was that none of those free-spirited warriors desired to be burdened with such responsibility. That, and they weren't as adept at planning a military offensive as they were at, say, pilfering and burying treasure.

oooooo

With leadership firmly established, the lion commenced commanding the 'new' Boogies, which now included — in addition to Sandovar and the original Boogies — Shel, Joy, Izzy, the flying boot gang, Taudello and the pirates, and Alice with a smattering of her loyal, royal guards.

"As capable as you all are I'm sure, we can't just show up on the Gambrine doorstep without a plan. We need to be strategic and coordinated. Whoever is expecting to be part of the mission will need to be at least somewhat trained and fit for duty. There will be no room for mistakes and no room for anyone not assigned to a specific task. All that aside, there is something I need to make clear before we go any further." The lion began to pace back and forth like a true general addressing his troops. "I will fight alongside you. I will fight

III – The Missing Piece

to save Manny and I will fight to save the king. They both are worth fighting for. But let's get something straight right now, I will never fire another gun so long as I live. My shooting days are over."

"What!?" cried Sandovar. "But that's why…" *we sought to get you out of prison in the first place*, the chief was going to say but caught himself, realizing that would have been terribly callous. Plus, that sentiment was not entirely true.

Izzy approached the lion. "Yams, if I may. I understand why you feel the way you do. After everything you've seen and been through, I don't think anyone can blame you for wanting to retire the gun. But I can't see how we're going to wage war against the Gambrine without weapons. I mean, do we just expect them to roll over and let us pat them on their bellies?" Those within earshot chuckled.

Ingo also let a slight smile slip across his face momentarily. "No, Izzy. I do not think that is realistic, unfortunately. As much as I would like to simply show up with gift-wrapped concessions and reason with our scaly neighbors, I don't see a diplomatic resolution here. Being stubborn and short-tempered as they are, making them all the more dangerous, I doubt they're likely to give up their prisoner without a fight. Still, I must believe there is another way than bloodshed. If violence is the answer you can count me out. Just put me right back in the cell where you found me."

Grumbles and mumbles of disappointment and disapproval emanated from the crowd. But there were also

III — The Missing Piece

those who felt relieved at the lion's admission and his insistence on a peaceful resolution. Namely, Joy and Shel.

Izzy rallied. "Okay. So how do you propose we fight without violence?"

"I don't have that answer just yet, Izzy. But if you'll permit me some time, I would like to consult with the queen, and with Alice and Joy too. All three of them are leaders, respected by their people for their level-headedness and compassion, and for their ability to find peace and cooperation where others see conflict and competition. As a warrior, I tend toward the latter and could use some counsel on seeking alternative solutions."

Izzy nodded, turned, and walked away, perhaps disappointed in the lack of a concrete plan; perhaps relieved that Ingo was adamant about a nonviolent solution. Perhaps he was contemplating what Manny must be going through after so many days in captivity. Perhaps he was going to speak privately with the Flying Boot Brigade. Perhaps he was just going to look for something to eat.

At his departure, others followed, catching on that it was time to give Ingo some space to plan the mission. Thus, the crowd dispersed, leaving only three in the company of the lion. Ingo and the queen mother looked at one another and, with a nod, locked arms and strolled off to discuss important things, leaving Joy and Shel alone in the garden of life.

ooooo

III – The Missing Piece

It had been some time since Joy and Shel had a moment to themselves. A lot had changed for each of them. Shel had made all sorts of new friends and had experienced many challenges, injuries, threats on his life and freedom, opportunities to demonstrate his worth... He did not feel like the same naive kid who hopped on that ridiculous raft and set off across Champion Lake, let alone the shy wimp from Chicago who ran away from home a week ago.

As for Joy, since meeting Sheldon, she too had made many new friends and spent more time away from home than usual. Like Shel, she had never crossed the desert with a caravan of gypsies, never spoken directly to the Peanut Butter King and negotiated for the release of a famous prisoner; and she had never plotted an attack on a neighboring community. She too felt distant from the Joy she knew only a few days ago. She felt less sure of the world and less sure of her own inner joy.

"Um, hi," she spoke shyly to her friend.

"Hi. You okay?" he replied. He desperately wanted to ask about her mom, another queen. Did that mean Joy was a princess? But he'd learned enough about Joy to know she'd prefer he ask about her, that she'd bring it up when she was good and ready to discuss it.

"I guess so. Thanks for asking." She sighed. "It's hard to believe all that's happened since we left the beach."

Ah, the beach. Both were reminded of their brief time together at the edge of the sea, before life became complicated with the plotting of jailbreaks and the planning

III – The Missing Piece

of war. Thinking of the sea, Joy knew she needed to return soon, her presence at the Costeros Palace long overdue.

"And you? How are you holding up?" she asked. It seemed small talk was all they could manage.

"I'm okay..." He wanted to tell her that he missed her company. With so much going on, the two of them hadn't had any time to just relax together, to sit and talk, or just walk like they did together on the beach and through the desert. Although he'd found the courage to stand up to a king, he still lacked the courage to tell this girl how he felt about her.

She tried to fill the awkward silence. "Well, it appears we have our army. So that's good."

"Yeah... So..." He began his inquiry of her family just in time for her to cut him off, possibly sensing what was coming.

"You know, Shel, I'm happy for you. You really seem to have found your voice."

Shel shrugged. "I guess." *If only she knew. If only I could find the words to tell her how I feel.*

"And your flock," she added.

"My flock?"

"Yeah, you know, the group of friends who take you in and care for you. Like the family you pick... or that picks you, instead of the one you're born into."

III – The Missing Piece

"Huh. Yeah." He paused and then bravely asked, "Are you… part of my flock?"

She hesitated. She was nervous, like him. But she also wasn't sure if there might be some ulterior motive behind his question. "Would you… like me to be?" she asked.

Shel opened his mouth to answer but was interrupted by Alice and the king's guard storming into the garden. For a moment he thought maybe they'd been tricked by the king and that they all were going to be arrested and hauled off to prison. Thus, he and Joy sighed in relief when Alice took off her helmet.

"We've gathered reinforcements for your mission," Lady Alice spoke with a bow.

Shel's eyes went wide. He didn't intend to be a leader of the mission. Why was Alice bowing to them?

Seeing that Alice was waiting for a response and Shel was hesitating, Joy stepped forward. "Thank you very much, Lady Alice. Your support is much needed and much appreciated. Have you yet spoken with Ingo? He is the commander of this mission."

"Not yet. As this is a mortal matter for the king, we are both obliged and honored to join the fight. You can expect our full support in whatever capacity you require."

"Splendid!" A voice blustered from the far end of the garden. Ingo was looking renewed, Queen Ruth still on his arm. "I'm sure we can use all the help we can get."

"Ingo! I—"

III — The Missing Piece

"Nothing need be said, Alice. You're loyal to the king and I do not hold that against you. You were following orders as any knight should."

"Well, I thank you for that kindness, Ingo, but... king's orders or not, your imprisonment was wrong, and I am so very sorry for my part. If we make it back from this mission and the dentist is able to save the king, we intend to make a few changes around here."

"We?" asked the lion, just as a loud cackling roared across the sky. A gang of witches flew overhead on brooms; one of them on a vacuum.

"Head's up!" yelled Don the bear, joining the group in the garden. "It's the witching hour!"

"They've come to join the fight," explained Alice. "Katya feels considerable guilt, being the chef who concocted the sandwich."

Shel scoffed in Don's direction, not forgetting the bear's comment about Shel being responsible for the king's predicament. Don grinned back sheepishly.

"And... she too is tired of being ordered to do things she knows in her heart aren't right," Alice concluded.

"I see," said Ingo. "Well, they are most welcome."

"Speaking of," Don interjected, "are you certain this invasion of Gambrinsville is the right thing?"

III — The Missing Piece

"I don't believe we have any other choice, Don," answered Ingo, "especially now that the king is in dire need of the dentist."

"But the Gambrine are many! Not well trained for war, but they have the numbers to put up quite the resistance, I'm sure." Don grabbed Joy's hand and spun her in a pirouette.

"The numbers aren't what worry me. I have a few tricks to even those odds. My concern is their leader, Supreme Chancellor Hume. From what I hear, *she* is a formidable adversary if there ever was one!"

"Indeed she is!" agreed the queen mother. "Underestimate the chancellor at your peril. Not likely to negotiate, is Hume. She has brought prosperity to the Gambrine, there's no denying that, but at the steep price of freedom. For Hume, it's her way or nothing; a dictator through and through. Good luck dealing with that one!"

"Plus, she's terrifying!" added Don. "Bigger than the two of us if you were on my shoulders, Ingo!"

Ingo laughed, though he knew it to be true: Chancellor Hume was, according to legend, one of the largest brocosmiles to have ever walked the land of Arcania. "I believe you, Donatchtuk. I haven't seen her in person but I know the stories. I haven't yet decided how I'm going to deal with Hume. They say she has only one weakness and I'm no good with flour and sugar."

"Banana tarts," spoke the queen.

III — The Missing Piece

"Exactly. And how a banana tart is supposed to help us win a fight, you got me," Ingo sighed.

Shel was suddenly hopping with ideas. He didn't feel it was his place to say anything, being amongst such experienced and wise leaders, but he couldn't ignore the obvious. He just had to ask, "What if we just baked a wagonload of tarts, gathered up some of the king's gold — he's got gold, right? I mean, he's got to, he's a king! ...Wait! No! His jewels! All the riches from the jewel farm. We could load up a heap of jewels and whatever else the Gambrine like, and take it to them to bargain. Couldn't we just *trade* for the dentist?"

"That would be the best option, Master Sheldon," answered Ingo. "Problem is, the Gambrine don't barter. They contend that they already have everything they could ever want or need."

Shel balked. "Wha? How could they not trade? Everyone trades!"

"Not in Arcania," Ingo replied.

"What does that mean?" Shel challenged.

"Think of it this way, Shel," chimed Izzy, who had sauntered into the garden somehow undetected. "Sandovar's Boogies live a nomadic life, right? Everything they do appears to revolve around their interacting and trading with other communities, cultures, creatures... yeah? Well, the Gambrine — and certain other tribes in Arcania — are pretty much the opposite. They pride themselves on being self-sufficient if not wholly self-contained. The

III – The Missing Piece

Gambrine are one of the more extreme examples. Not only do they refuse to engage in trade, but they've essentially developed a culture of isolation. As you've heard many times before, they're only really dangerous when you—"

"Bother their crop. I know," Interrupted Shel. "And?"

"And, well, just because they're not dangerous much beyond that, doesn't mean they're friendly. They're not."

"So... what you're saying is—"

"You show up on their doorstep with a bunch of gifts, no matter how amazing you think your gifts are — and believe me, many, *many* have tried — the answer is always, will always be no."

"But, what about the tarts? If they're really the chancellor's weakness, she won't be able to say no, right?"

"Well, that's possibly true," answered Ingo. "In that case the chancellor would simply take the tarts then slam the door in our face, because, as Izzy pointed out, the Gambrine don't barter." The lion turned to address the group at large. "Please, everyone," the group quieted down and looked at Ingo. "As Nanook announced, it is indeed the witching hour and that means we all need to be getting ready for bed."

"Wha?" said a voice. "Bed?" said another. "What are you, our dad?!" said a third.

"Calm down! I know I'm not your dad and you're not my kids. But I am your commanding officer so long as this

III — The Missing Piece

rescue mission is in play. As such, I must insist that you all get a good night's rest, for tomorrow we start our training."

Well accustomed to receiving orders, the Boogies got to work, scrambling in various directions, quickly erecting a camp just outside the queen's garden. Soon a massive cauldron was set over a roaring fire, emanating an intoxicating aroma of lentil puttanesca gumbo. A team of chefs, including Picklepots from the shoe crew, Katya from the king's kitchen, and Sarah Karynthia and Sylvia Kats from the Boogie caravan, worked diligently, chopping, mixing, sauteing, and serving.

Wanda was saved from the culinary burdens because she was, by all accounts, a right terrible cook; but also because Ingo had pulled her aside to ask about the spaghetti debacle at the palace. While she was ashamed at having created the mess, she was also an honest witch, and thus she told the lion everything.

"Thank you, Wanda. This information is very helpful," stated Ingo. "It gives me an idea for the battle which might help avoid any real injury. At this point, until we depart for Champion Valley, I feel you and Katya, and any other witches you may know, ought to return to the palace and help the king in any way you can. Try to get any sustenance into the king's belly lest he perish before we're able to return with the dentist."

"But, how?" Wanda asked.

"Try prying open a small section of his lips at the back of his mouth. If you can just open it a little, perhaps you can slip a straw through to get some water or juice in." Wanda

III — The Missing Piece

nodded and turned to depart. "One more thing before you go," Ingo added. "After you've finished tending to the king, I have a special onion dish I need you to cook up..."

○○○○○○

"Goodness me!" exclaimed Shel, dipping a finger into the concoction brewing over the fire then sucking the glop off his finger. "This soup is even better than your flying shoe stew! Pickles, what's your secret?"

"Aha! You noticed!" Pickles rejoiced. He retrieved a small vial from his pocket and handed it to Shel, proud as a president. "Clearly you've a taste for the finer ingredients in life. That little darlin' right there's what I call sky seasonin'. Scooped a bit o' the sunset into a canning jar one evening as we were settin' off to polish some stars. It doesn't look like much, on account of bein' so airy. But, a pinch of sky goes a long way, especially in the compliment of lentils."

"Ah, polishing stars... That fiasco," scoffed Shel. "Don't remind me." Shel twirled the canister in his fingers and nearly dropped it.

"Careful! That there morsel ain't easy to come by. Took some skill retrievin' that, it did!"

Tickles laughed at her brother and commenced to ramble on about the Boot Brigade's myriad celestial errands. Meanwhile, the aroma from the cauldron began attracting a real crowd, and soon the queue wrapped around the

III — The Missing Piece

campground twice over. There they all stood, a rag-tag gang of misfits, waiting, mostly patiently, in the periphery of the magical firelight for both their dinner... and their destiny.

Chapter Four

The Big Sleep

"All right you Dungries, dish up your chow. After you've had your fill, it's lights out. Training starts at dawn," directed General Ingonyama before shuffling off to attend some errand...

IV — The Big Sleep

"Dungries?" Shel asked Joy as they fell in line.

"Mmhmm," she nodded. "There's a legend in the Land of Happy about a giant who was called Hungry Dungry because he ate absolutely everything he saw."

"Everything? Really?" asked Shel, skeptical but intrigued.

"Everything. Food, rocks, houses... people."

"Ugh! Is that true?" he asked, looking around at the others, hoping Joy was just kidding.

"Of course!" butted-in Sandovar as he handed the two youngsters each a bowl of chow. "I knew him."

"Really?" questioned Joy. "Nooo. This is just one of your silly Sandy stories, isn't it? Hey, what's this?" she asked as Picklepots handed her a pair of chopsticks.

The chef laughed, "We ran out of spoons. Good luck eating your soup with these!"

Sandovar booed at Pickles then resumed his story. "Well, I didn't know him *personally*. We had a mutual acquaintance."

"Is that so?" pressed Joy.

"'Tis so indeed!" replied the chief. "When I was a kid I had a pet giant and he knew Dungry pretty well."

"A pet giant?!" challenged Izzy, carrying his own bowl of gumbo. He didn't need any chopsticks... or a spoon. He

IV – The Big Sleep

had a built-in vacuum hose. "That's preposterous!" he punctuated with a sonorous slurp of stew.

"Preposterous rhinoceros!" defended Sandovar, awkwardly scooping gumbo with his chopsticks. "It's true! I was young and King Longsmiles had just started putting the giants to sleep. I happened upon one slumbering down near Frenchman's Crick. I didn't know any better so I slung a rope 'round his neck and woke that big guy right up." He leaned aside to Shel and with an elbow jab, added, "I wasn't the brightest kid, you know." Then, sitting up he turned back to the group. "Anyhoo, not realizing the danger, I yelled at that giant; 'up-n-at-'em,' I said, 'You're mine now!' Haha!" Sandovar laughed.

"Really?" Izzy questioned skeptically. "And how did *that* work out for you?"

Still smiling, Sandovar scratched the back of his head and lifted his brow. "Well, lucky for me he turned out to be quite docile and sweet. He wasn't terribly happy that I woke him up but he was endlessly grateful that I woke him in time to save him from being put to sleep... if that makes any sense." Laughter bubbled up from the crowd. "I mean, I wasn't necessarily trying to save the poor guy. I just thought it would be fun to have a giant companion."

"I know the feeling," Shel smirked at Izzy.

"Hey! I'm not *that* big!" Izzy choked on his stew, eliciting more laughs from the audience.

"Anyway," Sando yawned, retrieving his story. "We steered clear of Longsmiles and most everyone else for

IV — The Big Sleep

months... as long as we could anyway. I kept that giant hidden under the Corcutt-Malley Bridge by day—"

"The Corcutt Bridge?!" Izzy interrupted. "That's just down the clearing, on the other side of the woods."

"Yup, that's right. I adhered to the old adage, keep it close to the king and they'll never suspect a thing. Anyway, we'd stay out of sight during the day and at night we'd go mischievate all over the countryside." Sandovar sighed and paused in memory. "Yup, he was my best friend... that summer anyway." There was another moment of silence then Sandovar began to laugh. "Ha, ha, ha! It was funny, when he was standing up I could never understand what he was saying because he was so tall, so far away... that and he talked so darned quiet." A wave of silent nods made its way around the campfire. "And my tiny words were too quiet for him to hear. So—"

"How did you talk to each other then, if you couldn't hear each other?" asked Shel.

"Yeah, I was just getting to that. We worked out a way of 'talking' where I would scratch on his toes to tell him things and he would tap his toes on the ground to tell me stuff in return."

Joy chimed in, "But, he was a giant. Eventually someone had to see him."

"Better believe it. One day, a couple of Longsmiles' guards found Charlie sleeping in his spot, down in the marshy sands of Frenchman's Crick," Sandovar pointed toward a forested area. As he did, he purposefully avoided

IV – The Big Sleep

making eye contact with Alice and the guards. "Charlie. That was his name, I think. It was either that, or Chattanooga or Chili Beans or Cha-cha Cherote. It was hard to tell in taps. Anyway, eventually he was discovered and they put him to sleep, just like Dungry and all the other giants in this *happy* place." Sandovar sarcastically emphasized the word 'happy', obviously upset about losing his friend.

Joy leaned over and put her arm around the chief. "Actually, that's not entirely true." Sandovar squinted at the girl. "Dungry was never put to sleep." A few chuckles, scoffs, and gasps came from the group, some thinking Joy was jesting, others thinking she didn't know what she was talking about, and still others believing her through and through.

"What are you talking about?" replied Sando. "Of course he was put to sleep, just like all the others who refused to leave."

"Not all were put to sleep," Alice chimed in. Sandovar spun around and glared at the royal guard with a squinty pucker. "In fact, Joy's right. We tried to capture the beast but Dungry was one giant who seemed unaffected by the onions."

"What? Why?!" asked Sandovar.

"The onions had no effect on him," replied Alice. "They say it was because he ate absolutely everything. So the king's guard had to find a different way of dealing with that troublemaker."

"So, what did they do?" asked Sando.

IV — The Big Sleep

"They sunk him, like an old boat," Joy answered, before placing her own inquiry — "Wait, onions?" But her question was buried beneath a timely interruption from Shel.

"Sunk him? You mean they drowned him?" he asked uneasily.

"No, Shel. Giants can breathe underwater. Not great, but they can when they need to." Joy explained. "So drowning wasn't an option. They anchored Dungry to the bottom of the sea."

"Like, permanently?" he added in disbelief. Joy shrugged.

Shel looked shocked, as did others hearing the story for the first time. After a chill jolted through the camp, Izzy chimed in. "They call it Hungry Kid Island. But Hungry Kid Island isn't an island, it's the top of Dungry's head."

"What?!" coughed Shel.

"Yeah, normally just the top of his scalp sits above the water line, looking like a deserted island. He's been there long enough that some grass, bushes, and even trees have taken root on his head. Sea-goers will stop there from time to time to rest and what-not, seeing as how he's in the middle of the lake. Most never make it off the island. Sometimes when the lake is low, Dungry's face becomes exposed, even his mouth. When that happens, from a distance it looks like a cave. That's when you *definitely* want to steer clear."

IV – The Big Sleep

"Is that why they put the giants to sleep?" asked Shel. "Because they were eating people?!"

Sandovar was nodding slowly but shook his head when he realized what Shel was asking. "No, no. Giants are generally not so dangerous. But there were a few who caused some problems for the kingdom. Dungry was probably the worst of 'em. You know the saying, 'one bad apple spoils the bunch'? The king decided he couldn't take the chance of the bad behavior spreading and decreed all giants leave the Land of Happy. Some left. Others refused to go. So, he ordered the ones who stayed to be put to sleep."

"Wow!" sighed Shel.

"But, they put them to sleep using onions?" Joy asked again.

"That's right. Onions cooked up by the witches!" the Sandman answered. "Onions steeped in a potion with an aroma altogether irresistible to the giants. So incredibly strong were these onions that one bite made the giants weep uncontrollably for days on end, exhausting the poor creatures to the point that all they could do was sit down and go to sleep. Once asleep, the potion prevented the giants from waking."

"I thought it was the wild strawberry jam?!" replied Joy, astonished and confused.

"Ha!" Sando laughed. "No. That's a myth, just something they tell people so they'll steer clear of those wretched berries. The jam from a wild strawberry isn't dangerous, it's phenomenally delicious. The bite, on the

IV — The Big Sleep

other hand, can be fatal if not treated. So, Longsmiles devised a plan to keep the people of Happy safely away from wild strawberries."

"Safe?" Joy queried, glancing at Shel.

"Well, could you imagine if everyone was out there trying to get at those delicious berries? We'd have a massacre on our hands! Just look at your Sheldon there. He barely survived and he only had a scratch."

"Barely survived?!" Joy choked on her stew and looked at Shel who was staring intensely at Sandovar.

"No sense in getting you all worked up at the time, so we didn't say anything. Why do you think he passed out so easily on the sand? Taud didn't drop him *that* hard. Yup, poor kid was knocking on death's door pretty loudly. It's a good thing death was out fishing, or whatever death does in his spare time."

Joy interjected, "But, I thought I did a good job treating—"

"Oh, you did! You did indeed," reassured Sandovar. "If you hadn't wrapped his hand in that salve of yours my dear, he would've likely been taken by fever, incapacitated in some way or another. And losing your faculties in the Sonrisa Desert is a sure path to disaster." Joy reached over and grabbed hold of Shel's hand. The two of them locked eyes. Sando continued, "Most likely he would've perished were it not for your attentive care; the talented and resourceful Joythea Costeros!" Joy stared at Sandovar, concern swirling in her eyes. "They're not to be trifled with, those berries," the

IV – The Big Sleep

chief added. "And now you understand why Longsmiles spread that little white lie."

Joy nodded slowly as she looked again at Shel, who'd obviously been considering his close call, evidenced by his pale face. Joy smiled reassuringly then turned to Sandovar. "I still don't agree with putting the giants to sleep."

Sando sighed. "Many people don't. I'm not certain I'll ever understand it entirely. I mean, I understand the need to do something about the bad apples, and I know Longsmiles gave them the option to leave and some refused. But I'm not convinced forced hibernation was the right solution."

Shel inquired, "You couldn't have gotten Charlie and his giant friends to resist? To rally against the king?"

Sandovar shrugged. "Charlie wasn't violent. Not at all. Plus, most of the other giants had already been tranquilized by the time I found him. He would've been knocked out too but he hadn't yet been discovered, probably because he took so many naps under the bridge, out of sight. And he always slept during the day... and I mean *all* day long."

"But why?!" Shel blurted.

Sando looked crossways at Shel and hollered back, "I don't know! I assume he was really tired!"

Shel looked away and smiled. "No. I mean, why did the king have to put the giants to sleep? It just seems... I don't know... cruel."

IV — The Big Sleep

Sandovar's eyebrows stood up in ovation as he nodded his head. "Couldn't agree more, kid! Ohp! Look what the cat dragged in!" coughed the chief as Ingo walked briskly back into camp. With a loud clap, the commander interrupted everyone's conversations. "All right, team. It's time for lights out!"

"But Ingo," cried Tickles, "it's taking forever to finish this soup with these darned chopsticks!"

"It's not soup," corrected her brother with a smile. "It's gumbo!"

Tickles smirked at the unwelcomed correction.

"Well do your best to wrap it up as quickly as possible," replied the lion. "We need to stay focused on saving Manny and the king. There'll be plenty of time for soup, gumbo, bonfires, and chit-chat after we get back. Fair enough?"

As people began to clean up and prepare for lights out, Sandovar stood to confront his commander. "Ingo, I'm not so sure about Alice. I mean, after what she and her team did to the giants… and to you. Do you really think we can trust her when push comes to shove? Do you really think she has what it takes to—"

The lion halted Sandovar with a raised paw, stroking his beard like a true man of thought. "Sando, I know you to be a gentleman. I see the way you care for Miss Karynthia and Miss Kats, how you treat them with the utmost respect. Let us not now abandon our sensibilities under the pressure that precedes a great battle. You and I both know she was

IV — The Big Sleep

acting on the orders of her king, trying to save her people. One cannot hold judgment over her for that. Her motives were valiant and honorable."

Sando pursed his lips. The pain of loss that he felt for his giant friend made his heart resistant to Ingo's words. "Honorable? Valiant? Putting the giants to sleep was not—"

"No. You misunderstand me. We're not in a position, due to a lack of time and lack of information, to debate the validity of that particular decision, which was a decision made by the king, not Alice nor any of the guards, mind you. Those guards are sworn to carry out the king's commands. The charge of a knight, sacrificing one's own liberty, sometimes life, for the good of the kingdom… that is what I deem honorable and valiant. Right now, Sandovar, you are as a knight of the realm. And right now your Boogies need your leadership. And I need your friendship. As for Alice, she is like the wind: lovely yet unpredictable, glorious yet dangerous; very hard to pin down. She's been an adventurous soul all her life, always up for trying new things and adapting gracefully with change. Yet, she is dedicated to her king and that is why we can trust her to serve the mission. As for her capability, she could likely best any man in this rabble, including you and me… and she could probably do it blindfolded. I assure you, Alice is as capable as they come. Now, if that is settled, I have a favor to ask regarding Sarah and Sylvia. If it is amenable to you, I would like to borrow your lovely attendants for a few hours tomorrow, if I may. I have a special errand for them, which I think you will find most rewarding."

IV — The Big Sleep

Sandovar replied as the gentleman he was. "How can I refuse?" With complimentary nods, the two bid one another goodnight and parted ways.

Ingo didn't get far before he was interrupted once more. (Being the commander came with the responsibility of listening to the concerns of his troops, regardless of the hour.) This particular distraction, however, was one that Ingo himself was anticipating. If he'd not been approached by her, he would have done the approaching. And so it was that Ingo and Joy took a walk in the late evening to discuss Joy's role in the impending conflict.

"I believe you know my family," Joy began as they walked. "And you know that our people are peaceful folk." The lion nodded. "I certainly hope for the safe return of the dentist and a healthy recovery for the king, but I cannot participate in an attack on the sovereign Gambrine colony. I know there are those in your company who believe that might makes right, that the best way to achieve peace is through a strong show of force — what they would call 'a good, old-fashioned fight' to decide a winner. But I feel differently." Her lofty brows punctuated her point. "I realize I may have sounded a bit militant when I was leading the charge to confront the king on your behalf, but—"

"Is that so?" Ingo interrupted and stopped walking. "I was not aware."

Joy looked down. Her assertive tone shifted to a softer key. "I may have gotten a little carried away," she smiled guiltily. "I suppose I was boasting in the moment. I would not have condoned violence against the king, but it did work to rally the cause." She smiled, and so did the lion.

IV — The Big Sleep

"Well, I'm flattered. Thank you for rescuing me."

Joy smiled then got back to the matter at hand as they continued walking in the warm evening. "My point is that you and I both know that so-called losers of a conflict never just go away and disappear. When the loss suffered is sufficiently humiliating or devastating, conflict always has the potential to provide fertile soil for sowing the seeds of revenge. My mother taught me that."

"The Mermaid Queen is very wise."

"She used to tell me the story of General Cray and General Korr, about how they had the option for peace but insisted on war; and how their war raged on for years and years, long after the two Generals had perished, all because of the pendulum of revenge." Ingo stopped walking so Joy stopped too, though she did not look at him, preferring instead to marvel at the stars. "She used to say, 'revenge is a seed planted by the victor' in her lessons on diplomacy." Joy looked Ingonyama in the eye. "Ingo, if conflict is necessary, as you seem to believe, and if you should prove victorious, I would caution you to be careful how you treat the Gambrine when the dust settles. Yes, it is they who captured the dentist, but that is not an invitation to war. I believe you would do well to ascertain their motives for detaining Manny in the first place and be prepared to offer concessions for any past transgressions. For, while the seed of revenge may never germinate, the threat is always there. It can take years, sometimes even generations to grow. Meanwhile, the possibility of retribution will loom like a cloud over the Land of Happy, darkening her otherwise clear, glorious skies. I know I don't have to tell you, living in

IV — The Big Sleep

a state of constant paranoia does not make for a peaceful life, even for those who are mighty and victorious on the battlefield."

The lion looked at Joy. *How wise she is!* he thought, slowly resuming his walk. He pulled a stalk of grass that was soft and white, and chewed on it while strolling at a pace measured and slow. Of course he knew she was absolutely right. But what was the solution? They had to retrieve Manny; and knowing the Gambrine would not negotiate, he knew they were going to have to use force. The lion already had a plan in motion that would, fingers crossed, minimize any violence, but Joy's words were true: he had to consider reconciliation; he had to consider this campaign from the perspective of the Gambrine, and he had to consider the kingdom's long-term relationship with the Gambrine nation. "Heavens, I wish I had your wisdom when I was your age, young lady. Your mother will be proud when she hears of how you saved the life of a stranded boy, then went on to rescue an old lion from a life of incarceration, and then protected an entire colony of Gambrine while quite possibly saving the life of the king himself!"

"Well, that's all a bit of an exaggeration," Joy replied modestly. "That last bit will be up to you, Ingo. When your army departs for Champion Valley I will not be going with you. I must return home, at least for now. I fear my time here in the Land of Happy has taken a toll on me... and on my heart, in more ways than I can recount here."

"I think I understand," said the lion. And he did.

Chapter Five

Runners

V — Runners

The next morning came much too early when Ingonyama began waking everyone with a series of loud roars, for he knew there would be plenty of training, planning, and organizing required to ready the troops for the mission. The king, with his jaw stuck closed, would not have many days left before he starved and withered away. With any hope, the witches would ensure that didn't happen. As for the dentist, it was anybody's guess how long he would hold up in the 'care' of the Gambrine. Time was very much against them.

Ingo had, with help, spent a good portion of the night building a crude obstacle course, complete with rope swings, tree climbs, and treacherous pitfalls. As it turned out, spending months on end in a small prison cell gave Ingonyama an abundance of pent-up energy and he was going to make the most of every second of his new-found freedom. Unfortunately, many of his recruits weren't so keen on running that morning. So, he found a way to motivate the troops, which included Izzy, the shoe crew, Sandovar and his Boogies, Taud and the pirates, Alice and a few members of the king's guard... nearly everyone but Shel.

With Ingo's permission, Sheldon left that morning to confer with Katryna, the cook witch. He did not divulge specifics, only that he had, "an idea how to help with the king's situation." Since it involved the king, Ingo let him go, to assist Katya in whatever way he could.

Everyone else stood at attention while Ingo, with a wide grin full of sharp teeth, warned, "All right. Listen up you duffers. You'd better start running or I'm going to take a bite out of your butt! I may look sophisticated in my

V – Runners

pressed shirt and trousers, but I'm still a lion. If you forget that, I'll be happy to jog your memory!" The group stood and stared at their commander, not sure if he was serious or trying to be funny or—

"Yeowww! You just bit me!" cried one of Alice's knights as the lion sunk his teeth into the warrior's leathers.

Ingo roared, reaffirming that he meant business. His ferocious growl sent the group scrambling through the obstacle course at breakneck speed, the lion giving chase. If anyone slowed down or tripped and fell, he was quick to remind them why they were running in the first place.

By the end of the day, Queen Ruth and her monkey, Joy, Sarah, and Sylvia, all had their hands full bandaging wounds and passing out bags of ice for the warriors to place on injuries sustained in the obstacle course, many of which came from Ingo himself. The lion drove his disciples hard. As a result, it only took two days to toughen up the motley crew and make them work and move together like cogs in a greased wheel.

"They look like real soldiers!" Shel observed upon return, channeling his fascination with the military. He'd spent one day in the kitchen with Katya and therefore got one day to train in the field with Ingo, which was plenty of time for him to feel like a warrior. Ingo smiled at the kid before looking over his regiments with an approving nod. His fighters were ready. It was time to go get Manny back.

oooooo

V – Runners

Ingo had planned to set sail that very night. "There's no time to spare. We'll sail through the night and attack at first light," instructed the lion.

"But we have no ship!" Taud the pirate asserted as they sat around the bonfire eating supper that evening.

"Taud's right. How are we supposed to reach Champion Valley without a boat?" challenged Izzy.

"Let me worry about that." Ingo stared off into the night as if the answer were hidden somewhere in the darkness. Seeing nothing, he turned back to the campfire and his troops. "The Boot Brigade will take as many as Delilah can carry. Shel, you will accompany the air attack. If they're able, the witches will cover your flank on their brooms."

Enthusiastic as he was about the idea of soldiering, Shel was suddenly frozen by the word 'attack', struck with the realization that they were really headed into combat. This was no drill, nor dream. Was he ready to fight? He wanted to save Manny but he was not a violent person, and he had nothing against the Gambrine. He didn't even know the Gambrine.

"Ingonyama, sir?"

"What is it, Sheldon?"

"I don't want to hurt anyone."

"Well it's a little late for that, don't you think?" replied the lion. "You've traveled a long way and accomplished

V — Runners

much, including freeing me from prison, all for the mission to recover the dentist. Correct?"

"Well, yeah, but, it's just—" Shel found it hard to put his feelings into words.

"Change of plans," Ingo spoke to the group. "Alice, if you would, I'd like you to take my place leading the ground attack. I'll ride with the Boot Brigade. We'll cover the air." The lion winked at Shel and the kid immediately felt relieved. But he still didn't want to see anyone harmed.

"Ingo," pressed the elephant, "there's still the problem of how the rest of us are going to get there."

Ingo looked at Captain Fickleface. "Can Delilah carry all of us," he waved his paw over the group slated for the boot, "all of the weaponry and ammunition, and the elephant too?"

Looking less than calm, Fickles slowly shook his head side-to-side.

"Okay, that's a no-go," Ingo concluded. "Looks like you're sailing with the pirates, big guy."

Taudello was fast to reply. "Oh? And just how might ye be plannin' this grand sea voyage without a ship?"

Suddenly, a salty voice bubbled up from the deep, from somewhere in the darkness behind them. "Arrr! Who says ye got no ship?" The entire group spun around to see a black figure lumbering toward the firelight. A wooden peg under his left leg and a hook in place of his right hand immediately gave away the identity of the scurvy barnacle.

V – Runners

"Well bless me beard and call me captain!" cried Taud.

"You're no captain!" scolded the crotchety Captain Jarby, unaware of what was afoot.

"No, I ain't! But he is!" replied Taud, pointing toward the large silhouette clomping closer and closer.

The figure raised a rusty hook into the air and with a growl, stepped into the red glow of the fire, eerily illuminating naught but his face beneath his oversized black hat.

"Did me old ears hear someone call for a black-capped buccaneer with a black heart, a mighty sail, and even mightier cannons?" The figure scratched out a terrifying laugh and a cough that sounded like death.

Ingo stood to greet his old friend but Taud and Morty stood faster and with an "Aye!" and an "Arrr!" and a "Yo, ho, ho!" The pirates embraced in a roasting Jolly Roger reunion that threatened to steal the flame from the fire itself.

"Who be there?" gruffed Captain Jarby. "Don't ye know to greet the captain first? I'll have ye strapped to the mizzen for this mutiny!"

Taud and Mort laughed at the old man's whining. Then, out from the pirate huddle emerged a large hook and a long face with a curved mustache.

"Be good to see ye too, captain! If ye don't recognize the hook, perhaps ye recognize the leg!" He stuck his wooden leg right in Captain Jarby's face, as if he were attacking with a sword.

V – Runners

"Arrr! Back ye beast!" Jarby yelled, stabbing at the peg leg with his fork. The entire group burst into laughter.

"Hold the spyglass!" barked Morty. "Who be that youngster ye got with ya, Hook? Did ye finally land a proper first mate? A young buck who ye be groomin' to take yer place when ye finally meet ol' Davy Jones?"

Captain Jarbison interjected, "That ain't no sparky young lad! That there be a pretty lass if I ever saw one. Hook, ye old dog, ye finally settled down! And who be the lucky lady there?"

"Them's be fightin' words!" cried out Hook's companion. "I'll have yer head fer that!"

Suddenly the evening air was filled with the clanging of metal as swords and scimitars were drawn and flung about in a frenzy. The pirates and the Boogies had suddenly all turned on each other and no one was certain why.

"Hold it!" cried Ingo. "Calm down, everyone! Please! Save your fighting energy for the Gambrine."

As the ruckus quieted, the hook-handed captain reached behind him and ensnared his companion-in-question by the collar, dragging him into the light. "This here be no woman o' mine nor anyone else! Best be careful with yer blabberin' ol' Jarby! This here be none other than Blackbeard himself! The most dangerous of 'em all!" The crowd gasped and everyone stood frozen with jaws dropped nearly to the ground.

V – Runners

"Blackbeard?!? Where is his black... beard?" scoffed Jarby, poking fun at his fellow captain. Instantly swords were raised again, and again Ingo called for calm.

Hook thought the exchange was rather amusing and tried to contain his laughter. "Blackbeard lost a bet, he did. Had to shave his chin clean, else it would've been his throat what been cut 'stead o' his whiskers!"

The crowd began to unravel in laughter and side chit-chat, prompting Ingo to impose order so as to keep the group focused. He roared loudly and the crowd fell silent. Eyes shifting through the lot, the lion bent down in the sand beside the campfire and began drawing with a stick. "Friends, please! Let's settle down. Captain Hook and Captain Blackbeard have come to help us in our crusade to retrieve the dentist. They've offered to let us use their ships."

A brief moment of celebration and embracing, now that swords had been thoroughly sheathed, threatened to disrupt Ingo's order once more.

"All right! Settle it and gather 'round. We need to go over our plan of attack." The lion began talking through his plan as he drew a map in the sand that identified the location of the Gambrine village in relation to Champion Lake and the Land of Happy. "The wind is in our favor tonight, so we ought to make good time crossing the lake. Captain Hook and Captain Blackbeard, we'll look to you to lead the marine attack. Your ships will sail through the night and travel up the Champion River in the early morning, arriving at the southwest end of the Gambrine village with the sunrise. Captain Jarbison and Mortimer will travel with Hook, along with Alice and the king's guard. Taud, you'll be

V – Runners

on board Blackbeard's vessel with Sandovar and the Boogies. I'd like the pirate captains to stay with the ships, along with anyone else wishing to stay out of the trenches. The ship's cannons will come in handy during the fight and we'll need both ships ready to launch for a swift departure when the time comes.

"At dawn, when you see my signal, the ships will fire all cannons on my target, while Alice and her troops, together with the Boogies, will attack on foot from the west." Ingo looked around to see silent nods affirming that everyone was following along closely.

"Blackbeard, you'll drop Sandovar and his companion at the mouth of the Champion River, here," the lion pointed to the battle model he'd constructed from sticks and rocks. "From there, they'll make their way through the mountains and forest to cover the eastern front. His Boogies will stay on board the ship with you until you make port."

"My companion?" squawked Sando. "Are you talking about Taud or—?"

"Chief, I have a special task for you," Ingo replied. "You are to guide your companion, a secret weapon if you will, up Champion Ridge and approach the village from the east. At dawn, on my signal, you will descend from the ridge and meet up with the rest of us. Blackbeard's ship will carry you to your destination. He has by far the largest ship in the seven seas—" Just then, the ground shook and the group could hear the snapping of branches in the distance. "...And you're going to need every inch of it!"

V — Runners

On cue, the booming of something very large stomping across the countryside made the group fall silent and everyone stiffened, unsure of what was happening. Sandovar stood, then Ingo, then the rest of the group. The pirates drew their swords and the king's guard followed suit.

"There'll be no need for that," exclaimed Ingo with an upcast paw. "This one's a friendly."

Shel squinted. "Is that?! No! Ingo, is that..."

"A giant!" Sandovar finished Shel's sentence.

"Not just any giant, my friend," replied the lion, as the enormous man came into view. Sandovar stared in utter disbelief as his caretakers Sarah Karynthia and Sylvia Kats stepped into the distant glow of the fire, carefully leading a giant by a soft rope tied around his index finger. Joythea, Katya the witch, and Queen Ruth accompanied the giant as well. Sarah and Sylvia bowed as they reached their chief. Joy nodded, indicating that all was well.

Ruth stepped forward. "May I present, Chester the giant." It was Sandovar's childhood friend, only the giant's name was not Charlie or Cha-cha Cherote; it was Chester.

"But... how?" was all that Sando could get out.

"I had some help," replied Ingo as he stretched a paw in the direction of the group of women.

"But... how did you find him?" pressed the Chief. "How did you wake him up? How did you get him to follow you? How did you—"

V – Runners

The queen raised a hand to halt Sando's questions. "Charmed onions put them to sleep. It was charmed *garlic* to wake this one. We had help from the witches, naturally. Turned out, waking him was the easy part."

"Let me guess," said Sandovar, "the hard part was keeping him calm after you woke him. I'll bet he was in a right fit—"

"Actually, he's been very decent, a real sweetheart. Aren't you, Chester?" The queen looked up at the giant and scratched out a rhythm on his toes. A low grumble and giggle came from high above. "The difficult part was getting him moving. As you might imagine, muscles and bones grow rather tired after resting for so many years. Thankfully, a giant's metabolism is extraordinarily slow, being built for long periods of hibernation... though usually not forty years of it. You may be aware, it wasn't unheard of for the giants of old to hibernate for decades at a time... which, incidentally, was why Longsmiles approved the proposition of long-term slumber in the first place. Not that I condone the act... Anyhoo, after Miss Karynthia and Miss Kats told us where to find him, I conscripted a modest regiment of the king's guard to help excavate him from the cave. With Katya's spellbinding, we were able to resuscitate him and walk him back to the castle for rehabilitation."

"But... all of that would have taken *days* to accomplish!"

"Indeed, Sandovar," replied Ingo. "Which is why we began the process a couple of days ago, only hours after I was released from prison. Addressing the plight of the giants was my first objective as a free man." Izzy raised eyebrows,

V – Runners

asking Ingo to clarify. "What happened to the giants has been on my mind for some time. I've given the issue a lot of thought while sitting alone in my cell. When you all charged me with commanding the invasion of Gambrinsville, I knew we were going to need a proper miracle. As soon as you mentioned your old giant friend," Ingo spoke to Sandovar, "and how he was somewhere nearby, I knew Chester could be that miracle."

"Do you intend to wake the others? Or... you already have?!?" asked Izzy, looking around nervously for more giants.

"No. Well, yes. That's, the plan: to wake them eventually. For now, we've only raised Chester. If this resurrection proves successful, we'll proceed with the others, *after* we return from Gambrinstown. Now listen, I need you to—"

Ingo had been prepared to launch into his plan for the giant, but Sandovar burst into hoots and cheers like a kid at Christmas, running to Chester and embracing the giant's ankle. Chester wasn't as happy to see Sandovar, however, given the grogginess still clinging to him after his forty-year nap. Plus, although Chester recognized something familiar about the Boogie chief, on the outside this Sandovar looked very different from the boy Chester knew so long ago.

As Sandovar hugged Chester's leg, the chief could sense the tangible rift that time had opened between the two pals. They were just kids when they knew each other last. Now, they were both grown. But unlike Sando, Chester didn't know how he'd come to be so old, and a fair bit larger. He did not have the memories of an experiential life as

V – Runners

Sandovar did. All he had were fast-fading memories of random dreams.

"He needs time," the queen said to the chief as she picked up on both Sandovar's disappointment and the giant's confusion, which was turning to sadness as Chester slowly became aware of just how many years had passed him by.

"Unfortunately, we don't have time," Ingo replied quietly to the queen but loud enough so Sandovar could hear. "Sandy, I can only imagine what this moment means to you. But we must stay focused on the mission in order to save the king in time."

Sandovar looked at Ingo disapprovingly. Despite what the chief might have been thinking at that moment, the lion did not have a heart of stone.

"I know what you must be thinking, Sando. The decision to wake him was not just for your benefit, nor was it solely for the benefit of the mission." Sandovar's expression relaxed a bit. "Longsmiles was wrong to put them to sleep in the first place. Certainly the dangerous ones, namely Dungry, needed to be dealt with. But the peaceful ones, like Chester here, ought to have been left to live in peace. Upon our return, we intend to initiate a great awakening, raise the giants from their slumber — those that can be awakened anyway. We will need Chester's help to make sure his kinfolk do not seek retribution against the kingdom. This means that between now and then, we need to do all we can to show Chester we mean him no harm, that we are friends, and that we are very sorry for what we did to him and his kind."

V – Runners

"You mean what *Longsmiles* did!" Sandovar replied coldly.

Ingo looked at the queen mother then back to the chief. "*We* are the kingdom, as one or not at all. We all must take responsibility for this injustice and work together to correct it. It is hardly sufficient to put the blame on one person alone. Because, then what? We have the king exiled, or worse? That would not serve justice for the giants. That would not assuage the pain and anger they no doubt will feel… that Chester must feel now. No, we must show them that the entire kingdom understands their plight and that we are full of remorse and regret; all of us. We must demonstrate that we wish to live alongside them and work alongside them once again. We must show them, one day at a time, that we intend to correct our mistake and heal the wounds of the past."

Sandovar took a breath and looked at Chester. He felt he could see, even at the giant's great height, the sadness in his friend's face. After a moment of thought and reflection, he replied, "All right. What do you need me to do."

"Sandovar, you and I are men of the sword and of the gun," replied Ingo. "We have known battle and conflict all our lives. This moment requires deep skill in the healing arts. For that we need kindness and empathy, but we also need inspiration and creativity, as we are — in a sense — introducing new life to the giants."

Sandovar nodded, giving Ingo his endorsement, so the lion proceeded while motioning to a young lady in the crowd. "If you'll permit, I would ask that you let Joythea guide you through your reunion with Chester and the healing

V – Runners

process." Sandovar's eyes widened in surprise, begging for an explanation. Ingo placed a gentle paw on Joy's shoulder. "I was very surprised to see Joythea Costeros among you when you came to collect me from prison, given that she is royalty herself."

Shel looked over at Joy in surprise. Their eyes connected. He couldn't help but feel let down in learning such important things about her from public discussions. But, he had to remind himself, she did not belong to him, not in the least. *What did you expect?* he challenged himself.

Joy could see Shel struggling with difficult emotions, whether frustration or confusion or disappointment, she wasn't entirely sure. But she knew the time to have an honest talk was now overdue. And yet, it could not be now, on the eve of battle. Especially now that she'd been charged with the important task of helping Chester reunite with his old friend and with the world. She looked away and Shel could feel the distance between them expand.

"But since we're lucky enough to have such a kind-hearted and creative resource in our midst," Ingo continued, "I have asked her to help and she has agreed. I have also asked Sarah Karynthia and Sylvia Kats to accompany her, as their healing skills are unmatched. Also, their kindness and compassion will go a long way to help Chester feel at ease. I suggest the five of you spend some time away from the group working on basic communication and getting the giant re-acquainted with his new reality. When you're ready, connect with Captain Blackbeard and see what you can do to help prepare the ship. I would like both marine regiments to be loaded and ready to set sail in two hours."

V – Runners

    Joy stood up and walked over to where Sandovar was standing with Chester. Sarah Karynthia and Sylvia Kats rallied to their chief and the five of them walked into the night.

o o o o o o

    "Okay Yams, you have the troops," noted Izzy. "Now what? You said your fighting days are over and I don't see any weapons except a few swords. I heard you mention the cannons on the ships... Where's all the ammunition? Where are all the guns?"

    "Not to worry, old friend. I have a plan to get Manny back. It's not ideal but it's the best I could do on such short notice. If all goes according to plan, we won't need guns or swords. If this works, no one will get hurt... much." The lion spoke up to address the crowd. "Wanda informs me that... You all know Wanda, right? The witch who flies on a vacuum and studies under Katya?" There were nods in the group and glances around the circle as people looked for the witches but didn't find them. "Well, anyway, Wanda has told me—"

    "Where did the witches go?" interrupted Don the bear. "They were just here."

    "I'm getting to that, Don," replied Ingo patiently. "Wanda tells me that right now, a good bit of the king's palace is still overflowing with spaghetti."

V – Runners

Some eyes in the group widened, others squinted, recalling the pasta avalanche.

"Did you know," the lion continued, "there are many good uses for spaghetti other than eating?" Looks of confusion were had by all. Ingo expected nothing less. "I have asked Wanda to re-create the mess she made in the palace... albeit in a more controlled manner. Soon we'll have enough pasta to feed a good portion of the people of Kantytown for a month."

"Are the people hungry?" asked Donachtuk, in surprise. "That would be weird because—"

"No, no," replied the lion. "The spaghetti is not for the people. It's not for eating. Sorry for the confusion. I just meant that we'll have a lot of it. Anyway, speaking of the people of Kantytown, I have asked the good citizens to collect as many fruits and vegetables as they can spare and we now have a considerable stockpile of watermelons, grapes, cherries, cantaloupes—"

"Yuck!" coughed Shel without meaning to.

The lion stopped and looked at him. "You okay, Shelby?" Shel nodded in embarrassment. "Right then. Where was I? Right. Food. So, you'll all have plenty of snacks for the trip... But most of it will be ammunition for the battle."

"Ammunition?!" barked Izzy.

"Ammunition," replied the lion coolly. "We have installed catapults on the ships, and the king's armory has

V — Runners

prepared various sizes and sorts of slingshots as personal weapons for you all."

There were both outbursts of protest and cheers of excitement from the group. Others remained quiet in contemplation or confusion as they tried to wrap their heads around what Ingo was indicating.

As usual, Izzy was the first to raise his trunk and ask, "Sooo, we're going to throw tomatoes at them? Do I have that right?"

"That's precisely right, Izzy," replied the lion. "You've heard of a food fight? Well, this is a food war! A few of you experienced just how debilitating it was to be stuck in that mush of spaghetti greeting you at the palace steps. Well, once we locate Manny in the fields, we'll overwhelm the Gambrine with enough pasta to create a veritable marshland. They'll be like flies in a spider's web. We'll hold them off long enough to extract the dentist and then get out of there before they have a chance to retaliate."

The cries of protest diminished to mumbles of consideration as the group slowly conceded that this crazy idea might just be crazy enough to work.

"My friends, I told you that my shooting days are over. I've had my fill of guns and bullets, swords and sorrow." Ingonyama hung his head for the destruction and sadness he'd seen during his lifetime, then added quietly, "Violence only begets violence. I know that now." He lifted his head, took a breath, and continued, recalling his role as the group's leader and thus the need to stay strong. "The plan is to debilitate, not to harm. Everyone got that?" He looked

V – Runners

around and locked eyes with as many in the group as he could. "In the end, we do not want to make an enemy of the Gambrine. They are not our enemy. Let me repeat that. The Gambrine are not our enemy. They are simply in the way of something we want. So, we only need to get them out of the way, temporarily. That's all."

"But Ingo, watermelons and cantaloupe thrown hard enough could still really do some harm. No?" Donachtuk pointed out.

"Indeed. That's why I need to ask you all to be cognizant of the fruit you throw. There will be plenty of over-ripe options. Those are okay to toss in the air. Rotten stuff will only cause discomfort... and maybe some nausea. That's exactly the sort of debilitation and distraction we want. But if you come across something hard, even something small like an apple, either mush it up before you launch it or set it aside... or maybe eat it. Because don't forget, it'll be important to keep your strength up, right?" Ingo smiled and people smiled back.

"Or, I don't know..." he continued, "let's say you have a hard watermelon. Instead of tossing it up in the air, try tossing it at ground level, rolling it like a bowling ball." He shrugged. "I don't have all the answers. You'll have to judge for yourself, so long as you keep in mind that ultimately the Gambrine are not our enemy. Historically, we've enjoyed a peaceful relationship with our scaly neighbors to the west. That peace has held because we keep our distance and do not disturb their way of life, especially their crop — a crop that has fed the people of Champion Valley for as long as any of us can remember. Right?"

V – Runners

Nods and mumbles affirmed his sentiment.

"Right. We won't be leaving without the dentist, that's a given. But we also don't want to leave behind insult and injury to inspire retribution. We don't want to return to save the king only to bring conflict and war to his doorstep in the future," the commander concluded.

A great murmur rumbled from the crowd, followed by a cloud of silence as everyone weighed the lion's words and his unorthodox proposition. In that moment, the only sound that could be heard was the crackling of the bonfire. This was the moment of truth when the group would accept Ingo's crazy plan or not.

Sheldon was so excited at this nonviolent solution — which actually sounded rather fun — that he burst into laughter. "Haha! Yes! I love it! Let's do it!" He stood up, walked over to Izzy, and gave his friend a hug. His enthusiasm ignited a fire in the group and others began to cry out in celebration.

"Okay. I'm in!" bellowed Izzy. "Let's give those Gambrine a taste of what we're serving up. Something *other* than broccoli!"

"Well, I'm glad you're on board!" exclaimed the lion. "Now, get on board! *Haha*," he laughed. "Delilah is being outfitted with catapults as we speak. I'll finish giving orders to the rest of the group and meet up with you all in one hour." He then turned to address Captain Blackbeard and the Boogies. "Captain, Sandovar and Chester should be back soon. Go ahead and prepare your ship if you would, please. We launch in one hour."

V – Runners

"Aye!" was all that Blackbeard said and he and the Boogies set off for the clean-shaven-pirate's ship.

That left Captain Hook, with Alice and her king's guard.

"Hook, you know what to do!" said Ingo. "As for you, Alice, I'm counting on you to keep the peace."

"Sir? The peace? I thought this was war."

"Indeed it is, Alice. And war must always end in peace, else, by definition, it does not end. Correct?"

Alice nodded, slowly. Impossible to deny, that logic was.

"And for all our sakes, we need peace to hold."

Alice continued to nod as she slowly came to understand where the lion was headed.

"This battle needs to be fought with good humor and result in as few injuries as possible. And once the battle is over, we'll need to mend relations with the Gambrine."

"I see," replied Lady Alice with a slight bow.

"The Gambrine will need to be compensated for the trespass we are about to endeavor against them."

"I see your point," she said.

"This campaign — the attack itself and the retrieval of the dentist — is going to put us in considerable debt to the Gambrine, not to mention the mess we're about to make

V — Runners

with the food. The mess will need to be cleaned up and the debt repaid. I intend to set things right with the Gambrine, and this is how..."

Ingonyama proceeded to explain his post-operations plan to bury the hatchet between the Gambrine and the kingdom of Happy. One hour later, Ingo's troops were packed and ready to set course for Champion Valley.

Chapter Six

Storm

VI – Storm

The fiery sunrise brought more than just a new day to Champion Valley, it brought a new world. Aboard the Flying Festoon, soaring above the landscape, Sheldon looked eastward in the direction they'd come, watching the evening blues blend into a rich blood orange.

"With any luck, that will be the only blood spilled today," Ingo nodded at the sunrise. Shel smiled hopefully.

As if thrown by Apollo before his grand entrance, thin spears of gold shot from the horizon, piercing the remaining stars still clinging to life in the highest corners of the sky. The brilliant green of the valley could already be seen glowing through the dense morning fog blanketing the basin. The scene unfolding was so magical Shel felt as if he'd leaped right onto the pages of a storybook.

"What a magnificent place," he whispered to himself. Turning north to look where they were headed, he spotted small figures bustling in the landscape. They looked like small lizards with miniature picks and hoes, rakes and shovels. "Brocosmiles?" he asked aloud to no one in particular, without taking his eyes off the land.

"Mmm hmm," someone replied, and at once Shel became nervous, for he knew the battle for Manny was about to begin.

The Gambrine were already out in the fields tending their crops in the twilight when Delilah came sailing slowly over the horizon, flying low in the dawn sky, concealing their arrival behind the blinding light of Apollo's sheen.

VI – Storm

"Eyes up! Stay alert!" commanded Ingonyama, who had dressed the part in an old military uniform Falconovich had given him for circus performances. It was an outfit from the Eastern Europe of old, every button, every stitch as authentic as the blood stains on the collar and sleeves. Ingo's otherwise wild mane was tucked as neatly as possible under a large, metal helmet whose brim sunk just above his dark eyes. His suit was pressed neatly, shoes polished, gloves starched. Every bit of this commander looked as a man, tall and broad and stoic. If Shel didn't know there was a lion under the uniform, he would've guessed Ingo was just another one of the king's men. In fact, in this particular suit, Shel thought Ingo looked nearly identical to the soldier he'd run into on the streets of Chicago!

Noticing Shel's examination and reading his mind, Ingo smiled. "Good! That's exactly the response I'm going for. The fewer who know Ingonyama is here, the better. Today I am just another military man."

Shel smiled and nodded.

"What about you? What's that thing slung around your chest?" Ingo asked.

"You mean my pack?" Shel replied. "It's a satchel I borrowed from Sandovar. It's got a few things I thought might be useful for the battle. I brought a gift... for Chancellor Hume."

Ingo raised a brow in curiosity but did not inquire, sheer surprise at the youth's boldness scraping the words from his tongue. Instead, he just smiled and turned to

VI – Storm

Captain Fickleface, making ready to signal the first attack. "Ready cap-i-tan? Hold her slow and steady now..."

Somewhere below Delilah, the pirate ships sailed silently up the Champion River. Meanwhile, Katya and her cousin, Wanda, having completed both the lion's tasks, recruiting three more of their Wiccan sisters in the process, bringing the flying broom (and vacuum) contingent of Ingo's army to an even five, flew on ahead of Sandovar and Chester, escorting the Boogie chief and his giant through the Gambrine forest to their battle station at the top of Fallshugger Ridge.

With his chessboard set, all pieces in place, the Nifumo storm was nigh upon the valley.

oooooo

A flying boot is a hard thing to miss. And so, as the Festoon crested the hills encircling the valley, the brocosmiles in the fields began to perch on hind legs and stretch their necks, giving them the look of curious meerkats on the savannah. One by one, the crocodile-like creatures stood up, forgetting their tilling and weeding and planting, as if they could sense something wasn't right about the incoming vessel. When they heard the warning calls from their kin working in the swamps down by the river, alerting them of more foreign vessels approaching, this time from the sea, their hunch was confirmed. This was not a friendly visit. This was not Grandma Gambrine bringing fresh-baked

VI – Storm

broccoli calzones in her antique pirate ship. No, this was an invasion!

Shel turned with a nervous smile to his comrades, his anxiety now joined by excitement, heart pounding out of his chest. As Delilah sailed over the fields, Shel marveled at the brocosmiles crawling around, scrambling about, fleeing and hiding. A few of the bolder ones stood and stared, while others pointed up at them with various things in their hands. *Could be just farm tools*, Shel hoped.

The battle stage was set. All that was needed was for Fickleface, who was frantically scanning the countryside with his trusty Evil Eye spyglass, to locate Manny so the lion commander would have his target. Suddenly, a premature war cry from Chester let the cat out of the bag, a giant warning echoing through the valley like thunder.

The brocosmiles jolted, turning away from the flying shoe to confront the invisible monster howling at them from somewhere in the forest. The grip of fear clenched its fist and brocosmiles scattered like flies, buzzing this way and that, bumping into each other, tripping over anything and everything. They now knew beyond doubt that they were under attack. Many of the brocos began throwing things like spades and pitchforks into the sky at the passing airship, signaling to Ingonyama that it was time to strike.

"Where's Manny?!" yelled Ingo. "Did we arrive on the wrong day? Is he still locked away in Gambrinsluk?"

Fickles shrugged nervously from behind his telescope.

VI – Storm

Just then, Pickles cried out, "There! I see 'im! It's Manny! I can't believe it! There he is!!"

Shel leaned over the side of the ship, straining in the direction where Pickles was pointing, and immediately had to duck to avoid a head of broccoli sailing over the bow.

"Lookout!" cried Tickles. "They're onto us!"

Although he was still far away, the dentist was rather easy to spot since he was of considerably different shape than any of the gangly reptiles. His white dentist coat stood out like a sore molar against the green of the brocosmiles and the valley.

Satisfied with his target, Ingo turned and nodded to Chef Picklepots, who instantly brought down a mighty cleaver, cutting through the rope restraining a catapult full of pasta. As the catapult spun with a force that shook the ship from bow to stern, a massive tangle of goopy spaghetti flew high into the dawn, blocking out the rising sun.

WHOOSH!

Thick strands of noodles, twenty feet long and tangled together in a bramble only a witch could weave, swirled through the sky like earthworm storm clouds, raining down drops of marinara as they flew. Meanwhile, waiting in their mighty ships, the pirates saw the starchy signal and scrambled to their battle stations.

"Spark the cannons!" wailed Captain Blackbeard, and a wild ruckus roared to life.

VI – Storm

BOOM! BOOM BOOM! The cannons hollered one by one, sending mushy watermelons, cantaloupes, and grapefruit sailing like a flock of wingless birds over the fields of Gambrinstown. As the fruit landed with echoing splats and splishes, the Gambrine scattered, running for shelter wherever shelter could be found.

The witches also saw the writing on the wall once the spaghetti was in the air and began flying around like gnats, encircling Chester's head, calling out instructions. In response, the giant reached into a large satchel at his side, laughing with glee as he pulled out handfuls of omelet mush and began tossing bunches of breakfast over the treetops, down into the farmland below.

Before any brocosmiles had time to grab their forks, tuck in their napkins, and give thanks for the meal they were about to receive, the skies became overcast in food fireworks of green onions, red carrots, yellow peppers, and purple cabbage. Not knowing what to make of this bizarre, never-before-seen onslaught, the brocosmiles' response was anything but unified — exactly the sort of chaos and confusion Ingonyama had hoped to create.

oooooo

Some brocos stood still, bewildered and mesmerized by the colorful fare… "ooh-ing" and "aah-ing" as it flew through the air, until the mess descended *smack*! onto their spellbound stare.

VI – Storm

Some laughed and danced in the rain of cuisine, mad as hatters, rejoicing in the splatters, if you know what I mean.

"What is this ridiculousness?!" they yelled in fright. "Who knows?! But sure is marvelousness!" they answered in delight.

Others scattered and scurried to avoid being buried.

"Look out!" they cried.

"The sky is falling!!" they lied.

And still others took the flying grub as a welcomed invitation, eager for a good, old-fashioned, healthy altercation.

"Bring it on, you food-tossin' floobies!" they taunted, growing ever more sick, as more and more brocos became schtuck in the schtick; smothered in sludgy, rotten, slickity-ick.

o o o o o o

At the water's edge, Alice and her knights sprang from the pirate ships to commence the ground assault along the western front, fighting not with their usual swords and staffs but with oversized stale bread sticks and sourdough baguettes.

VI – Storm

"Ahooo! Look! The salt from the pretzel bombs... it's irritating their skin," called out one of the guards.

"More salt!" yelled Alice. "Pass the message to all the troops! Salt is the key!"

At the same time, from the north came a great crashing of trees and bushes. With the Boogie chief clinging fast to his shoulder, Chester the giant came bounding down from Fallshugger Ridge, smashing everything in his path. As he reached the valley floor, howling with delight, he found enormous blooms of broccoli sitting like teed-up golf balls on top of their long stalks. The jolly giant rejoiced in booting the vegetables across the fields and into the heart of Gambrinstown. In this way he'd found a cathartic outlet for his pent-up frustration at having been put to sleep for so many years. After such a considerable nap, once he got moving, he discovered that he was overflowing with energy!

oooooo

The riotous onslaught coming at the Gambrine from all directions was absolutely overwhelming. Never before in Arcania had an invasion like this been conceived, let alone carried out. Champion Valley was, after all, a mostly peaceful place. Accordingly, the Gambrine's military regiments were ill-prepared and out-of-sorts, especially during the season of sowing, which was historically very peaceful, what with communities coming together to help in the planting of seeds and all. On the morning of the great battle, the Gambrine's weapons were stowed and their

VI – Storm

armaments unmanned, and so Ingonyama's invasion went almost entirely uncontested as the food piled up, around, and on top of the flailing brocosmiles.

On any given day, the Gambrine might experience the odd crop raid by wandering scoundrels. Some brocosmiles working in far-away fields late at night might stay a hair more vigilant against possible rogue Worst beasts lurking in the bushes. Sure, they had to remember not to accidentally start reciting poetry while pulling weeds, lest they attract a hungry Banzakoot. Other than all that, Gambrinstown was quite safe — that is, if you happened to be a Gambrine. Visitors were not so welcomed. Then how did a dentist end up in the Gambrine village, one might ask? Indeed, that was the question on the mind of everyone fighting for Manny that day.

oooooo

The lion's strategy was first to create utter chaos by throwing everything they had at the Gambrine: fruits, vegetables, grains, fungi... Even old, moldy cheeses and chunks of curdled pudding were hurled into the fray to add an extra element of yuck.

The pirates, meanwhile, ever seaward-thinking, tossed some fish they'd caught during the voyage over. The seafood, unlike much of the other stuff being thrown, was perfectly fresh, and brocosmiles love fresh fish, perhaps above all other food, including broccoli! With sardines,

VI – Storm

salmon, and sea bass now on the menu, holy mackerel was there ever a feeding frenzy!

The 'shock and awe' campaign was unfolding like clockwork. Once the Gambrine were sufficiently confused and distracted, the boot brigade worked to surround Manny with a moat of mushy macaroni while Chester made his way to snatch the dentist from captivity. Easy as pie.

(Heads up! Flying pie comin' through!)

But, just as the giant was closing in on Manny's position, something unexpected ensnared Chester's attention. He stopped, turned ninety degrees to the right, and began walking briskly away from the farm fields in the direction of Gambrinstown, sniffing the air as he went, like a bloodhound suddenly catching a scent.

"Chester!" yelled Sandovar, still fixed to the giant's shoulder. "What are you doing?!" The giant didn't answer; he just kept sniffing the air and twitching his nose like Ingonyama's little mouse. "Chester! We have to get down there to save Manny! Chester!!" Even the witches, still flying in formation around the giant, tried getting through to him, but Chester wasn't listening to anyone. Like a rat called by the Pied Piper, Chester the giant stumbled from the battlefield and marched right into the beating heart of Gambrinstown. A speck on the giant's shoulder, Sandovar considered abandoning his ride, but there was no safe way to get down from such a height. So, the chief just held on and watched the witches in the air and his fighting comrades on the ground, fade into the distance, unsure of what would be waiting for him in the Gambrine capital, other than a city full of irate brocosmiles.

VI – Storm

oooooo

As the fight closed in on Manny's position, Delilah's crew feverishly tossed fistfuls of fettuccini, bucketfuls of bucatini, and tankfuls of tagliatelle over her bow, doing whatever they could to create a barrier around the dentist. Meanwhile, two brazen brocos, seeing where the conflict was headed — literally and figuratively — ran directly into the fray, braving the milieu of marinara, and swiftly snatched the dentist from where he was eagerly awaiting his rescue.

Manny looked up at the flying shoe passing overhead, locked eyes with Captain Fickleface, and cried out, "Fickles! Hellllp meeee!" as the two Gambrine goons dragged him away. Fickles' eyes grew red with rage, and he tore at the Festoon's laces, desperately trying to position Delilah for another bombing run, barking at his crew to, "Put everything we have in front of those brocosmiles! Cut them off!! Stop them from escaping!!!"

The crew responded without delay. Like the chiming bells of Notre Dame, the wooden catapults of the Flying Festoon rang out a blitzkrieg of feed, fodder, lunch, and larder. And as the airborne smörgåsbord choked the skies, scavenger sea birds began flocking to the mess, adding to the chaos. Gulls, petrels, and terns swarmed, followed by their larger cousin, the giant albatross. Fickles had to swerve to avoid colliding with the birds and keep the Festoon afloat. Jolted by something other than a bird — and other than Fickles' mad zig-zag steering, making everyone aboard feel ill — Delilah rocked and churned uncontrollably, tossing her crew like corn kernels popping in a pan. *BANG! BOOM!*

VI – Storm

POP! Delilah was hit again and again. Stumbling, Ingo grasped the side of the ship and looked overboard to see what was attacking them. Catapults lining the forest's edge were flinging huge broccoli crowns into the air as fast as the Gambrine could load them.

"They're firing back!" he yelled, as if his mates weren't already aware.

"We need to set 'er down!" Picklepots yelled. "We'll be blasted out of the sky!"

"Fickles! Pots is right!" cried Tickletoes. "The Festoon ain't no fightin' bird. She's not built to withstand a proper broccoli beatin'!"

When a dark shadow passed overhead, blocking out the light trickling through the fog, food, fowl, and fray, the Festoon crew looked up to discover what was descending upon them. Did the Gambrine possess their own fleet of flying machines? Were they prepared for an air assault after all?? Could this be the end for Delilah and her crew???

"Look, look!" cried Shel, pointing at the massive shadow. "It's Charlotte!"

The pelican winked at Shel and his shipmates before snatching a few broccoli bombs out of midair before they smashed into the boot. Two other pelicans joined in and together, their large mouths served as safety nets protecting the ship from incoming projectiles. Charlotte and her fellow pelicans flew in tight formation, encircling Delilah, catching broccoli crowns then dropping them over the catapults, giving the brocosmiles a taste of their own medicine. "You'd

VI – Storm

better get out of here before you're knocked out of the sky," she warned Fickleface before cutting sharply starboard to intercept another round of ordinance coming in hot.

"Phew! We're saved!" cried Pickles.

"Yeah, I thought we were in trouble! Figured we'd be grounded for sure! But ol' Jezebel flies again!" yelled a triumphant Tickletoes — who, it turned out, spoke too soon as a massive broccoli ball blasted through the floorboards of Delilah, leaving a gaping hole in her sole. Stunned, the bootaneers peered through the opening. Below, the Gambrine waved and smiled up at them, celebrating.

"Uh oh!" Picklepots assessed the hole pessimistically.

"That's not good!" Tickletoes agreed. Clearly Delilah concurred, swaying back and forth as if knocked silly.

"Nope. Not good at all!" concluded Fickleface with a final prognosis. He glanced at the lion with distress. "Sorry, Yams, looks like we're going to have to set 'er down... and fast... 'for she loses all her beautiful buoyancy."

Charlotte and her pelican regiment continued to circle the shoe, doing what they could to help, but it was clear they would be out of work soon and so they readied to retire. "She's asking to be set on solid ground!" called Charlotte to the crew, assessing the ship while snagging more incoming projectiles as she passed, doing what she could to make their impending disaster less disastrous.

VI – Storm

The lion grumbled, "Hmmm, all right then," and scratched his beard, trying to keep a cool head despite the mounting chaos. "Where's Manny now?"

Pickles quickly picked up the spyglass while Shel rushed to the bow to have a look around. Meanwhile, Tickles posted up on the deck of the ship, lying flat on her belly, sticking her head out of the gaping hole.

"Careful, Ticks," warned the captain. "Wouldn't want ya fallin' through. Might be the last we ever see of ya." Tickles backed away from the opening and grinned sheepishly at her brother.

"I don't see nothin'!" cried Pickles, squinting through the Evil Eye.

Fickles looked over, rolled his eyes, and wiped a glob of marinara from the lens. "There. Give that a try."

"Oh! Much better!" said Pickles, staring through the spyglass right at Fickles' face. "Have you always had that mole on your cheek?"

"PICKLES!" yelled Fickles and Tickles in unison.

"Manny's gone!" called Shel. "There's just a huge pile of noodles and glop down there."

"Oh no! We buried 'im alive!" yelled Tickletoes.

"Hey! There's Izzy and Alice and the king's guard!" Shel spotted friendly troops heading to where the Gambrine had set up the bulk of their defenses. The sheer number of brocosmiles was frightening. Despite the pelicans' best

VI – Storm

efforts, Delilah was slowly but surely being blasted out of the sky.

"See if you can land the ship as close as possible to those catapults," Ingo called to the captain. "Shel and I will join forces with Alice and Izzy while you three try and find Manny." Fickles nodded, maneuvering Delilah into position using the control ropes.

Ingo located Charlotte zigging and zagging through the obstacles filling the sky, and with a nod he thanked her and her friends for their valiant effort and acknowledged that the birds would be of little help now that the air attack was coming to an end. And so, Charlotte and her companions turned sharply back toward Champion Lake, their fight in the battle now over. "We'll have to finish this fight on foot!" Ingonyama roared. Seeing the look of fear in Shel's eyes, he comforted his young friend. "Do not be afraid, Shelby. Stay close to me. I will protect you!"

"Delilah, get us down there!" Fickles called to his ship. The captain was in a mad fit at seeing how close they were to getting his friend back. He yanked on the laces and, just like when Shel first landed in the Festoon back in Chicago, the ship pitched hard and began to roll upside-down.

"Ficks! We're going to crash!" yelled Ingo.

"Trust me!" Captain Fickleface called to his crew as they flipped through the air. Clearly he knew something they did not. A contingency escape plan for just such a catastrophe is, after all, the province of any good captain. Fickles reached into his coat and pulled out what looked like a bottle rocket. Holding it out toward his chef, he instructed,

VI – Storm

"Pickles, if you please?" The chef knew just what to do. With the book of matches he always carried in his pocket (a good chef is always prepared to light a cooking fire) he ignited the fuse then quickly plugged his ears and clenched his eyes. With hands full of ropes and rockets, Captain Fickles had no fingers left to spare, so Tickletoes made the sacrifice and stuck her fingers in her captain's ears. The valiant gesture was unnecessary, however, for when the rocket exploded into the air, it released but a gentle whistle — loud, sure, but melodiously attractive. That was, after all, precisely its purpose. The lovely sound, together with the brilliant red and green flashes from the explosion, worked their magic. Everyone in the vicinity stopped for a moment to gawk at the fireworks, oooo-ing and ahhhh-ing as if rehearsed.

"Now when I say jump, everyone let go uh the ship n' jump! Got it?!"

The boot was heading straight for the Gambrine catapults, forcing brocosmiles to scatter lest they be crushed like the Wicked Witch of the West (who, according to legend, was Wanda's third cousin). And speaking of Wanda... like genies from a bottle, a gaggle of witches suddenly appeared, having been signaled by Fickles' bottle rocket. The broomed bedlam encircled the descending boot, prompting Fickleface to yell, "JUUMMMP!!!"

As his comrades leapt from the careening Festoon, the witches, like spiders catching flies in midair, snagged the falling sailors, securing them atop their brooms. One-by-one, Ingo, Shel, Fickles, Pickles, and Tickles found themselves saved from disaster. Sadly, the same could not be said for their ship.

VI – Storm

CRASH! CLANG! BANG! BOOM!

Delilah came down right atop the Gambrine catapults, smashing the ramparts into splinters. The great flying shoe didn't fare much better. When Delilah finally came to rest, she took one last breath, her massive hull expanding then contracting, before going still and silent.

"DELILAH!! No!!!" cried Captain Fickleface, hovering just above the wreckage on the back of Wanda's upright vacuum — no brooms for that batty, old hag.

"Oh, no!" sobbed Picklepots, tears in his eyes as he flew by in what seemed like slow motion. The witches dropped him and Fickleface in a swamp of squash before flying off to engage in the escalating battle. Shel and Tickletoes, meanwhile, were set down in a nearby nest of noodles. Shel immediately had to restrain Tickletoes as she struggled to get back to Delilah to comfort her dying friend.

"There's no use," reasoned Shel. "She's gone!" But Tickles wasn't listening. "Tickletoes!" cried Shel. "Don't waste Delilah's sacrifice! We need to get Manny. Stick to the mission, Tick! We came here to save your friend, remember?! Delilah can be rebuilt but Manny can't. Tickles!" Heeding his words, Tickletoes crumpled in Shel's arms and wept.

Meanwhile, Izzy, together with Alice and the king's guard, fought their way toward the wreckage, to make sure everyone was alive and okay. But as the rescue mission surrounded the crash site, an army of brocosmiles surrounded the rescuers. The enemy was closing in.

Chapter Seven

The Search

"Hold 'em off!" cried a voice from above. "We need time to find Manny! He's buried somewhere under that mound of pasta!" Ingo was still leading the offensive from his new battle station, zooming above the fray on the back of Katya's willow-branch broom…

VII — The Search

A rusty voice rang out in response. "Arrr! If ye need be findin' buried treasure, a pirate be the right bloke fer the job!"

Ingo looked down from his perch. "Taud! Morty! ...And... Blackbeard?! Jarbison?! What are you doing here? I thought the captains were going to stay with the ships!?"

"Aye, that they were, but ships be damned!" replied Blackbeard. "Our hearties be in trouble, they be. And a pirate never leaves his mates tuh hang."

"Even if they be dry landlubbers! *Har, har, har!*" added Taudello, letting loose his indomitable laugh for all to hear; a deep rumble echoing through the valley, lightening the hearts of Ingo's army, dispiriting the enemy.

"Buhsides," snarled Jarbison, "the ships' cannons already clobbered the western flank. Ain't no targets left within range."

Ingo grinned. "Well, all right then! You pirates get to digging. Find that dentist! I'll help Alice hold off the Gambrine as long as we can. Set me down just there!" Ingo called to Katya, and so she did.

Once on the ground, Ingo grabbed all the fruit and vegetables he could carry and began lobbing them like grenades at the incoming brocos, before bolting like a hurricane to where Alice and her troops were fighting at the front. Jumping into the chaos of battle, the lion immediately began wrestling with the crocs, tumbling and flipping and rolling about in the slop, setting the example for others to follow.

VII — The Search

The food was still flying in a frenzy but no longer from high in the air. The ground assault was in full swing. Ripe, red tomatoes were a favorite given the magnificent *splish* that resulted when exploding over the face of one's opponent, the gooey red juice giving the fight a more authentic feel.

In contrast to the rotten vegetables being thrown by the invaders, the raw broccoli being tossed by the Gambrine didn't feel so soft. But that was the only projectile they had. Luckily for the invaders, the Gambrine didn't use advanced weaponry like guns and bombs. Instead, they preferred catapults and spears. They also had, however, a whole lot of sharp teeth and claws at their disposal. *YOUCH!*

Who knows why, but the Gambrine have always been naturally talented in the martial arts. Hand-to-hand combat against a brocosmile is almost always a losing proposition. For veteran warriors like Alice, however — who was handy with almost any weapon, even a stale loaf of bread — dispatching one broco after the other was only slightly more taxing than a brisk hike up the Champion Mountain range.

And then there was Izzy, a full-grown elephant with a nearly impenetrable hide (though the Gambrine were certainly trying to penetrate it). Izzy couldn't really grasp a weapon, having no fingers, but he didn't have to; he had tusks for moving things aside, other animals included. Though he preferred to use it for pondering life's curiosities, his thick head was pretty useful for ramming things. It was his massive body that proved the handiest, however, as he shoved (as gently as possible) his adversaries left and right, like a bowling ball knocking down pins, one after the other.

VII — The Search

If the Gambrine didn't leap out of the way of the pachyderm express, they were launched out of the way.

"Wahoo!" some would yell as they sailed through the air, enjoying the free ride.

The battle was proving a rather welcome change of pace for some of the Gambrine. It was more excitement than most had seen in ages. And since a good deal of the fighters were only getting entangled, buried, or otherwise overwhelmed by food scraps, as opposed to the more serious injuries commonly sustained on a battlefield, there was very little grief or sorrow involved. The biggest casualty that day was the Gambrine ego, and that's not necessarily a bad thing. This was, after all, war in Arcania, and war in Arcania need not be violent. Indeed, it ought not to be. In fact, a passage commemorating the battle would later be added to the Harvest Hymn, the anthem sung at the opening of each Champion Valley harvest season.

T'was some good, ol-fashioned food-tossin',
Swamp-shakin', double-crossin',
Slop-wrestlin', fruit-fineselin',
Get-down on the farm!

Do-si-do atop ol' spaghetti,
Toss a peach, it's compost confetti!
Cut loose, go wild, n' have no fear!
Smush a banana in yer partner's ear!

It smelled so wrong but felt so right;
Sure had-a-lotta fun at the ol' food fight!

o o o o o o

VII — The Search

"How's it coming?" the lion called to the pirates, who'd been joined by Shel and the boot crew, all digging like mad, trying to find Manny under the pile of pasta.

"Arrr! Does yer dentist friend be havin' a long, fluffy backside?" asked pirate Mortimer, holding up what appeared to be a large, furry tail.

Speechless, Ingo squinted at Morty while keeping a large paw wrapped around a brocosmile's mouth. (One thing's for sure, you don't want to let a broco's massive mouth clamp down on you if you can avoid it.) The lion shook his head in disbelief as Morty yanked on the tail, pulling what was attached to it out from the tangle of noodles. Sadly, it wasn't the dentist. But happily, it was the dentist's philosophy-loving friend: that big, fat cat; old mister Buddha Baggs!

Izzy did a double take, skidding to a halt and jaw dropping to the ground when he saw Baggs dangling from Morty's hand. As soon as he stopped, a gang of brocosmiles jumped on his back, trying to bring the great pachyderm down. But Izzy simply shook like a wet dog, sending the brocos, like drops of water, flying in all directions.

It was at that moment when a great commotion erupted in the distance, followed by a harangue of shrieks, wails, and cries. Izzy, Shel, Fickles, and everyone else, turned to see a mass of brocosmiles and Ingo's troops alike, scattering, fleeing something. A figure, impossible to make out, was moving through the crowd. Izzy knew straight away it must be a Worst beast. It must've been alerted by the ruckus of battle, which, no doubt, could be heard in every corner of the valley. It made perfect sense! Of course a Worst

VII — The Search

would show up to take advantage of the chaos. Whether rotten fruit, animal, or human, finding a meal in this mess would be like shooting fish in a barrel for a Worst. There was no time to lose!

"RUUUNNN!" cried Izzy. "Save yourself!"

Shel started to follow his friend but stopped when something familiar in his periphery ensnared his attention. "Hang on." Shel squinted at the approaching terror. "Can it be??" He squinted harder until the thing became clear. "Oh my gosh, it is! It's them! Izzy! It's them!"

Izzy froze mid-bolt. "What?? Them? Them who?!?" Izzy looked back at where the Worst would've been, but the beast wasn't there. In its place were three, mostly regular-sized folks, small compared to an adult Worst... or an elephant. Thus, Izzy's fear diminished. "That's not a Worst!" he announced to the crowd around him, quelling the fear he'd just incited. "Are those your friends, Shelby? The ones you told me about?"

"Izzy, those are my friends! The ones I told you about!" Shel repeated, paying scant attention to the elephant, let alone his rolling eyes.

Walking casually — one might even say strolling — through the crowd, scattering creatures left and right with naught but their looks, came Karl the ghoul, Dracula the vampire, and Walter the werewolf... pushing a red bicycle.

"Hey! Shelby!" Walter waved from a distance. "We brought your bike back! Heard you were in the neighborhood, so we thought we'd swing on by." Walter

VII — The Search

spoke as if there wasn't a war going on, not a care in the world. And why should they care? The three of them together were the most fearsome gang in Arcania. To be fair, a gang of a Worst, a Banzakoot, and a storm dragon would be far more dangerous and terrifying, but those monsters worked alone. These three on the other hand could paralyze a victim with a bite from poisonous fangs, then eat the poor soul alive, bones and all, and then haunt them in the afterlife... if they wanted, which they most certainly did not!

"Heya, Shel! How's it?!" greeted a friendly Karl. "Everything good with you?" It was as if they couldn't even *see* the battle raging on around them.

"Uh, hi guys!" said Shel, doing his best to pretend he wasn't amidst a heap of swirling chaos. "Yeah, I'm okay. Just, you know, fighting a war with the Gambrine. No big deal." Shel smiled smartly.

Izzy chuckled, till a succession of grapes pelted the side of his head like rapid fire from a fully-automatic machinegun — *zap zap zap zap zap!* — prompting him to bolt in the direction of the assailant. "I'll get you for that!" he yelled, stampeding through a mess of noodles and smiling brocosmiles.

"Soooo, you guys come to help us fight? Orrrr..." Shel queried, holding out an abandoned rake he'd found lying on the ground.

"Oh, no, probably not," replied Dracula. "We don't really go in for that aggressive stuff so much these days; had our fair share of battles over the years; the many, many years... eternal souls and all. Besides, you may've noticed,

VII — The Search

we don't exactly have to fight. Our mere presence typically does the job. Sometimes a stereotype works in your favor. Haha!"

"Hey Drac!" called Walter. "Looks like you may have been a bit hasty. Check it out!" Walter pointed to a gang of brocosmiles heading their way, clearly intending to confront the paranormal pack, likely concluding — after witnessing their relatively docile attitude — that the monsters weren't as threatening as they looked. It didn't take long, however, for the brocos to realize their mistake. One loud roar from each monster was sufficient to send the Gambrine fleeing for their lives.

Farther away, another Gambrine platoon pushed their way to the center of the fight. Unlike most of the brocos fighting in the fields that day, however, this group was well-organized, well-armed, and led by what looked to be an armored tank.

Without warning, the tank stopped and stood on its back legs, revealing itself to be not a tank at all but a massive brocosmile, larger than any other, indeed larger than any animal Shel had ever seen in his life, save for the storm dragon. The dragon, by contrast, was bolstered by the power of the tumultuous sea, able to grow big as tidal waves. This beast came from the land and stood entirely on its own, for her own might was enough.

The broco tank paused when she reached the top of a hill of noodles, turning in a slow circle, surveying with a scowl the wreckage spreading over her land. Then, growing even bigger, she raised her arms, displaying a fearsome set of claws, and bellowed, "STAAAAAAWP!"

VII — The Search

Upon hearing her voice ringing across the land like an air raid siren, vibrating through the air and the ground in subsonic tremors — as was the Gambrine method of communicating over long distances — nearly all fighting came to immediate arrest. Food fighters everywhere froze in battle poses like wax figurines, daring not to move.

Surrounded by her royal guards, the Gambrine High Chancellor stood on her hill of noodles rising above the landscape, sizing up Ingo's army. She was darker and bore far more scars than any of her kinfolk, looking as if she'd clawed her way, tooth and nail, to the top. This monster struck fear into the heart of every one of the invaders, save maybe for Alice (whose absolute lack of fear incited many a rumor that she was actually a cyborg with literal nerves of steel — an absolutely ridiculous notion, of course).

The Gambrine leader, whose family name was Hume (a shortened version of Humungor, the original Gambrine clan who settled the Valley a thousand years prior, give or take) bellowed like the horn of a cargo tanker on the ocean, "WHO IS RESPONSIBLE FOR THIS TRANSGRESSION?! This OFFENSIVE invasion! Show yourself! I demand RECONCILLIATION! I demand JUSTICE!"

Her ability to stop the war on command was beyond impressive. Even Ingo thought so. Everyone did. A deafening grave silence settled over the fields, so absolute that when a flea on the western front sneezed, a caterpillar way over on the eastern flank replied, "Gesundheit!" In that moment of quiet, Shel sensed something, an inaudible buzzing in his bones, a whisper on the wind, nudging him to look down to his left.

VII — The Search

No, your other left!... Behind you!... Down here!

There in the food wasteland, looking like Sheldon when he was buried on the steps of the Kantytown palace, sticking out from under a pile of noodles and nectarines, broccoli and beans, was a hand.

As the moment of silence passed and Chancellor Hume resumed her demands of this, that, and the other, Shel's eyes widened, watching the hand twitch. He dared not move, however, lest he attract the attention of the reptilian tank, not more than twenty yards away. *She's as big as a house*, Shel thought. *Like the Worst beast... but bigger!*

Without taking his peripheral sight off the buried hand, Shel reached to his right and snatched Captain Fickles' shirt sleeve. Like everyone else, Fickles' attention was glued to the enormous brocosmile belting out a harangue of insults and ultimatums from her high post. Shel's incessant tugging was as a tenacious mosquito, irritating and unwelcome.

"What?!" Fickles whisper-yelled, annoyed that Shel would risk drawing attention to them both. "What is it?" He bent his head only slightly, frowning sideways at his friend. Shel gestured with his head, pointing with his eyes to a spot on the ground behind them. Fickleface glanced backward but didn't see anything right off. Shel persisted so Fickles looked once more. Upon closer inspection, he recognized the familiar-looking hand sticking out of the spaghetti. The boot captain couldn't help but let a squeak slip out before he caught himself, two hands clapped over his mouth, eyes shifting rapidly to see who may have heard. The coast was

VII — The Search

clear. Fickles collected himself, reached over, and began tugging on Picklepots' shirt.

Pickles had the same, annoyed reaction. Obviously they should all be still and silent like obedient students at a classroom lecture. "Knock it off, Fick!" But then he too caught a glimpse of the hand, and also squealed with delight. His reaction not only caught the attention of Tickletoes who scowled at her brothers, goofing off when they most certainly ought not to be, it also caught the attention of some nearby brocosmiles.

"Will you guys pipe dowwww..." Tickletoes stuttered as she caught sight of the hand. "Oh my goodne—urmph!" A pile of hands from her brothers smothered her mouth as several nearby brocosmiles crept toward them, intent on squelching what appeared to be a rebellion in the making.

The commotion also caught the attention of Ingonyama, however, who quickly deduced that a distraction was in order. Fine timing too, since he, as the leader of the invasion, was being called out by the Gambrine High Chancellor.

"WHO IS IN COMMAND OF THIS ASININE ASSAULT? THIS EGREGIOUS ERROR? This... This DERANGED and DEPLORABLE directive?? This unthinkable, ugly, utterly.. Ugh! WHO IS IN CHARGE HERE?!"

"I AM!" Ingonyama boomed like a fifty-ton gong on a mountaintop, swiftly untangling himself from a pack of brocosmiles and standing tall. All creatures within earshot looked his way, including the gang of brocos approaching the boot crew. Adjusting his helmet snugly over his eyes and

VII — The Search

tucking his mane into the base of the cap — once again assuming the look of a military man, disguising his feline identity — he casually made his way through the tangle of noodles toward the chancellor, flicking food scraps from his suit as he went.

With the crowd enraptured by the impending confrontation between their respective military leaders, Shel and the boot brigade proceeded with their task in anonymity, albeit slowly, carefully, quietly. After a great deal of digging and scraping away food slop, they finally extracted, at long last, their old friend, Manny the missing dentist!

Chapter Eight

War and Peace

VIII — War and Peace

"I am the one you want!" With a final shoving aside of a few stray brocosmiles, Ingonyama approached the hill on which Chancellor Hume stood. At least a dozen brocos were working diligently, lining the tall mush mound with meatballs and mash, shoring up the chancellor's makeshift command post. Upon Ingo's declaration, four guards leapt from their construction tasks and slithered up to the lion, quickly binding his limbs with noodles. With two brocosmiles on each arm, Ingo the prisoner was escorted up Spaghetti Hill — the name given to the mound from where the high chancellor (as would be recorded in the Gambrine history books), "defended the Realm during the Great Battle of Champion Valley."

"Kneel, you scoundrel!" The guards tugged at Ingo's arms, pulling him toward the ground. "Bow before the high chancellor!"

Ingo's army erupted in protest, shouting and tossing food at the hill. It looked as though the tenuous peace would not hold. In response, Ingo twisted and spun like a martial arts master, effortlessly lowering his captors to the ground. He took a few long strides toward the colossal Hume, who looked large enough to eat Ingo in one bite. Her guards readied their spears, intending to perforate the aggressor, when he quickly turned to the crowd.

"Boogies! Stay your fighting! Alice, still your guards! Pirates, at ease my hearties!" The lion turned to the chancellor and with a bow of his head, dropped to one knee. "Your chancellorship. I take it the Gambrine are not in the mood for a good-humored, old-fashioned, friendly food fight?"

VIII — War and Peace

"Guards!" commanded the chancellor, and instantly Ingo was recaptured — though this time his hands were bound with more than mere pasta. Some dark green twine reinforced the noodles, twine that looked and smelled of broccoli (of course).

"Friendly? Food fight?!? GOOD HUMOR?!?! Is that your idea of a JOKE?! I am *NOT* laughing! How dare you attack our sovereign land! Who do you think you are?!" The chancellor paused long enough to give the rebel commander the idea it was his turn to speak.

"Your Highness, we have come—"

It wasn't.

"I don't care *why* you have come. It makes no difference *why* you have chosen to attack us. You think just because you've chosen, in place of cannons and swords, to use— What is this nonsense?" The chancellor bent down, picked up a handful of food scraps, "...Rotten vegetables?! You think that makes it—"

"Beg your pardon, Your Highness, but I think it does matter. If you would hear me out—"

"I WILL NOT! You can't erase what you've done here with mere words! The only thing that matters now is that we have you! All of you! You work for the Gambrine now! Every last one of you! You will clean up this disgraceful, repugnant mess; you will regrow the crops you've destroyed; and then you will work in our fields as our prisoners... for the remainder of your days! I hope it was worth it!" With that, the chancellor motioned to her guards to, 'take him away,'

VIII — War and Peace

and — confident she'd successfully squelched the invasion — turned to depart.

In defiance, Ingonyama lifted himself off the ground, refusing help from his captors, cleared his throat, "Ahem," and announced, "I'm not finished."

The chancellor whipped around. "Oh, you are most certainly finished!"

Ingo nonchalantly ignored the lashing out of Hume's ego — "We *will* help clean up the mess..." — once again effortlessly ripping apart his bonds, eliciting cheers from his audience. The Gambrine guards assumed fighting stances and the chancellor squared off, readying for an attack that never came. Instead, Ingo stayed calm, casually brushing invisible dirt from his clothes. "...And we will help replant your crops. But we will not be staying beyond that. In fact, some of us will be leaving immediately." He winked subtly at Shel standing just in front of the boot crew, a drooping dentist clinging to the shoulders of Fickles and Tickles. This was their cue. Shel turned and nodded to Fickles, who nodded at his compadres, and they very slowly began shuffling their way through the soggy noodles, dragging Manny, who looked like a soggy noodle himself. Unfortunately, they did not get far.

"Leaving?! I don't think so!" Retorted the chancellor. "Perhaps you weren't listening; this is your new home! You all work for the Gambrine now. No one is leaving."

Upon hearing those words, brocosmiles everywhere adopted aggressive stances, doing their best to look like barricades against any possible retreat. Manny and the boot

VIII — War and Peace

crew found themselves surrounded by brocos brandishing farming tools, blocking their escape. Of course Ingo noticed the blockade, as did Izzy and Alice. *But did Hume see?* Ingo wondered. *Does she know about the dentist?*

It was clear the lion and the crocodile were at a standoff. Ingo knew he had to be more persuasive or, at the very least, create another distraction so Shel and the Boot Brigade could press on. Thinking quickly, he snatched a spear from a nearby brocosmile, twirled it in a circle, snapped it across his thigh, and tossed the broken shards at the feet of the shocked and offended chancellor. He intended the gesture to be symbolic of breaking the Gambrine stronghold, breaking Chancellor Hume's illusion of control. Most everyone watching, however — eager for any excuse to resume the epic food fight — took it as a sign that the battle was back on. And so the food went flying once more, both Hume and Ingo ducking to avoid being splattered.

"THAT'S ENOUGH!" The chancellor roared, resuming control. She raised an enormous claw, halting a good majority of her troops. "Enough of this *nonsense*! Everyone!" Once again the fighters froze. She took a few steps toward the lion, looming over the defiant brute, baring a mouthful of giant, pointed teeth. "I know your type, commander. You're the sort of malefactor that throws a stone at a window just to see if it's open!"

Ingo risked a quick glance in the direction of the boot crew and was immediately relieved to see the gang able to continue their retreat with Izzy clearing a path. Returning his attention to the chancellor, Ingo shrugged and bobbed

VIII — War and Peace

his head. "I've been known to throw a few stones in my day. Strike first and ask questions later, I always say."

Somewhere in the crowd Walter nodded at Karl bitterly. "He's clearly been spending too much time with humans."

Karl rolled his 'eyes'.

"I figure," Ingo continued, "It's better to ask for forgiveness than to ask for permission. Isn't that right my friends?!" Ingo addressed Alice and his fighters and they responded with cheers.

The chancellor's belly grumbled in distaste for the commander's audacity. "Hmmm. I, myself, have a slightly different version. *EAT* them first and ask questions later." She growled with a sinister smile and took a step toward the lion.

Ingo gulped. Though he knew the Gambrine weren't the sort to go around eating other creatures, they certainly could if they wished; this one especially. Hume had the most dangerous reputation of all, one that matched her intimidating size.

"Well, go on then," she challenged, "ask for forgiveness," adding in a slow growl, "see how that goes for you!"

Ingonyama straightened his back. "I think perhaps we'll skip that bit and get to the part where we negotiate peace terms. Shall we?"

VIII — War and Peace

"Peace?! You speak of peace, you war-mongering miscreant?! We *were* at peace before you INVADED!" Her farmers cheered in agreement.

"Ah, but that's not entirely true, is it?" Ingo roared above the crowd and the cheers calmed. "For how can you rest peacefully when the feathers that fill your bed have been plucked from stolen geese?"

The chancellor squinted.

"Three geese to be exact," Ingo clarified.

Hume scowled at the cheeky military man spouting riddles, wasting her time. Meanwhile, more Gambrine poured into the fields from the village as word spread that an invasion had been thwarted by the chancellor herself. Noting the engorged crowd, the chancellor rallied. "I don't know what you're playing at with your goose-feather gibberish, but as you can see, you're vastly outnumbered. Give up without any more of this food-fighting ridiculousness and we'll make sure you and your friends have a comfortable stay at the Gambrinsluk bed and breakfast."

(Of course, Gambrinsluk was no bed and breakfast. It was quite the opposite, known as the worst prison in Arcania: cold, dark, wet, stone cells, buried deep under the broccoli fields at the edge of Gambrinstown.)

Unafraid of the chancellor's threats, Ingo laughed. "You really have no idea who *we* are, do you?" With an outstretched, gloved finger, he pointed. "That there is Lady Alice, the most formidable knight in King Longsmiles' army.

VIII — War and Peace

Were she here alone she could vanquish fifty of your fearsome brocos."

"Ah, but there aren't fifty of us!" roared the chancellor. "There are five hundred! And more on the way."

Ingo nodded, "Indeed," though he knew the chancellor was exaggerating her numbers. "And just the same, Alice is not alone, she has her king's army at her side, with more standing by at our ships just over the hill, down at the harbor... and a thousand more who could be here tomorrow."

"Tomorrow! Ha! By then we'll have—"

"And she has Ingonyama!" the soldier interrupted with a blast. "The famous rifleman... who never misses his target. Perhaps you've heard of him?"

"Ingonyama?! The sharpshooting lion?" the chancellor replied, visibly shaken but trying to keep calm. Everyone in Arcania knew of Ingo's reputation as the most formidable warrior in the land. "That lion died a long time ago. That or he's long since departed these lands. Either way, no one's seen hide nor hair of that cat in years." Hume was distracted but doing her best to hide it, to believe her own words.

"He's here," replied Ingo. "I assure you. And closer than you think."

"Where then?! You're bluffing! He's hiding somewhere... In the bushes, perhaps?!" The chancellor looked around uneasily. "Show yourself you cowardly lion!" She shouted at the surroundings.

VIII — War and Peace

Ingonyama laughed from behind his uniform disguise. "Cowardly? Ha! Sounds like you have him confused with that stuttering dandy lion from our neighbor town, the merry old land of Oz. Arcania's version, I assure you, is no coward. In fact, he's standing right before you!"

Ingo swiftly removed his helmet and shook out his mane with a menacing growl. A tremendous gasp shot through the crowd. Several nearby brocosmiles jumped. Some even turned and ran. The chancellor herself nearly fell over backward. The Gambrine were up against the ropes, if only momentarily.

"Now that I have your attention... Hume!" Ingo proceeded, knowing full well that no one ever dared use the chancellor's given name. But Ingo also knew that his best option was to unsettle the formidable brocosmile, get under her skin, force her to make a mistake. Seeing her falter at the sight of him, then shutter at hearing her name, Ingo pressed his advantage. "That's right. I know who you are, Francis Pretmore Hume." The chancellor writhed, digging her claws into the surrounding food. "I know all about you and your insatiable pursuit of perfection. Nothing's ever good enough for Hume, is it? But, what I'm about to tell you is the best offer you're going to get. So, will you hear me out? Will you consider my proposal? Or will you choose all-out war and the destruction of Gambrinsville?"

The chancellor stared with daggers in her eyes. "The destruction of... hmpf! Is that your proposition, lion? Tell me, do you know what happened to the last visitor who arrived unannounced and uninvited, laden with his own proposal? He even dared to call himself a caretaker of the

VIII — War and Peace

Gambrine. A caretaker! How precious! Well... I ate him! Pipe and all! Poor mister Fredrick; tasty young chap with a fancy derby cap." The chancellor took a few measured steps toward the lion. "And do you know what happened to the next fellow who stopped by, demanding his lost cat, if you can believe that?"

Ingo risked another peek at the escaping boot crew, now a good distance away, Manny still clinging to the bootaneers like a soggy cape. The dentist was worn down but still very much alive. Still very much *not* eaten.

"As a matter of fact, I do," Ingo replied defiantly. "He's over yonder, in the care of my good friends. I believe you know the Flying Boot Brigade."

"WHAT?!" The chancellor spun around, following Ingo's eyes, aghast at seeing her prisoner in the hands of the enemy.

oooooo

Now, the Boot Brigade was not an actual enemy of the Gambrine, nor anyone else for that matter, at least not before the Battle of Champion Valley. The flying shoe crew had always been respectful of the Gambrine, at least their crop. If brocosmiles had friends — which they did not — the shoe fliers might have been considered among them. But after this little stunt, they would be lucky to ever be invited to the annual broccoli harvest festival again. Not that guests were ever really *invited* per se. During the festival, the

VIII — War and Peace

Gambrine would just sort of scuttle off and disappear back to their huts or caves or wherever they called home, making way for the greater Champion Valley community to trespass in the fields for a few days, harvest whatever broccoli they so desired, and leave handsome payments in honor buckets hanging throughout the farm. If no payment was left, the Gambrine would surely find out. Somehow they always found out if anyone failed to pay. But the Boot Brigade always left full payment, plus tip. And so they were always welcomed back, year after year; given priority notice in fact. But that was before the war.

As for Buddha Baggs, Manny's cat, it was a rare exception indeed for anyone to have been tolerated as long as he was — what with his aimless wandering through the fields without care; reclining on the grass, puffing smoke rings in the air; waxing philosophically till the day was well done; all while watching brocos slave away in the hot sun...

The Gambrine were known to be highly communal creatures, but only with their own kind. Baggs being allowed such liberty was a testament to the fact that he was so calm and peaceful, so curious and personable, so darned cute and fluffy!

oooooo

"STOP THEM!" Hume hollered, pointing at her escaping prisoner in the clutches of the boot crew. Her army, however, had no idea to whom she was referring, and so they just scrambled about, doing their darndest to stop someone

VIII — War and Peace

from doing something. As a result — and because the onlookers were bored listening to the two commanders swapping insults — the food fight resumed, much to the delight of nearly everyone; everyone except Hume.

Ingonyama knew he had Hume unhinged. His plan had always been to create chaos, and here was more chaos erupting. Now was not the time to let up.

"And in case you hadn't noticed the others in our party, chancellor," the lion continued, "we've brought with us the most feared pirate fleet in all the seven seas! Now, I concede that, like Ingonyama," he placed a paw over his own chest, "this man is hard to recognize, what with being clean shaven and all..." He stroked his own fluffy beard then pointed to the crowd, identifying a figure standing tall and menacing in all-black robes and bottomless black eyes. "But that man there is none other than the ruthless Blackbeard!" Gasps rang out, exactly the reaction Ingo was hoping for, expecting even. "And somewhere near Blackbeard... where is my good man?" Ingo squinted into the crowd. "Somewhere... is another black-hearted sea devil... Blackbeard, where's Hook?"

Blackbeard shrugged.

"Hook?!" The chancellor stammered. "As in *Captain* Hook??"

"The very same!" replied Ingo with a smile, confident that this news would further unsettle the chancellor. And it did... at first.

VIII — War and Peace

Hume stumbled and fell back into her makeshift 'throne' of broccoli, meatballs, melon, and celery. There she sat, looking around intensely, searching for the one called Hook, her fated nemesis. (Somewhere in the distance a ticking clock could be heard echoing on the wind.)

"I... haven't heard that name in...," she sputtered. The momentary shock dissipated and Ingo watched, to his dismay, as a sinister grin swept across Hume's enormous mouth. She collected herself, diminishing Ingo's advantage.

"Hooook... Yes, I think I recall him..." the chancellor growled, shifting in her throne to get comfortable. "Where is he then? Show yourself, Hook!" she spat at the crowd. "Is he also wearing a disguise? I might not recognize your face... it has been many years indeed. But I'd never forget that stench; the stink of worn-out, salt-soaked leather and fear! ...And there's something else," she feigned confusion. "Something else about you I'd never forget... What was it?? Oh, yes! Your TASTE!" Hume snarled, licking her chops! "I think I still have bits of your hand stuck in my molars... Someone bring me that dentist!" she blasted furiously. But Manny was well on his way to the pirate ships, unbeknownst to Hume. "Where are you, Hook?! Come out and face me!" she challenged. "I'm going to have my teeth cleaned and polished, ready to devour the rest of you, you pitiful pirate!"

Ingonyama was caught entirely sideways by this development, no notion that Hume and Hook had history. "Blackbeard," Ingo whispered as discretely as he could then shrugged his shoulders, silently asking, 'Where is Hook?'

Looking as dangerous as ever, mouth twisted in a snarl, baguette swords clenched in fists ready for more

VIII — War and Peace

brawling, Blackbeard whisper-yelled back, "Arrr! Stayed with the ships he did. Said he's against crocs uh any kind. Can't abide 'em, won't go near 'em. Said he'd man the cannons fer when things need blastin', an' the sails fer when folks need escapin'."

Ingo was stunned. He could sense a sudden, unexpected shift of power, could almost see his advantage slipping through his fingertips. The Chancellor sensed it too. She scratched her way out of her throne and stood tall to receive the dentist. Except Manny didn't reach Spaghetti Hill because the boot crew, thanks in large part to their elephant escort, never found their way back into the clutches of the Gambrine. Even if they had, Ingo was ready to defend Manny at any cost. Seeing that another distraction was in order but running low on options, he resigned to his fate as commander of the mission. "A captain must be prepared to go down with the ship," he muttered to himself, helping to gather his courage. Though he knew he could not win in a one-on-one fight against the chancellor — she was just too big — he leapt anyway.

With a mighty roar, Ingo launched himself through the air, landing squarely atop Chancellor Hume's shoulders. Instantly a frenzied wrestling match ensued, food scraps flying as the two commanders tumbled and thrashed about. The bold act reignited the food fight across the battlefield and the war was back on!

It didn't take long for Hume to subdue her attacker, however. Though he was fierce, her sheer size was impossible to overcome, especially in the slop where stable footing proved elusive.

VIII — War and Peace

"Such a shame," the chancellor snarled, pinning Ingo in the mire. "You've come back from the dead only to die again." She pushed him down into the noodle slop, a food-scrap sarcophagus, expiring the light of day as his head sunk below the surface. Each time he tried to take a breath his mouth filled with some rotten sauce or chunks of moldy mush. "This time I'm going to make sure you don't return. You should've never come here, lion. You should've known that I cannot be beaten. My Gambrine are too powerful! Now I'm going to teach you a lesson. I'm going to drown you in this filth of your own making." Hume rolled her body over Ingo, pressing her full weight into him. He would suffocate for sure... if he didn't drown first.

oooooo

Izzy, Shel, and the boot crew, who were by then a considerable distance from their commander, crested the last hill at the edge of the battlefield, ground no longer covered in food waste. Once Shel saw the pirate ships down at the harbor, he breathed a sigh of relief, a sentiment shared by the rest of the party. They'd persevered! They'd gotten Manny out! Mission accomplished!

Shel turned with a smile back toward where Ingo was still wrestling with Hume. His smile faded.

What if Ingo lost the fight? Will Chancellor Hume, like the jungle king, make Ingo her dinner? No way! That couldn't happen! Shel couldn't let that happen. After all, he'd gotten Ingo, and everyone else, into this mess in the first place.

VIII — War and Peace

Well, to be fair, Manny had a lot to do with it, he argued to himself.

Okay, sure, but the mission to recover Manny was my idea!

Eh, that was the Boot Crew... and Izzy.

Right. Fine. But who pressed the mission forward, across the sea and sand, all the way to Kantcomplainistan? I did! And who insisted on freeing Ingo and—

Well, that was Joy, really.

Okay. You're right. But who came up with the plan to invade the Gambrine village?

Ingo. Remember?

Argh! So, what have I done then? What have I even contributed since coming to Arcania?

Time on the battlefield seemed to stop as Shel quarreled with himself, pondering his significance, or lack thereof. He realized there were many characters sharing the spotlight on the Arcania stage, a plethora of protagonists in this play; a tale woven by many lives, many adventures all crossing paths at this point in history.

We've contributed quite a bit, actually. But we don't have time to get into all of that. Right here, right now is a great opportunity for us to contribute.

But... how?

VIII — War and Peace

Ingo. He needs our help.

He does? Are you sure?

Have a look.

Shel squinted until Spaghetti Hill came into view. There he could see Chancellor Hume attacking something, clutching a body, burying it into the noodled earth beneath her.

"Ingo!" Shel cried aloud.

Exactly! He needs help, his inner voice encouraged. *Come on!*

But... Hume is... HUGE! We won't stand a chance! She's too powerful!

All the more reason to help. If we don't, then why are we even here? Why have we come to Arcania?

I don't know! I've been trying to figure that out since—

Oh, don't give me that nonsense. You know exactly why we're here!

He immediately thought of his parents, of his father.

Dad.

Yup. We already decided we're not going to let fear rule our fate, decided we're going to make our own destiny. Now it's time to prove it!

VIII — War and Peace

"Shel! What are you doing? Let's go!" Fickles yelled, shaking Shel out of his head.

Shel looked at the boot crew one by one. "We can't just leave him!"

"Who?! Ingo? He'll be fine," contended Picklepots. "That lion's a fighter like no other. Besides, he's just creatin' a distraction, givin' us a fightin' chance at gettin' Manny out! He knows eh'zactly what he's doin'."

"Yeah," agreed Tickletoes. "If we go back n'try'n help 'im, we'll only make things worse."

Fickles added, "He wouldn't uh exposed himself, puttin' 'imself in harm's way like that if it weren't part uh his master plan."

"I don't know." Shel hesitated. With his shirt being tugged by Fickles and his back being shoved by Pickles, they started to move. "No! I can't!" Shel snapped. "He needs help!" And without another word, he sprinted off in the direction of Ingo and the chancellor.

"Shel, no! Don't!" cried Izzy, but it was too late. He was off, lost to the maze of tangled-up noodle warriors.

"Come on, Tick. There's nothing we can do. We gotta get Manny to the boats," commanded Captain Fickles, and the four dwarves retreated. "Izzy? You coming?"

ooooo

VIII — War and Peace

"Hey!" a small voice cried out in the distance. "Hey, YOU!" The small voice was getting bigger, and though it had been far away, it was approaching fast, faster than any human or crocodile could go, and it was bouncing up and down furiously. "YOU LEAVE HIM ALONE!"

Suddenly, out from in front of the voice came a large round thing, flying through the air like a Hail Mary soaring over a football field. As the overripe fruit splattered across Chancellor Hume's head, Sheldon — the small, faraway voice that was no longer small and faraway — cried out, "ME FIRRRSSST!" with tremendous satisfaction, reveling in his tomato-tossing triumph.

"Steee-riiiike! Right down the pipe!" announced Izzy, delighting in the terrific tomato mess all over Hume's face.

Though she was blinded temporarily in one eye, it was hardly enough to incapacitate her. It was, however, enough to shift her attention from Ingonyama to the elephant and the boy, galloping toward her at breakneck speed. The chancellor raised her massive torso using Ingonyama's limp body to steady her footing. Rising to her full height, she let out a ferocious growl, her razor-tooth-filled mouth screwed up in a menacing snarl. She wiped the tomato from her eye and roared from her bottomless soul, shaking the ground, making all within earshot halt their fighting and look her way. She was, at that moment, the most horrifying thing Shel had ever seen — worse than the Worst beast, worse even than the storm dragon.

The Worst beast was wild, out of control, driven by hunger. Hume, on the other hand, was lethally calculating and driven by revenge. While the storm dragon was deadly

VIII — War and Peace

— make no mistake — it was also indifferent, unconcerned with the plight of its victims. The chancellor was deadly for the opposite reason. For her, this was personal. She sought not only to dominate her enemies, she wanted them to suffer. There she stood atop Spaghetti Hill, triumphantly poised over her motionless victim, a demon-like savage enshrouded in fury, fiery wrath ablaze in her volcanic, beady eyes. She stared with malice like a missile, locked onto a young man riding atop an elephant. A new adversary approached, and she was ready.

As Shel and Izzy drew near, both felt at once rapped with horror and empowered by an unexpected resolve to destroy the evil thing staring them down. Without giving it much thought — which was how Izzy made most all his decisions — the elephant reached his trunk to the ground and scooped up an apple. He tossed it up to Shel, "Shelby! Catch!" then reached down once more to snag himself a cantaloupe. "On three! Ready? One, two, THREE!!" They fired the fruit at the massive brocosmile with as much force as they could, hoping for... well, they didn't really know what hitting Hume with more rotten food would accomplish, but they had to do something. They had to try, for Ingo's sake.

Hume had no trouble dealing with the onslaught, however, for she was laser-focused and quick to react. She opened her enormous mouth, easily catching the projectiles. Then, with no regard for ripeness, she swallowed the mess whole, worms, mold, and all.

The last assault of Izzy and Shel wasn't a total loss, however, as it gave Shel an idea. He reached down and pulled something from his satchel just as Hume leaped from

VIII — War and Peace

her high post, mouth agape, intending to chomp down on Izzy or Shel or whatever got in her way. It didn't matter to Hume. She was in a mood to eat the world if it came to it. The world would have to wait, however, for first came the pie!

Shel cried out, "Bangarang!" invoking the spirit of Peter Pan as he tossed a homemade banana cream tart at the descending crocodile. (He'd baked the dessert because he'd heard it was her favorite and he wanted to do something nice to thank her, you know, for everything she'd done for everyone, and... No, not really. The tart had a special ingredient. This was Shel's secret weapon!)

Despite sailing through the air, Hume could, with her heightened senses, detect the ripe, creamy banana filling and sugary sweet crust coming her way. Sheldon's aim — thanks to years of tossing a baseball — was spot on, and the pastry flew right into the brocosmile's mouth. Even if it weren't aligned perfectly, she still would've snatched it easily, unable to resist the banana cream, her one weakness. Her jaws clamped down and that, as the saying goes, was all she wrote.

The 1922 Peter Pan peanut butter — the special pie-filling additive — went to work straight away. By the time she hit the ground (Izzy had taken one step to his right and Hume landed *SPLAT!* just to his left), her jaw was locked tight. The chancellor would not be chomping down on anything for a very long time. It wasn't all bad for Hume, however. Despite being disappointed at missing her mark, distraught at failing to conquer her enemies, and dizzy from the impact, Hume couldn't help but feel overwhelming

VIII — War and Peace

satisfaction at her tastebuds bursting with delight. As she lay on the ground, writhing in both frustration and ecstasy simultaneously, Shel's delectable treat worked its magic, literally. In addition to the dreaded peanut butter, Katya the witch had added a pinch of her own special ingredient: a potion designed to incapacitate — not by rendering the victim unconscious, but by inhibiting their motor functions, immobilizing them.

"What in the world?" Izzy stared at the zombified chancellor. "Did she just knock herself silly?"

"Fruit tarts," Shel replied with a grin. "It's the one thing I learned to make in my father's bakery. They're quite tasty, if you like that sort of thing. Turns out they're great for hiding secret potions and stuff." Shel kind of chuckled at the twitching brocosmile lying helpless on the ground. "I suppose once Manny's finished working on the king, they'll need him to come back to fix this one. That oughta be interesting." His thoughts quickly turned to Ingonyama. He leapt down off Izzy's back and scrambled up Spaghetti Hill, as fast as he could go. Izzy wasn't far behind, followed by Alice, Blackbeard, Taudello, and a smattering of Boogies and king's guards.

"Ingo!" cried Shel, rushing to where the lion lay buried beneath the mush. He began digging, doing his best to expose Ingonyama's face, to get air to him, give him room to breathe. As he cleared away the waste, he lifted Ingo's head, cradling it in his arms. But there was no response. Members of Ingo's army began to congregate. Meanwhile, a regiment of brocosmiles also gathered. With both leaders immobilized, the fighting had diminished to minor pushing, shoving, and

VIII — War and Peace

name-calling. The ultimate outcome of the war had yet to be decided.

Though distraught over her fallen leader, Alice, who was second in command, knew the battle was not over. There were still important matters to conclude such as getting her troops safely out of Gambrinsville, getting the dentist back to the king, and orchestrating the cleanup effort. Now was not the time to delay or show weakness. Ingo would've demanded the same were it anyone else who'd fallen in his stead. She needed to stay focused on the mission. There was one problem, however: the Gambrine High Chancellor, despite consuming the wretched tart, was still stirring up trouble.

It took eight brocosmiles to drag her body back up Spaghetti Hill and place her once again atop her command post. Though her torso was flaccid as a child's stuffed toy and her jaws were stuck, she was far from harmless, for her wit remained intact, conjuring wicked notions that her lips were still able to convey, albeit in little more than growls, grunts, and hisses.

The chancellor squeaked slowly through involuntarily gritted teeth, "I don't know who you are or where you come from, Mr. Silvers..." — the chancellor had sorted out Shel's identity. The Gambrine were, after all, resourceful, sharp-witted, not ignorant by any means. "...But you and I will have plenty of time to get to know one another now that the lion can't protect you. ...And now that your little, bearded friends have crashed their flying shoe in my backyard... and you have no way out!" Two brocosmiles clutched Sheldon's arms. "A fair trade for the dentist, I suppose."

VIII — War and Peace

Shel was speechless. Was he to spend the rest of his days in Arcania, in Gambrinstown of all places? He'd always assumed he'd be going home, back to Chicago, eventually. Getting time away, finding his own path, that was one thing. He hadn't planned on never seeing his family again.

Satisfied, the chancellor's eyes drifted from Shel, falling on Alice. "I see you're in charge now that the lion has... retired. You have recovered your prize for your king. Now leave this place! I keep this one," — she indicated Ingo's body with the slightest nod — "...as my trophy. ...The boy's mine too, along with a handful of your troops... to clean up and replant." More brocosmiles captured some of the Boogies and the king's guard. "The rest of you may go," she concluded, but no one moved a muscle. They could sense something wasn't settled. There was a strange vibration on the air, a methodical, subsonic thumping. Each who felt it believed it to be their own heart, nervously pulsating as if anticipating some unknown event. No one dared move.

"I suggest you get going before I change my mind and keep the lot!" growled Hume. "What are you all waiting for? The other shoe to drop? Ha! The Festoon was the only flying shoe in Arcania. There's no one else coming to save you!"

The vibration was not just in the air now, it seemed to shake the very ground, ever so subtly. Out of nowhere, a soft yet deep, weak yet powerful voice crept up behind the chancellor, making her eyes triple in size. "I wonder... where might one... acquire... a giant shoe... in which to fly?"

If Hume could've moved, she would've jumped ten feet in the air, for that is the appropriate response when seeing someone rise from the dead. He clutched her cloak with a giant paw and pulled himself from Sheldon's arms, sitting upright in his coffin of noodles.

"INGO!" Shel cried out, embracing his friend tightly.

"Now that's what I call a resurrection!" noted Dracula to Karl and Walter, both of whom nodded enthusiastically.

Ingonyama ignored Shel and the others, for now. He had unfinished business with the chancellor. Staring with vengeful eyes, the great lion growled, "I ask again: Where would one get a giant shoe?" Hume was stunned silent. "Why, from a *GIANT* of course!" Thunderous sounds of trees being crushed punctuated Ingo's conclusion, the booming vibrations in the earth rising to a crescendo, heralding the advance of not one, but two skyscraping creatures!

"Chester!" hollered Alice, delighting in the arrival of Ingo's pièce de resistance.

"And I believe you already know Chester's sister, Charlie. Isn't that right, Hume?" growled Ingo.

"Chester? ...Charlie?" The chancellor choked, and that was all she was able to get out before collapsing unconscious at Alice's feet. The return of Ingonyama was shock enough. The appearance of the giants, signaling the end of her military counterattack, was beyond her ability to stomach.

ooooo

VIII — War and Peace

By the time she awoke from her 'nap' — an unauthorized slumber that would, no doubt, be investigated by Sir Marcus at some future date — a good deal of her farm fields had been cleared and her brocosmiles were back to their usual tasks of raking, weeding, hoeing, mulching... Only a handful of Ingo's army remained, assisting Hume's kinfolk with the task of replanting the broccoli — along with several other, new crops.

"So, they took my giant after all, did they?" Hume spoke aloud through stuck jaws, mostly to herself. Utterly defeated — physically, morally, and strategically — she sat, resigned, resting under a small broccoli tree where she'd been placed like a commemorative statue, until the time when she would be able to walk again. Keeping her company, making sure she remained captive, was the infirmed Ingonyama, also resting and recovering.

"You gave her a home when she had nowhere else to turn, saved her from the king's Nightshade campaign. She would be asleep, ten feet under the sand if it weren't for the Gambrine. But, her debt has been repaid many times over. She is free now... and reunited with her kin. Lady Alice is escorting Charlie and her brother back to the Land of Happy, for they are needed in the service of the king."

Hume growled in protest. It was just the two of them now, no reason to fight. Instead, it was a time for words, to reflect and make sense of the war, if any sense could be made.

"We're going to stay," Ingo coughed, choking on remnants of noodles stuck in the depths of his lungs.

VIII — War and Peace

"...Some of us anyway, for as long as it takes, working side-by-side with the Gambrine. We'll help clean up the mess—"

"Your mess!" Hume hissed but Ingo ignored the invitation to another argument.

"We'll help clean the mess, help rebuild and replant... and implement Mr. Silver's plan for expanding your farming enterprise, leaving the Gambrine better off than when we encountered you just this morning."

"Expansion?! What expansion?!" Hume whined.

"The Gambrine's ability to grow the best-tasting broccoli is unparalleled," Ingo explained. "With the right resources, there's no reason you shouldn't also be able to grow other vegetables; food that will be just as sought-after to the entire community as your beloved broccoli has been; ultimately bringing you even greater prosperity. The kingdom of Happy is prepared to provide said resources for this expansion."

"And what if we don't want it?!"

"Don't be foolish, chancellor. More crops? More revenue? More land? Don't pretend the Gambrine wouldn't like more land."

"More land?" Hume was unable to hide her curiosity.

"More land," Ingo nodded, "and the resources to cultivate the land: tools and labor. Then, after the Gambrine are sufficiently established in their new enterprise, we shall part ways... as friends, having given the Gambrine much in return for what we've taken today."

VIII — War and Peace

"What a lovely sentiment," Hume scoffed. "But the fact remains, you can't just invade a sovereign nation, take things that don't belong to you, and change their way of life!"

Ingo remained calm. "Hume..."

"Don't call me that!"

Ingo sighed. "Chancellor, you and I both know that Charlie, Manny, and Buddha the cat — the three feathers of which I spoke, if you recall — do not *belong* to anyone, least of all you. They are free souls who deserve to live in peace. Beyond them, slavery has no place in Arcania. Not that it ever did, but those old ways are long gone. You must renounce your practice of imprisoning people into slavery."

"Oh, I suppose you think your methods are better? Stash prisoners away in windowless cells, let them wither and die in the damp dark? At least my prisoners get to breathe fresh air and feel the sun on their skin. And they eat what they harvest, wholesome, nutritious, fresh—"

"Chancellor," Ingo interrupted, "I am not in a position to give you alternative policies. I am only delivering the message of the nations of Arcania: slavery is over. Ignore this message at your peril. Conform, and King Longsmiles will honor the long history of friendship between the Land of Happy and the Gambrine. That is the promise of the king... and the word of Ingonyama."

"Your word? Your word is no better than the garbage you've left all across our valley. Someday we'll repay you properly for this transgression; you and the *Happy* King!"

VIII — War and Peace

"And what would that prove, chancellor?"

"It would prove that we're better than you!"

"It wouldn't. More violent perhaps. Not better. Winning doesn't *prove* a victor better than a loser, chancellor, you know this. There are simply too many variables, too much chance at play. Winning is not only ephemeral — victor one day, loser the next — it is also relative. Sometimes when you think you win, you lose; and sometimes when you think you've lost, you've actually won."

"You think of yourself as quite the philosopher, don't you? Tell me, what sort of enlightened being goes around stealing other's honor?!"

"Enlightened?" Ingo laughed. "No. Experienced. And I can honestly tell you, I did not take away your honor. So long as you choose to respond with honor, you retain yours. If you decide you've only lost three prisoners — not your dignity, not your honor, not your sovereignty — then peace is already within your grasp." The chancellor squinted defiantly. "You must realize, chancellor, we could have come with *real* weapons, started a *real* war. We knew you wouldn't give up your 'prisoners' without a fight... right?"

"Of course not! Charlie came to us for protection... from *your* king! The cat came uninvited, meddling in our affairs..."

"Yes. I'm aware of all of that. But as I said, the practice of indentured servitude, for any reason, will no longer be tolerated by the other nations of Arcania. You're lucky we only brought rotten food. There are others who, no doubt,

VIII — War and Peace

would've brought cannons and razed Gambrinsville to the ground. You're lucky I understand that violence breeds violence. No one needs to suffer for your stubbornness, chancellor. You're lucky my directive was to free your prisoners without anyone actually getting hurt."

"I got hurt!" a distant brocosmile voice whimpered.

"Mind your business, Jerry!" chided Hume, and the brocosmile got back to raking. "Lucky!?" Hume growled. "Hmpf!"

"Lucky," answered Ingo conclusively. "We all are."

Chapter Nine

The Whale-eater and the Dreams of Tomorrow

IX — The Whale-eater and the Dreams of Tomorrow

"Where is my lion?!" read the king's sign in red crayon, his mouth still stuck shut, of course. After days of not being able to eat anything solid — water infused with soluble nutrients keeping him alive via a straw at the back of his mouth — Skippy was in no mood to see Shel standing before him empty-handed. It wasn't that Shel was literally empty-handed. He was, after all, carrying a small, ornately carved wooden staff, the remnant shard of a Gambrine rake — a souvenir from battle. He just didn't have with him the king's prisoner whom he'd promised to bring back.

"Do you not recall the king's story of the silver fish?" asked the king's official spokesperson. With mouth sealed tight, the king thought it prudent to appoint a royal speaker to give commands on his behalf. For this task, the king chose none other than Marcus the pleaseman, on account of his unfailing, though oft overbearing, loyalty.

"And what of Alice? And the king's royal guards?" Marcus continued. He looked at the king and the king nodded in approval.

"Your Highness," Shel bowed, "Ingo and Alice have elected to stay behind to help clean up after the battle, in order to ensure the peace between the Gambrine and your kingdom holds into the future." Shel had rehearsed precisely what Ingo had instructed him to tell the king upon return. Ingo knew the king would not be happy, but the argument in favor of keeping the peace could not be refuted, even by Longsmiles — especially by Longsmiles.

Shel, Izzy, and the Boot Brigade, along with pirates Taud and Hook, had returned from the battle exhausted, hungry, and stained from head to toe in the remnants of

IX — The Whale-eater and the Dreams of Tomorrow

every sort of food imaginable. The last thing any of them wanted was to stand in front of the king and be interrogated by his royal mouthpiece. But, there was no avoiding King Skippy or the pleaseman. The king was the first stop after docking Hook's ship, for more reasons than ceremony.

As Izzy approached Shel and the king, Marcus noted with great interest the package balancing uneasily atop the elephant's back. There sat a disheveled-looking old man with dark eyes suggesting he hadn't slept in days, and he too was covered in the stench of rotting food.

"Your Majesty," Izzy began, "may I present Doctor Manfred Faffen Jr., the world's premier dentist." Izzy bowed his head, allowing Manny a path to ground. The dentist jumped onto the elephant's trunk, tripped, and tumbled down what had intended to be a slide, flopping to the ground with a thud and a moan. "Oops!" coughed Izzy. "Sorry, Manny. You okay?"

Manny jumped up, tossed an 'all good' wink at Izzy, then turned his attention to the king.

"Your Royal Sovereign! Sure is a pleasure to meet ya... finally. Heard a great deal 'bout the famous King Longsmiles and his wonderful Land uh Happy." Then Manny the bold decided to test the king's patience. "Always wanted tuh visit, but, 'dentists not allowed' an all."

At that point, the king would have interrupted if he could have, put the dentist in his place, or in a place of the king's choosing rather (someplace like the dungeon). Longsmiles' fidgeting, which indicated he wished to speak, went entirely unnoticed by his spokesperson who was

IX — The Whale-eater and the Dreams of Tomorrow

distracted by the energetic dentist. Marcus scrutinized the little man, trying to predict his intentions.

Thus, Manny continued his rant uninterrupted. "It is lovely here, sire. I can certainly understand yer obsession with sandwiches, given all the sand an' all the witches in the place... Buuut, I advise against the extra sticky peanut butter varietals." He widened his eyes and pointed two index fingers at the king's mouth. "Case in point... with all due respect... Your Highness."

The king did not look pleased. He grabbed another piece of paper and began scribbling something. As he did, the dentist leaned back and whispered to Izzy that he was going to need something large and flat with which to pry the king's mouth open. Manny looked back at Longsmiles just in time for the king to present his sign, but Manny wasn't interested. He swatted that sign right out of the king's hands. "Oh, there's no need for any uh that! You just sit back 'n relax. I'll have ya fixed up right quick! ...Aaand while we wait for Izzy to return with ma tools... how 'bout a little story, eh?" The dentist stared at the king then glanced around at his audience, nodding as he scanned their faces.

Turning back to the king, Manny began, "Have y'ever heard the story of Bindala Bale? The little girl who ate a whole whale?" Longsmiles scowled at Manfred and Manfred happily ignored him. "That lil' miss sat at her table for eighty-nine years. Eighty-nine years! Can you buh-leeve that?! Never even left thuh house!"

Some people in the audience gasped, some chuckled, others mumbled or grumbled, and the rest either quietly

IX — The Whale-eater and the Dreams of Tomorrow

reveled in astonishment or scowled in solidarity with the king.

"Yup! I used to visit Bindala, work on her teeth while she sat right there at her dinin' table. I'd be fillin' in cavities in between her bites, I would! She was the most food-obsessed person I'd ever met. That is, till I heard tell uh the great Peanut Butter King!"

The king pounded his fists on his chair furiously and began sweating. He couldn't recall the last time someone talked to him in such a manner.

Sympathetically stunned, Marcus looked around for something to pound *his* fist on. A thin branch protruding from a willow bush was leaning toward him, teasing for trouble. So, Marcus slapped that branch in a show of royal support. Marcus felt rather pleased with himself for a half-second until the bendy branch came swinging back, slapping Mark across the face. Touché!

Frustrated beyond words, Marcus hastily drew his sword, intending to cut the branch down to size. His frustration was only fertilized, however, when his fencing arm was stayed mid-swing by the royal gardener, who, with a slow, silent shake of his head, reminded the pleaseman it was not yet pruning season. Discomposed, Marcus fumbled to sheath his blade then bit his lip to blood as he waited in desperate anticipation for the order to haul the defiant, disrespectful dentist to the dungeon; teach him some good old-fashioned manners. But Manny wasn't going anywhere, least of all to any dungeon. He had other plans.

IX — The Whale-eater and the Dreams of Tomorrow

"Relaaaax, Longsmiley," (the king nearly exploded at the abuse of his name), "Ever'un knows yer obsessed with peanut butter. But you took it too far this time, didn't ya? Just like Bindala. Gave up her life for her obsession, she did." He paused for effect and then pointed two fingers at the king again. "And you almost did too!"

Longsmiles' scowls grew in marked intensity. But what else could he do besides scowl? Manny let the king have his contempt, which was, eventually — as Manny knew it would be — followed by a moment of reflection, at which point Manfred continued.

"But, no! This king's not gonna perish. No sir indeedy! We're gunna git you squared away right quick, we are!" Seeing a lumbering pachyderm heading his way, Manny called to the elephant at the far side of the crowd. "You bring what I asked fer?"

"Um, well, I know you said you needed some sort of dental spoon extractor thingy, but this is the only spoon I could think to grab." The elephant held his trunk high above the crowd to present the giant silver spoon which Sandovar had gifted to the king only recently.

Manny was a tad stunned. "Uh... huh. Well, I s'pose that'll have to do. I was hopin' to go about the job a little more... sensitive like, with a finer tool to chip away at the clay-like nutcrete. But, I s'pose you're right. Why beat around the butter? Let's just jab that spoon in there and pry on it until his face cracks wide open, shall we?"

IX — The Whale-eater and the Dreams of Tomorrow

The king's eyes nearly popped out of his head. Mark saw the look on Longsmile's face and eagerly stepped in front of Manny. "Now just a minute you—"

"Oh, I don't have time for this." The dentist stopped Mark short. "Izzy, do something about this party pooper will ya?" Manny ordered as he snatched the large spoon from the elephant.

With his trunk now empty, Izzy needed something to fill it. So, he grabbed hold of the pleaseman and tossed him aside without delay.

Meanwhile, Manny, being of small stature, was struggling with the oversized spoon. "Goodness! This thing weighs a ton!" Eventually, he was able to lift the spoon up onto his shoulder. With a shuffle of his little feet he approached the king, who was squirming in his throne. "Now just hold still Yer Royallness," (Manny winked at Shel), "Just imagine this spoon is filled with peanut butter. Open them lips wide as ya can an' show me them chompers. Come on now, smile fer papa!"

The king was not the least bit sweet on the dentist's instructions — Manny's bedside manner lacking manners, as it were, and he refused to comply. So, Manny did what any good dentist would do: he had his assistants, the shoe crew (and Sheldon too), hold Longsmiles' arms while he shoved that spoon right into the king's mouth despite all the fidgeting and groans of protest. Being a skilled tooth doctor, Manny quickly found a proper spot to wedge the utensil.

The dentist glanced back to see if Izzy had managed to subdue the pleaseman. Mark appeared to be resting

IX — The Whale-eater and the Dreams of Tomorrow

comfortably on the lawn about fifteen feet away. No one needed to worry about interruptions from *that* man anytime soon. So, Manny got on with his work. Using the king's overbite as leverage, the dentist pressed the spoon as best he could in between the king's maxillary and mandibular incisors — that is, between his upper and lower teeth.

"Izzy, would you be so kind as to press up on the end of this spoon, ever so gently, with your most capable proboscis?" Izzy did as Manny requested. "Okay, now hold it right there for a moment." The dentist employed a pressurized bottle to spray a jet of tonic into the king's mouth, attempting to loosen the peanut butter cement. The tonic, concocted on the boat ride back from Champion Valley, consisted of salt water mixed with various spoiled foodstuffs, plus some herbs they'd collected from various inlets along the way, topped off with a good helping of Katya's dismembering potion. And with that, the king's head popped clean off...

(Only kidding. The potion was a *dissolving* potion, not dismembering. Bit of a thesaurical slip there!)

As Manny generously sprayed a waterfall of the *dissolving* elixir into the king's mouth, Izzy pried on the spoon. Katya, meanwhile, got on with waving her hands about, mumbling incantations to help grease the wheels of the crazy charade.

At first nothing seemed to be happening, except for the king shedding a deluge of tears, presumably from pain but could've been humiliation. For that matter, he could've been crying at the prospect of these nutty people trying to remove his tasty peanut butter mortar. Manny, for one, got

IX — The Whale-eater and the Dreams of Tomorrow

a kick out of seeing the king so despondent. The dentist had been less than pleased about being banned from the Land of Happy simply because his chosen profession was considered a primer for anxiety and stress (which, as everyone knows, is!)

"If this doesn't work I'm going to need a hammer and chisel. We'll just knock his teeth out one by one until there's nothing for the butter to cling to," Manny jested with a chuckle. He wasn't serious, of course, but after the interrogation of the brocosmile, there was no telling of what this dentist was capable. The king, for one, had no idea Manny was joking, so he began moaning and crying even harder, providing even more moisture to the mortar. As his tears flooded his mouth, threatening to drown him, suddenly, a very faint *crack* could be heard.

"Hold it!" Manny commanded, a skosh concerned they may be starting to crack the king's jaw... or extract his teeth. "Just hold it right there, Izzy." Manny stretched his palm in Izzy's direction while inspecting all around the king's mouth. He looked back at Izzy with a rascally grin and a wink. "Well," he said, feigning resignation, "looks like there's no hope for *this* king. Anyone else want to try on the crown?"

Boy, did that send the king and crowd into a frenzy! Manny couldn't help it. He burst into a fit of laughter. Instantly, Longsmiles tried to wave his arms and stand up but the Boot Brigade kept the king solidly in check. With a twitch of his fingers as if signaling someone to come hither, Manny directed Izzy to press up just a hair more on the spoon.

IX — The Whale-eater and the Dreams of Tomorrow

While the dentist flushed the king's mouth with more elixir and the king's tears flowed like the great Zambezi over Victoria Falls, Katya intensified her chanting and waving into a stomping dance — at which point Wanda attempted to join in but Katya waived her off, fearing that the batty, old hag might accidentally turn the king into a newt.

Seeing bits of peanut butter begin to dislodge from the king's gums, Manny knew right then that he was going to prevail. He motioned for Izzy to press up just a bit harder and *creeeaaak!* went the king's jaw ever so slightly, ever so slowly. "Checkmate! I've got your king now!" he derided the peanut butter spirits. Like an excited grasshopper, Manny leaped up onto the handle of the spoon. "Let's go, Izzy! Elevator up!"

The elephant pulled up on the handle, lifting the dentist and prying on the king's mouth with elephantine force. And then, with a final *KE-RACK!* that could be heard all the way across Champion Lake, over in Gambrinstown (incidentally, waking up Marcus the pleaseman — who would now have to prosecute *himself* for taking an unauthorized nap), the peanut butter finally gave up its herculean stick and surrendered once and for all. The king's jaws were free!

Instantly, the crowd erupted, cheering and clapping for the dentist, and for their king (of course). Meanwhile, Longsmiles, exhausted and overwhelmed with pain, slumped in his throne and passed right out... but not before uttering one, last command in the slightest of whispers. The poor, starving, delusional king, in a labored ghost of a breath, requested... another peanut butter sandwich.

IX — The Whale-eater and the Dreams of Tomorrow

oooooo

"Let's get this poor guy to bed." Manny looked at Katya. "He can sleep it off. That'll be best for everyone, I'm sure." Katya nodded at some nearby servants and they got straight to task.

"Wow! That was really something, Manny," said Izzy.

"Couldn't've done it without you, big guy," replied the dentist. "And thanks to yous guys toos!" he motioned in the direction of the boot crew.

"Manny, I can't tell you how good it is to have you back! I really thought you were a goner," Izzy confessed. The boot crew agreed with various expressions of "Yeah!" and "For certain!" and "Tally ho!"

(Tally ho?)

"Me too!" confessed Manny. "Let's hope Longsmiles is in good spirits when he wakes up, else all the trouble I put him and his kingdom through will come back at me like a fifty-ton boomerang."

"Trouble?!" reeled Fickleface. "What trouble? You just saved the king's life for goodness' sake!"

Manny chuckled. "Maybe. I just meant that if I hadn't run off to Gambrinstown in the first place, like a darned fool, y'all wouldn't've had tuh come rescue me, wastin' all that time, not to mention all that good food!"

IX — The Whale-eater and the Dreams of Tomorrow

"Oh, pish tosh! Put a cork in that bottle!" Fickles retorted.

"Busides, the food was all rotten tuh begin with!" added Pickles.

Izzy laughed. "Yeah. Searching for you, traveling all over, and fighting to get you back... that's been the adventure of a lifetime! Isn't that right, Sheldon?" While the bootaneers nodded in agreement, Shel stared blankly as if he'd been hit over the head.

"What is it, kid?" asked Izzy. "What's wrong?"

Shel shrugged. "I dunno. I guess... I just hadn't really thought about it before."

"'Bout what?" asked Tickles.

Sheldon sort of shuffled his feet. "Well, the end of the adventure, I suppose."

"Hmm. Right," remarked Izzy pensively.

"You're walkin' on a cloud, kid. Don't look down! Just keep on goin'!" Shel looked up and met the old eyes of the dentist, eyes which had seen a thing or two. Manny was holding Buddha Baggs in his arms, looking content, though he was clearly straining under the weight of the big cat. He looked at Baggs and added, "When one adventure ends, another always begins... so long as you're open to it. Just don't look down or you'll fall right back to the ground. And that's when you grow roots! Before ya know it, you're an old tree like me."

IX — The Whale-eater and the Dreams of Tomorrow

Shel smiled and nodded. There was a brief pause and then he said to no one in particular, "I need to see Joy."

oooooo

On their voyage to Gambrinstown, on the eve of battle, Ingo had sat Shel down in the boot and gave him the news that Joy had gone home, that she was not going to be joining the fight to free Manny because she did not wish to fight; even if it *was* a food fight. Not only was she a peaceful soul, the Gambrine were neighbors, allies to the Costeros clan. It would not be right for Joy to involve her family in the dispute since it was not their quarrel.

Ingo didn't have an answer for Shel when the kid asked when Joy would be returning. The lion didn't know if Joy would be coming back at all. "But she wanted me to tell you that you are with her, in her heart, Sheldon. ...And she wanted me to give you this." Ingo handed Shel a small book, the pages of which were blank. Poor Shelby looked perplexed, and so the lion explained. "She said you're a storyteller, Sheldon, and that you have an incredible story that needs telling: the story of Arcania."

Shel wasn't sure what to say. He didn't think he and Joy would part ways like that, without words, without goodbyes, nothing to show for their friendship but a book of empty pages. He hadn't considered the possibility that they *would* part ways. Something inside of him was sure she would always be with him. Now that they were back from

IX — The Whale-eater and the Dreams of Tomorrow

battle, back in the Land of Happy where he'd met her, Shel knew he needed to tell her just how he felt about her.

oooooo

"I have to see her. But... I don't know where she is," he confessed.

Izzy and the boot crew remained silent, unsure of what to say. Then, with an audible inhale and sigh, Izzy relented. "I'll take you." The elephant knew the journey back through the Sonrisa desert would be long and dangerous, especially if the giants were being woken up, as was the plan according to Ingonyama. Regardless, he figured helping his friend was the least he could do after Shel saved his life. To him, helping Sheldon was worth all the trouble in the world. Izzy was adrift in thought when a gruff voice butted in.

"Arrr, there'll be no need of that!"

Shel and the group jerked around to see a dark figure standing behind them.

"Blackbeard!" Shel blurted. "Where'd you come from?"

"Ah! I be comin' in from the sea, as pirates tend to do now and again." The pirate — whose beard stubble was growing in nicely now, reuniting him with his namesake... and his villainous appearance — exchanged hugs and handshakes with Shel, Izzy, the boot crew, Manny, even Katya.

IX — The Whale-eater and the Dreams of Tomorrow

"Where's everyone else?" asked Shel. "Where's Ingonyama? And Sandovar, and the giants?"

"Alice and the king's guard?" added Katya.

The black pirate stared blankly back at the group for a moment, taking a deep breath before looking down at the ground. His drooping head shook back and forth as he spoke slowly and softly, well out of character for such a bawdy pirate. "I be afraid not everythin' went 'cordin' tuh plan."

"What?! What do you mean?!" exclaimed Shel. "What happened? Where is everyone?!"

"There were Glunks in the trunks and Zawfees in our coffee! There were Snitchens in the kitchen and Vaths in the bath!"

"What?!" Izzy tried to make sense of the black pirate's babble, but Blackbeard just kept babbling.

"We tried to hide behind doors, under dressers... Even hid under a pile of clothes..."

"Yeah, I tried that. It doesn't work," mumbled Shel.

"...We hid in garbage pails..."

"Ewww. Gross," commented Pickles.

"What in the monkey's rump are you blabbering about?" Izzy pressed, growing impatient.

"*I've* found," chimed Manny, stroking the mane of Buddha Baggs and staring into oblivion, "that the only place

IX — The Whale-eater and the Dreams of Tomorrow

to hide is in the dreams of tomorrow." The group, including Blackbeard, squinted at the dentist, everyone trying to sort out what was just said.

Finally, Izzy blurted, "What... is... happening?! Has everyone gone mad?! Blackbeard, you'd better stop riddling nonsense and tell us what happened or I'm going to plant you like a rutabaga, headfirst, right here in the sand."

"Alrighty then," replied the pirate, hands up in surrender. "Calm yerself ya big bludder wuffer." Blackbeard's salty demeanor was back. "Ye friends be slow to disembark's all. So I figured I'd make sure the coast be clear 'fore we all got into a mess of boilin' oil with the king. But looks as though things be settled right proper if the dentist be wanderin' 'round free as a polly in paradise." Another wave of silence washed over everyone as they translated the pirate speak.

"Black, just tell us where Ingo is." The elephant cut straight to it.

"There! Look!" cried Fickleface, pointing in the direction of the seaport.

Marching over the horizon came a silhouette of various colors, shapes, and sizes, preceded by the pungent stench of decaying food.

"Arrr, my apologies." Blackbeard fumbled his soiled fingers through his coal-black hair. "Hadn't much time for pleasantries like bathing or scrubbin' rags, we didn't."

IX — The Whale-eater and the Dreams of Tomorrow

"Scrubbing rags? Oh, you mean washing clothes?" Shel interpreted.

"Aye, that too," replied Blackbeard.

It wasn't long before the silhouettes became distinct. A wild mane whipped pridefully like a triumphant flag in the wind.

"Ingonyama," whispered Izzy in relief.

Next to the mane moved a figure walking with grace and purpose, as if on a mission.

"Alice!" announced Katya.

On the other side of Ingo walked a smaller figure whose mane danced on the wind like Ingonyama's only not as bushy; longer and more playful. The figure moved across the sand with a flowy elegance, like Alice only without the unyielding determination and drive. This one, although walking with the group, appeared to be marching to the beat of a different drummer. Or, not marching at all, rather, but sort of sashaying with some intermittent skipping. And then... a twirl.

Shel's heart skipped. He felt for a moment that he was imaging everything. The sensation that he was in a dream washed over him like a rainstorm and he shivered. When the faceless silhouettes were close enough to come alive, identities slowly appearing on faces like a welcomed sunrise over a dark valley, all was confirmed. There next to the lion stood the strong and beautiful and whimsical mermaid princess, Joythea Aquarius Costeros.

IX — The Whale-eater and the Dreams of Tomorrow

Shel was instantly jolted by an invisible bolt of lightning affixing his feet to the ground. He felt immobile, bronzed to the earth, a statue for all of eternity to marvel at. (Goodness, how dramatic he was!) After a moment, he decided this was not a dream, this was real, as real as it gets, anyway. She was not a mirage and he was not a statue. He broke free of the shock and ran to her, engulfing her in a tremendous embrace.

This time she was not afraid. He picked her up and swung her around and around, and she laughed and laughed... as she does. For a moment they were back on the shore of Isla de Sonrisas, just the two of them, cool sea breeze in their hair and warm sunshine on their skin.

Joy looked down at Shel and began singing something in French as she flew in the air. He looked up at her with adoring eyes, eyes of longing, and fondness; eyes that had no idea what she was saying... and that did not go unnoticed by the perceptive and wide-eyed Izzy.

"Don't tell me you don't speak Spanish, Artilan, OR French!" the elephant teased, and everyone laughed, especially Shel.

Chapter Ten

Namesake

"Ingo, where's Sandovar? Where are Chester and Charlie?" Izzy asked after the initial excitement died down, embraces were had, and the laughter quieted...

X — Namesake

"Yeah, where's Sandovar?" asked Pickles.

"And Alice?" asked Tickles.

"And the giants?" asked Fickles.

"Friends! Friends," Ingo held up a paw, invoking calm. "Sandovar and his Boogies are leading Chester and Charlie along a different road. They're passing through the desert, waking the Snoozants as they go. And they have plenty of help, including some of Katya's witch friends, who, as I understand, have recruited a few more of their paranormal brethren. I believe Shel knows 'em: Walter, Karl, and Dracula."

"Really?!" erupted Shel excitedly.

"Yup. They said they weren't so interested in the food fighting party, but that they wanted to do something to help nonetheless. I figured their experience with resurrecting things could come in handy. Drac certainly thought so." Ingo and Shel laughed together.

"So it's really happening then; the giants are returning to the Land of Happy?" Joy sounded positively enthusiastic. (But when did she not?)

"Yup!" answered Ingo. "Our friends are assisting Chester and Charlie in making sure the giants are reoriented properly, slowly, and with plenty of compassion. A new day is dawning in the Land of Happy, my friends. Things are about to change in a big, big way!

Izzy nodded slowly, taking it all in. "Okay! Wow! Well, Ingo, in your estimation, do you foresee peace for the Land of Happy?" Did Hume finally relent? Will the giants seek retribution?" He was really grilling his commander.

"Slow down there, buddy. First off, as for the giants, we'll have to wait and see if they have any demands, see where they want to live, what they want—"

"Well, yes, of course, all of that," Izzy cut him off. "But what about the Gambrine?"

"Well, Izzy," Ingo replied slowly, "I suppose only time holds that answer. But for now it seems we will have peace, yes. The giants made quick work cleaning up the food mess and replanting what crops were destroyed... Incidentally, the food scraps proved to be good compost—"

"Soil amendment!" whispered an astonished Pickles, snatching a handful of sand and letting the dry granules trickle through his fingers. "Makes perfect sense!"

"Exactly," Ingo replied. "And we contributed, best we could, to the acquisition of more land for the Gambrine, per our agreement. ...By the time we left, Hume seemed at least a little accepting of the changes. Of course she's never completely satisfied. But, short of perfection, I think we did a good job of getting the Gambrine back on track, ahead of schedule, even, according to the farmer's almanac."

Still holding big 'ol Buddha, Manny poked his head into the conversation. "Well, in that case, I believe there's cause enough for celebration, eh?!"

oooooo

X — Namesake

The revelry celebrating the reunion of friends and recovery of the king was unparalleled, made all the more fun by the return of the king's silly disposition and general good nature — an unexpected but welcomed bonus. He almost instantly forgave all past transgressions, realizing everyone had made tremendous efforts on his behalf. Rather than accusing anyone of any crimes, he attributed his ill-temper to his own ego, an ego sorely in need of a good humbling, which he received in spades thanks to the Peter Pan sandwich. Now on the mend, the king threw a grand picnic on the palace lawns, complete with a buffet, a band, several bonfires, and, of course, some badminton.

King Longsmiles loved the game of badminton. Unfortunately, he was still too frail to participate. Instead, Skippy sat in his wheelchair near one of the bonfires, munching on a sandwich (of ham and cheese, mind you), and cheering a team of his guards as they challenged various members of the extended Boogies.

Despite his jovial attitude and newfound appreciation for life, the king's passion for peanut butter had not subsided. Not one bit. He was still demanding sticky peanut butter sandwiches. His requests were, thankfully, thus far being carefully dodged using a combination of logic rooted in sound health practices, a smidge of manipulative psychology, and a pinch of pagan hypnosis administered by Izzy and the witches. Still, all were fast coming to their wit's end with the king's ridiculous obsession.

"Why doesn't he just add some jelly?" Shel casually suggested as they stood around a campfire, the witches complaining to no end about their stubborn king.

X — Namesake

"What's that?" Katya challenged. "Jelly? On his peanut butter sandwich? Yuck!"

"What do you mean 'yuck'?" Shel defended. "You've never heard of a PB and J?"

"Pee-bee and what?" the witch asked.

"A peanut butter and jelly sandwich," Shel replied in the key of *duh* major.

"Never heard of such a ridiculous thing," concluded Katya. She looked at Picklepots and raised her brows, silently asking the flying shoe chef if he'd ever heard of this P B and J nonsense. Pickles shook his head, no.

Shel noted defenses being fortified. "Look, don't knock it till you try it. For all you know, the pee-bee-jay could be the best thing you've ever tried. Aaaand, it might just be the answer to your problem."

Katya squinted. "Ugh! Fine. How does it work then?"

"How does it...? What do you mean, how does it work? You put some jelly on the sandwich, along with the peanut butter. Done." Katya stared back at him. One could see Shel beginning to drift, dreaming about his glorious peanut butter and jelly sandwiches back home. Wanda snapped her bony fingers in front of his face and he came back to the bonfire, recalling that they were working on a solution for the king. "Well, anyway, I think it'll help."

"How's that again?" the witches asked in unison.

X — Namesake

Shel shrugged and gave Katya 'obvious' eyes. "Becaaaause, it makes the peanut butter less sticky." Realizing it would just be easier to show them, he sought out Joythea. "Hang on. Where's... Ah!" He found her playing nearby and yelled to her. "Uh, Joy, I'm pretty sure cartwheels aren't allowed in badminton." Joy smiled back. "Hey, so that toast you gave me when we were in the desert... where'd you get the jelly?"

"What's that? Jelly?" She called back, swinging her racquet, smacking the shuttlecock and sending it zooming through the air. "I don't know..." *Swing! Swoosh! Twirl! Jump! Smash! Point for team Joy!* "Oh! The jelly on toast! I don't know. It was something Sandovar had."

The Boogie chief was of course away on his giant mission. His first mate, however, was keeping company with some Kantytown locals, just nearby.

"Hey, Taud," interrupted Shel, "got any more of the Sandman's special jelly stashed somewhere? I need to make a sandwich."

Taudello looked up curiously from his iced, wild-strawberry lemonade. "Arrr, whatever fer? There be plenty uh rations 'round here. Don't need a sandwich you nubbin chucker." Taud's audience chuckled at the mockery.

Shel paid no mind. "Nubbin chucker... That's a new one... Uh, no, I need it for the king. I want to try something." Taud squinted, paused, then hopped up, walked to a nearby tent, retrieved a jar, and handed it to Shel. "Thanks!" Shel then turned to Katya. "Lead the way."

X — Namesake

The witch adopted a skeptical expression while slowly reaching for her broom. "Okaaay. Hop on, I guess."

Shel's previous and less-than-pleasant experience on a flying broom, zooming over the battlefield, was enough to make him hesitate. Katya was not feeling very patient.

"Look, either get on and let's get this done or give it up. I don't have all day. I'm next in line for badminton and I've been waiting all morning." Shel hopped on the back of the broom. "Now, hold on tight, young man, I like to fly fast!"

They arrived at the palace kitchens in no time. Katya collected Skippy's favorite peanut butter along with his favorite sprouted grain sourdough bread and Shel made quick work of assembling the sandwich. (The convenience and glorious flavor, coupled with the nutrition of the fruit and the protein of the peanut, is precisely why a PB&J is arguably the greatest invention since, well, sliced bread. Shel knew this. Indeed, all great adventurers know this. But King Longsmiles did not know it. Not yet.)

Katya flew Shel and his sandwiches (he took the liberty of making himself one too) back to the picnic party, right up to the king. The royal audience included Ingonyama, Donachtuk the bear, the queen mother with her husband Simonson and their kangaroo and monkey, Lady Alice, Mark the pleaseman, and a heaping handful of Kantytown villagers. They were all listening to the king's stories — he was very talkative after having his mouth glued shut for several days. They were also entertained by a lively dialogue between the king and the lion, the two of them having come from very different lives, both of which were extremely fascinating. Since Ingonyama's return, the king had made sure to keep the lion within sight at all times, for he had not yet made up his mind about Ingo's imprisonment. The lion had certainly proven his worth securing the dentist's return, and he had proven his loyalty by returning despite the uncertainty of a pardon for his 'crimes'. The king, however, still grieved the loss of his friends and brother, and still felt betrayed. And so, Ingo's future still hung tenuously in the air like the smoke from the campfires that warmed the faces and the hearts of the many friends on the palace lawns that day.

Longsmiles looked up as Katryna advanced with Shel in tow. "Ah, the hero approacheth," announced the king, locking eyes with Shel. It was clear to everyone that Ingonyama was a hero for leading his troops to victory and saving Manny. It was also clear that Manny was a hero for working his dental magic and saving the king. But many others contributed in essential ways and Shel was no exception. Katya stepped out of the way, and with a bow, Shel presented the sandwich.

"What's this?" asked Longsmiles with kingly kindness and curiosity. Before Shel could answer, however, the king's disposition shifted to almost uncontrollable excitement. "A peanut butter sandwich?!" He then tried to stand but fell into the arms of Donachtuk, who had to resist the urge to swing his feeble partner round and round (which would have been a royal mistake). Longsmiles was thrilled to see a peanut butter sandwich again, and he had intended to say, 'Thank you.' But, haunted by the trauma of his near-death experience, he instead shouted, "Are you trying to kill me?!"

X — Namesake

All was well, however, for Shel, now battle-hardened, was unphased by Longsmiles' theatrics. After all, it was common knowledge that the king could be a bit of a drama queen.

"It's a peanut butter *and jelly* sandwich, Your Highness. Back home we call it a PB&J." Don sat the king in his throne-on-wheels, allowing the king to catch his breath and compose himself. "Katya provided me with your favorite peanut butter and bread, and Taudello provided me with Sandovar's prized jelly. I put them all together and now you have possibly the best sandwich the world has ever known! ...I can't believe no one here has ever heard of a PB&J!" The king squinted skeptically, as Katya had. "Sire, come on! Don't you trust me? Haven't I proven myself? If I wanted to harm you, would I do it with another sandwich? And in front of all these people? Would I have risked my life to find Manny and help bring him back to save you?" Shel let the king come to his senses. "Just calm down and try a bite!"

The king pursed his lips and examined the sandwich. "A pee-bee and jay, eh?" he finally said, then looked over at Mark the pleaseman. "Here!" he held out the sandwich. "You go first!" Mark jerked his head back in defiance. It wasn't so much that the combination of peanut butter and jam sounded terrible. It was just something new, and people can be funny about trying new things. Mark, who thrived on routine, was just such a person.

"Oh, for Heaven's sake!" exclaimed Alice, snatching the sandwich and biting in. Mark and the king stared wide-eyed at the brave knight who was famous for her

X — Namesake

adventurous spirit. She was, beyond a doubt, the boldest and most daring soul in the kingdom. But being bold and daring can come with its share of risk. Unfortunately, her impetuous act spelled disaster for the brave knight, for Shel was indeed trying to poison the king! As Alice fell to her knees, succumbing to the toxic snack, she struggled to pull her sword from its sheath in one last valiant act of upholding her sovereign duty to protect her king. But it was too late!

Just kidding.

What really happened was that Alice loved the sandwich and, being a bold woman of action, after taking her bite, she shoved that sandwich right in the king's mouth! After getting over the initial shock of the unorthodox force-feeding, Longsmiles could not ignore the amazing flavors invading his tastebuds. Within seconds, his expression shifted from utter surprise to ultimate satisfaction. Right then Shel knew he had a winner.

Following a moment of not-so-silent chewing, the king making all sorts of "mmm" and "ohhh" and "ahhh" sounds, Longsmiles finally swallowed... then opened his not-stuck mouth. "Peee beee and jayyy," he said slowly.

Shel smiled. "Not bad, eh?"

Longsmiles nodded and beheld the remaining sandwich that rested comfortably in his hands. "Not bad, indeed. All the flavors of my beloved peanut butter... and more!" He looked at Katya with big eyes. "And no danger of stuck mouth syndrome!" The witch nodded, satisfied with the result: a happy, and safe, king.

X — Namesake

(Let us now recall the royal dog to whom the king fed a nugget of Joy's peanut butter sandwich in book three, for this dog — whose name also happened to be Skippy — nearly brought the picnic party to a grinding halt, almost losing his life in the process.) As the king brought that glorious sandwich to his lips for a second bite — this one of his *own* feeding — Skippy the dog jumped up and snatched that PB&J right out of the king's hands! Forgetting that it was he who'd trained the dog to also love peanut butter, the king barked furiously at the foul-mannered canine. "You come back here with that! Else I'm going to make myself a PB&D!!"

"PB&D, sire?" Katya squinted.

"Peanut butter and DOG!"

The crowd broke into an uproar.

Longsmiles, however, was livid. "'Man's best friend', my eye! Skippy, if I've told you once I've told you a thousand times: the only way you and I are going to get along is if I tell you what to do and you do it!" he derided the canine but Skippy the dog wasn't paying any attention.

More laughter erupted from the crowd, the contagiousness of which eventually got to Longsmiles too as he realized he was only getting angry at a dog for simply doing what dogs do. His fledgling smile grew a thousand times bigger when Shel pulled the second sandwich from Katya's satchel and handed it to Skippy (the king, not the dog). As he did, the king yanked Shel's arm and pulled him in for a hug.

X — Namesake

The laughter and commotion caught the attention of the other partygoers and, seeing that their king was engaging in something momentous (he wasn't a big hugger), they began to migrate. Soon, a large crowd gathered. With a mouthful of food (he continued to feed himself with his left hand while hugging Shel with his right), the king stood up and placed a hand on Shel's shoulder to steady himself. From there he began delivering a speech to the enlarged crowd.

"It took me some time to see it. Perhaps I was blinded by grief, perhaps by fear. But I see clearly now that I am surrounded by friends who not only care about me..." He made eye contact with one friend after another, "You all care deeply about one another as well." The crowd nodded and smiled. "What's more is you care about the Land of Happy... and the whole of Arcania... and even unknown lands beyond our borders." He looked at Shel and then at Izzy. "I recall that the virtues of kindness and empathy do not have borders, are free of judgment, do not discriminate; things I knew long ago but had forgotten. Thanks to old friendships reignited," the king found Joy in the crowd, "I am recalling just how important it is to maintain good relations with our neighbors; not just for keeping the peace in our communities but also for keeping peace in our hearts. And, thanks to all of you, I recall the importance of keeping our bodies healthy." The king took a few steps, a little wobbly but entirely without help. "...And strong," he added, taking two more steps toward Ingonyama and placing a hand on the lion's shoulder, a gesture of kindness... and balance. Although he continued to address the crowd at large, he spoke softer, leaning in toward the lion, yet staring directly at Shel. "Isn't it incredible how a visit from a perfect stranger

X — Namesake

can bring about so much change?" The king paused in reflection. His eyes shifted from Shel to the ground, then over the crowd, finally coming to rest right next door on Ingonyama. "That young man over there fought for your freedom, against a *king* no less! And he didn't even know you." Then the king looked at Joy. "And this young woman here fought for your freedom too. As did Izzy and Sandovar and the Boogies..." He looked straight at the lion. "Who am I to deny the will of the people?"

"You are the king, Sire! That's who," replied Ingonyama with conviction.

Longsmiles shook his head. "No. A king does not hide behind his throne, using his crown to enforce his will. A king does not use his might to push his people toward some grandiose ideal, no matter how noble the cause. A true king walks alongside his people, through the muck and mire, using his power to clear pathways through the most challenging terrain, the fiercest storms, and always in the direction his people wish to go." He paused and looked around, inhaling deeply the cool, spring air. Then he looked squarely at the lion. "The people wish you to be free, Ingo, and so you are."

"Sire?" the lion sputtered.

"I should have been there to fight the Gambrine alongside you. Instead, you had to fight on my behalf. It is finally clear to me that you are good, that you fight on the side of good, and that you will continue to do good in this world. So, go. Be free. Go and do good things."

X — Namesake

There was a moment of reverent silence while the crowd waited to see what would happen next. But nothing happened. The lion stared at the king, likely making sure this wasn't some game, a cruel joke. But the king said nothing more, just stared back at the lion. Finally, with nothing left to do, Ingonyama bowed and turned away. He took a couple of steps from the king — Alice quickly stepping up to take his place as Longsmiles' crutch — but then he paused and turned back to Shel.

"It wasn't so long ago that I had given up hope of ever roaming the free world again… until you and your friends came for me." The lion looked at Izzy and winked, then back at Shel. "But even then I wasn't sure I had anything left to offer." He reached in his pocket and pulled out the puzzle piece. "But you helped me imagine life beyond my jail cell, and finally I saw that I *did* have more to give. And for that, I can't thank you enough. For that, I honor you." He handed the piece back to Shel. "This belongs to you. I won't have need of it where I am going."

Shel looked down at Ingonyama's open paw and took the puzzle piece slowly, noting that it had once again become dirty while in the care of the lion, with the ending of the word 'imagine' smudged somewhat. As Shel was distracted trying to clean the bit of wood, the lion pulled something else from one of his other pockets. It was a large Gambrine tooth he'd presumably picked up during the battle. He had wound copper wire tightly around the base of the tooth to make a pendant, which he'd then affixed to a chain. He held it up.

"My pendant!" Shel blurted out.

X — Namesake

"Yes. This also belongs to you," said Ingonyama. "A knight should always carry a reminder of the deed that won him his honor." The lion placed the necklace over Shel's head as he bowed in gratitude.

"But how did you—"

The lion cut him off with a raised paw and a shake of his head. "That is a question you will have to answer for yourself. Now, you are not yet a knight, officially... only the king... or queen mother — he winked at Ruth — can remedy that. ...But there is more to being a knight than holding title. You have shown your quality as a courageous and honorable man, one who is willing to put the well-being of others before his own. Those are the core qualities of any good knight."

Still uneasy about how the necklace came back to him, Shel protested. "But, Yams, I don't need anything to help me remember you and everyone, and I—"

"No," Ingo interrupted again. "This is not for you to remember any of us, Sheldon. I'm confident you won't forget your friends here. This is for you to remember who *you* are, who you *really* are, deep down, and the deeds of which you are capable. Don't forget the man you have become here in Arcania."

Shel was humblestunned. "But... what about you? You should be wearing this. You're the one who—"

Ingo shook his head. "The reminder of my deeds I carry with me in my heart, and in my heart alone. Those memories are too painful to wear on the outside." He looked down at his clothes and fidgeted with the shirt buttons. "Not

X — Namesake

unlike these clothes, actually." He looked up at Shel and smiled, turned to Izzy and nodded, then bowed slightly to the king. And then, Ingonyama the lion turned and walked away. Everyone stood and watched as the lion made his way across the palace lawns, removing his pressed shirt and pleated pants in stride, letting the clothes fall to the ground, then letting himself fall to the ground, landing on all fours. Without looking back, the lion ran into the fields beyond the groomed lawns and disappeared into the tall grass.

oooooo

Staring into the distance, pondering the wake of Ingonyama, the king held out a hand toward Mark the pleaseman. Mark was startled by the gesture as he knew what it meant but wasn't sure why the king would need a sword at that moment. Still, not being one to ever refuse a Longsmiles command (unless he wasn't paying attention), Mark pulled his sword from its sheath and placed the hilt into the palm of the king.

"Ingonyama is right. Any man or woman who has endured what you have who has certainly earned a place in the service of a king. And while my company would be honored to have you, I suspect the day is fast approaching when you will make your journey home, back to Chicago." On instinct, Shel glanced at Joy. She smiled sweetly then looked down. "But before you go, as a gesture of gratitude for saving this king's life…" Longsmiles paused and stiffened himself up. "Kneel, Master Sheldon."

X — Namesake

Shel looked at Izzy, who smiled and nodded as if to say, 'Do as the king commands, you knucklehead!' And so, Shel did. As he bent on one knee, King Longsmiles placed the sword atop his shoulders and spoke some faint words in the language of the flowers. Shel of course didn't know what was being said until the king spoke once again in English.

"It is against our customs to knight children, as that would place undue burden upon the child's head. However, I think we can all agree with Ingo's assertion that you are no longer a child, not after what you've been through. Still, you are not yet a man. Close, but not quite. Thus, until you are of age to receive your well-deserved knighthood, rise, Sheldon Silvers, royal *teen* of the realm, protector of the king, and protector of the lands of both Happy and of Champion Valley, and of all the good people and creatures that live under these skies, forever and ever."

And with that, Shel stood up to a great roar of the crowd, cheering, "Shel Silvers, teen of the realm! Shel Silvers, teen of the realm!" Izzy plucked Shel from the crowd and held him up high and Shel felt on top of the world.

Longsmiles looked up at the young man. "Now then, what gift would you ask of your king? If it is mine to give, I shall give it... But please do not ask for a television set. That I do not have." (Somewhere in the background Kish Khet could be seen kicking rocks.)

Shel tried to think of something but his mind was blank, overwhelmed by all the attention. Since his mind was quiet, his mouth decided to blurt out, "Falconovich's bat!" Longsmiles squinted, as did Izzy. "I mean... No, Izzy, what I meant was... I don't *want* it. I don't want your bat. I just

X — Namesake

meant that we could use it... we *should* use it, and the ball... and the glove too, I suppose."

Longsmiles interjected, "Sir Sheldon, what are you going on about?"

Shel collected himself. "I'm sorry, Your Highness. What I'm trying to say is that I would really love to play a game of baseball... with all of you. I mean, we have more than enough players... and we have Shoeless Joe's bat for goodness' sake! Are you kidding me?! We should get a game going!" Then he added more quietly, "Don't you think?" The crowd looked around at one another, not sure what to think.

"I love it!" Joy exclaimed as she jumped up and threw her arms high in the air. "But I don't know how to play," she added as she came back down to the ground.

"Does *anyone* know how to play?" asked Izzy. They looked around at each other a second time, shrugging and shaking their heads.

"That's okay!" interjected Shel. "I can teach you. I can teach you all how to play!"

Joy saw the enthusiasm on Shel's face, a look she'd never seen before. In that moment he was visibly filled with the love of the world. And in that moment she knew, without a doubt, that she loved him too, wholly and completely.

Chapter Eleven

The Ball Game

Sketch by S. Silvers, teen.

XI — The Ball Game

The next day, after breakfast, the baseball game was on! Shel had Izzy playing second base, on account of the long reach of his trunk being useful to cover the gap between second and first. On first base, Shel put Alice because of her keen reflexes and all-around natural abilities. Joy played shortstop as that position requires a lot of energy. Next to her, on third base, was Sandovar of Sandeen, recently returned from his journey through the desert.

oooooo

"The job of waking the giants has proved much easier than expected," Sandovar reported to the king and crowd. "Dracula and his lot have provided invaluable expertise on how to properly resurrect a soul. Once awakened, Sarah Karynthia and Sylvia Kats turn on their charm, keeping the giants calm while Chester and Charlie reorient their brethren. With this approach, the giants seem to be accepting their new reality with grace, or at the least, understanding. They are, of course, not pleased with having been put to sleep in the first place, but they seem happy to be awake again."

oooooo

"Now remember, no swords in the belly, Sandman," warned Shel, much to the chief's disappointment.

XI — The Ball Game

Fickles, Pickles, and Tickles took the outfield slots while Manny, despite his age, decided he wanted to play catcher — with a designated hitter to take his place when it came time to bat.

Shel, meanwhile, assumed the pitcher's mound (don't mind if I do!).

"Now, Izzy, you sure you got this?" Shel challenged his oversized pal at second. "Your dad being from Chicago and all, and being friends with Shoeless Joe, I figure you know what you're doing out there. I'm counting on you to manage the infield."

"Fuhgetabowdit!" Izzy replied, mistaking Chicago for Brooklyn. "I'm a natural! After all, who can kick a football from here to Afghanistan? I can!"

"Okaaay," Shel mused. "You do realize that football is *not* baseball, right?" He glared through his bushy brows at the elephant before turning back to his mound to toss a few practice pitches at Manny.

For the opposing team, the pirates were assigned to the outfield: Taudello in left, Mortimer in right, and Blackbeard — who now looked more passable as a pirate with three-and-a-half-days of coal-black stubble on his chin — playing centerfield. Katya and Wanda, the cook witches, took first and second bases, while Sarah Karynthia and Sylvia Kats took shortstop and third base. Don the bear dared to mount the pitcher's mound, and his queen's kangaroo sat in as catcher.

XI — The Ball Game

Others, such as pirate captain Jarby, on account of his age, and Hook, on account of his, well, hook, filled the important roles of base coaches — although all Jarby did was berate his runners with taunts like, "Arrr, ye run like a dried-up jellyfish!" and, "me ol' granny be runnin' faster than ye, and she be dead by a hundred years she be!"

The stands were filled with King Longsmiles, Ruth and Simonson, and all sorts of Kantytown citizens, some with spaghetti stains still on their shirts, and all with great big smiles on their faces. Most of the smiles were in anticipation of the game, but some were in anticipation of the lunch that Katya had planned. She'd permitted Wanda to use some of her eccentric cooking methods to whip up the world's biggest hot dog. Until that was ready, there was plenty of peanuts and popcorn to go around. And for those lucky enough to sit close to the king, Longsmiles had a picnic basket full of gourmet peanut butter (and jelly!) sandwiches, which he gladly shared.

The king cried out, "Play Ball!" in his best umpire voice, as Shel had instructed him to do upon the signal: a wink and a nod from the pitcher's mound. Shel performed a tidy wind up and tossed the ball toward Donachtuk at home plate, the lead-off batter for the home team.

"Strike one!" called the umpire, who happened to be none other than Mister Rulebook himself, Sir Marcus O'Rillynice Gladface McGee. Don looked back at Mark and growled. Shel laughed, as did many of the other players. Mark did not.

Shel decided he'd take a little walk to home plate to remind the temperamental bear of a few fundamentals.

XI — The Ball Game

"Okay, Don, try to keep calm. You have a few more tries. Just remember, you don't have to swing if the pitch is bad. But, if you do swing and you miss, like that last one, that's an automatic strike. Three strikes and you're out. Okay?" Locking his eyes on the bear, Shel cocked his head high then let it fall slowly to drive his point home.

"Hey Tooky, why don't you take some practice swings?" came a voice from the dugout.

"You need to tighten your grip, Don!" came another.

"Yeah! And choke up on the bat!"

"Straighten your shoulders and swivel your hips!" cried yet another, at which point, Don had just about enough advice, and with a mighty roar he chucked that bat clear into left field.

"...And work on your sportsmanship, too!"

The crowd laughed. Don did not.

By the time Fickleface returned from the outfield with the bat, Donachtuk had cooled down thanks to an ice cream cone, courtesy of Joythea.

"Ice cream? Where'd you get ice cream?!" cried Izzy. "I want some."

"Me too! I'll take chocolate," barked the queen's kangaroo.

"Vanilla for me!" wailed her monkey.

XI — The Ball Game

As Joy departed the field, happy to oblige the sweet-toothed animals, the bear gripped the bat firmly, thanks to his ice cream-soaked — and thus sticky — hands. He took a couple exaggerated practice swings before stepping back into the batter's box with a carefree whistle and a ten-pound smile. "Bring it on, pitcher!" he yelled at Shel, acting the part. With his bat positioned atop his right shoulder, he ground the ball of his back foot into the dirt a good inch or two, ready for the showdown.

Not heeding the bear's temper, Manny decided, poorly, to give Don something to think about other than the ballgame: namely, the bear's sister. "You're sister looks like a racoon, and smells like an armadillo!"

Now *that* was not nice!

Donachtuk, standing squarely in the batter's box, looked down at the foul-mouthed jaw jockey and growled between smiling teeth. "If I weren't a vegetarian I would take a bite out of your—"

"Steee-rike two!" yelled Marcus as a heater of a fast pitch came zinging over the plate. Marcus threw his right arm out to the side and extended two fingers like he was flinging a yo-yo. Instantly, Don whipped around and leaped at Mark while Manny jumped out of the way, not wanting to get clobbered. Shel doubled over in laughter and Alice took off from third base to meet Sandovar at home plate in the nick of time to keep Don from doing any real harm to the pleaseman — who was doing his best to remain polite, asking, "Please do not chew on my arms. Pretty please!"

XI — The Ball Game

oooooo

Donachtuk wasn't normally malicious, but he already didn't like Mark on account of the pleaseman threatening to arrest the bear the previous summer for allegedly stealing the oversized refrigerator out of the palace storeroom. Now, did Don steal the refer? No! Of course not! ...Well, maybe just a little.

You see, Donachtuk was a polar bear, in case that wasn't already made clear. And boy did it get hot in the Land of Happy during the summertime. So, Tooky simply *borrowed* for a bit the only oversized ice box around, so that he would have a nice place to rest and get some relief from the heat. He was going to return it, honest he was. But since it wasn't even being used at the palace, it was just sitting in storage, he figured he'd just hang on to it for a while until someone asked for it back. That was three years ago.

But why would a polar bear move from the Arctic to the sweltering Land of Happy, you ask? Well, poor Don was afraid of the snow. Who ever heard of a polar bear being afraid of the snow?! Meet Donachtuk Nanook.

oooooo

Shel walked to home plate once more, Don sufficiently restrained. "Don," Shel was trying to keep from laughing,

XI — The Ball Game

"you have to try and stay calm. Remember, this is only a game. We're just here to have fun. Yeah?"

Don nodded somewhat shamefully.

"Look, out of everyone here, *you* ought to be the most cool-headed, being from the land of ice and snow. No?"

Don nodded, somewhat shamefully... again.

"And don't worry, Manny isn't going to say anything else to distract you. Isn't that right, Manny?" Shel scowled at the dentist. This time Manny was the one who nodded shamefully — but only after sneaking in a sideways grin. "Just try to relax, Don. Think of something that makes you happy — like dancing!"

Don looked confused.

"Think of me as your dancing partner," Shel continued, "way out there on the mound. You and I need to connect, just like two people dancing. And the way we connect is through this little ball here." Shel tossed the ball up into the air and caught it again. "So, when I throw this ball to you, it's like I'm reaching out for you to swing me around. But instead of swinging me you're going to swing that bat. You want to give *that* a try?"

One of Don's eyebrows stood up to get a better look at where Shel was coming from. Satisfied, the bear shrugged and nodded, "Sure. Okay. It sounds kooky but I'll give it a shot."

XI — The Ball Game

"Okay! Good." Shel walked back to the pitcher's mound. "Just remember, you and I connect through the *ball*. So keep your eye on the ball. Okay?"

"Yeah, okay. I got it!" Don replied.

"You sure you got all that, Fred Astaire?" teased Manny.

Donachtuk whipped around to face the dentist, looking as if he were going to tackle him.

"Don, just focus on the ball," Shel called to him. "It's just you, me, and the ball. That's the dance: you, me, and the ball. Here it comes now. Ready? Watch it!" Shel wound up and tossed the ball at the bear. Once Don saw the ball coming, he spun in a circle, a pirouettish twirl, and *crack!* — he smacked that ball way out into centerfield where Fickles and Pickles fumbled around attempting to recover it. The bear rounded second base and made it all the way to third by the time the ball got to the infield.

Joy tossed the ball gleefully back to Shel, who snatched it out of the air with a wink to Don, who was now grinning like a jester and dancing in circles, having the time of his life. The half-ton lug was almost floating he was so happy. And so was Shel, because now he had himself a ball game!

"Next at bat," called Mark in his loud, authoritative announcer voice, "Tauder the Marauder!"

o o o o o o

XI — The Ball Game

The game continued as any amateur baseball game might, with errors, mishaps, players running the bases in the wrong order, arguments culminating in the kicking of dirt onto other players' shoes, bats being thrown in all directions, hats being turned upside-down for good luck, endless laughs, cheers, and of course plenty of cartwheels (mostly from the visiting team's shortstop)... until finally it was time for lunch.

"Yay! Halftime!" Joy yelled as she ran off the field toward the makeshift kitchen set up to serve everyone.

"Actually, it's called the seventh-inning stretch," corrected Shel. "But it looks like we're going to take a food break. So, sure, you can call it halftime if you like. Whatever."

The sound of rolling battle drums announced a regiment of the king's guard carrying something on their shoulders. It looked like the trunk of a large redwood tree that might be used as a battering ram to knock down a rival's castle gate. The regiment set the log atop a large picnic blanket laid over the grass and began pouring what looked like ketchup and mustard on top.

"Goodness! It IS the world's biggest hot dog!" salivated Picklepots.

"Yeah," replied one of the guards. "But apparently they forgot to make the bun to go with it. Plus," he added with overt chagrin, "it's not even a *real* hot dog. It's a veggie dog! Can you believe that?!"

XI — The Ball Game

Well, that was music to Shel's ears... and to Joy's and Izzy's, none of whom were fans of eating meat. And then there was the king, who was plenty content with his PB&J sandwiches. For the rest of the crowd, starting with Pickles, the communal feast of the largest (faux) hot dog in the world commenced with a frenzy! Sandovar was so impressed with both the cuisine and the enthusiasm of the crowd, he vowed to open a hot dog stand of his own someday.

After a good hour or so of epic feasting and dialoguing, the crowd grew tired and the celebratory atmosphere quieted to a midday lull. Small groups wandered off to collapse in the shade of sycamore and maple trees. Others snuck back to more comfortable caches in houses or barns, wherever a bed could be found, as the seventh-inning stretch stretched out into a full-blown, proper siesta. After all, as Manny put it: "Ain't nothin' so glorious as a good after-meal nap!"

"Quite right!" agreed the king (with Marcus in the background double-checking the royal nap ledger).

oooooo

Later that day, when the nappers began slowly waking, enthusiasm for this new game Shel had introduced was thoroughly renewed. What a day! In fact, that was the best day many in the Land of Happy could recall in a very long time. Sure, the dinner party with the avalanche of spaghetti was a blast, but the clean-up afterward was a real drag.

XI — The Ball Game

The home team ran and jumped and skipped onto the field to take their positions while the visiting team lined up to bat. Leading off was the fabulous head knight of Kantytown, Lady Alice. Don the bear glared at Alice with a grizzly stare. He wound up like a top and tossed a fastball straight down the pipe. Alice didn't even flinch. She just let that pitch sail right on by without even looking at it, as if it were some lowly admirer and she were a famous star of the silver screen.

"Steee-riiiike one!" cried Marcus, grateful to be umpiring for someone other than Don.

Alice's aloofness rattled Donachtuk, who didn't understand why she wasn't engaging, why she didn't swing at such a perfect toss. But Alice had a secret, a secret Shel had shared with her. "Never swing at your first pitch. This will allow you to size up your pitcher's style and help soothe the jitters." But Alice didn't have jitters. She was unphased, cool as a cucumber. She had fought all sorts of foes and battles, and the only thing that rattled her was the thought of settling down to a quiet, peaceful, provincial life.

There she was, a beauty at bat. And there was Don, the beast atop his hill. The kangaroo catcher threw the ball back to the mound and Don did a little dance before winding up again, again throwing a fastball right down the pipe. But this time his dancing partner did her own little wind up and *WHAM!* Alice rang that bell so loud the ball didn't know what hit it. Everyone in the stands cheered as the old leather and twine sailed clean out of the field. Meanwhile, Alice casually jogged triumphantly through the infield. As she rounded

XI — The Ball Game

third base, the entire visiting team cleared the bench and went out to greet her at home plate.

Mark waited until the celebration died down and the players returned to the bench before announcing, "Next at-bat: Sheldon Silvers."

"Ahem!" the king cleared his throat.

"Oh! Excuse me. Sheldon Silvers, teen," corrected the umpire.

"Silvers teen! Silvers teen!" came the cheers from the crowd, encouraging the young man to recreate Alice's magnificent performance.

"Silvers teen," Shel repeated softly as he picked Joe Jackson's bat up out of the dirt, reveling in the attention and the sound of his new extended surname. He stopped smiling after a couple of practice swings when it struck him that Alice's performance would be a tough act to follow. His legs stiffened and his heart began to race. Up to this point, he'd been enjoying the game, errors and all. Now, he suddenly felt pressure to perform, as if he would let his team down if he didn't pull off something spectacular. Worse, he felt as though everyone were now looking at him as the *inventor* of baseball, and as such, expected a performance *at least* as spectacular as Alice's. Out of nowhere, the old feeling of being a shy nobody on the school playground crept up on him — something he hadn't felt in a very long while. He looked around and instead of seeing Don and Katya, Sarah and Sylvia, the pirates in the outfield — all of whom were his friends — he saw school kids, bullies even, staring back at

XI — The Ball Game

him, waiting for him to strike out so they could laugh and make fun.

As he approached home plate he could feel his arms grow weak and his palms sweaty (which didn't help for maintaining a grip on the bat). *What in the world is happening*, he thought. *I thought I was past all this!* He thought he had grown and matured after everything he'd experienced since running away from school. But here they were, his fears and insecurities coming back to haunt him. But why now? Why here at the baseball game? He was so distracted and distraught that he forgot his own rule of not swinging at the first pitch.

"Strike one!" Shel heard Marcus call from somewhere in the distance behind him.

His vision blurred. He felt dizzy and stumbled out of the batter's box, stalling the game. As he looked back to the crowd behind home plate, he could see King Longsmiles watching him, disappointment in his eyes. In truth, it was concern but Shel was unable to see or think clearly. A moment later he no longer even recognized the king. His father's eyes, full of disappointment and disapproval, stared back at him. Overwhelmed, he lowered his head and dropped to one knee. As he did, he inadvertently stumbled back into the batter's box, clearing the way for Donachtuk to proceed — and he did, that ruthless dancer!

"Strike two!" called the umpire.

"That's not very polite, Marcus!" called Joy from the bullpen. Marcus shrugged. Was he supposed to lie?

XI — The Ball Game

Although it should have been obvious that Shel was struggling, he had been in such good spirits the past few days that Marcus and Don and most everyone else in the crowd figured the kid was just being silly and putting on a show, albeit a strange one. Since most of the people both watching and playing knew almost nothing of the game, many figured this was just some oddball ritual, beholden to the second batter in the bottom of the seventh inning.

What an odd game this is!

Some, however, could see this was no act. The king understood that Shel wasn't himself. Izzy could see it too. Joy knew it also. Almost simultaneously, Joy and Izzy, who had been sitting next to one another, stood up and rushed onto the field.

Don started his theatrical wind-up to what would surely by his third and final pitch, as he'd been throwing solid strikes all day. Time seemed to slow for Shel as he steadied himself against Joe Jackson's bat. Still on one knee, he looked up once more at the king, but the king was not there. The crowd too was gone. There, alone in the bleachers, stood Shel's dad, shaking his head.

"It doesn't matter what you think you've accomplished here," chided Patterson in a piercing, cold voice. "These people are not your friends. You're nothing but a dreamer." Shel could feel his father's words, like stones thrown at his weakened body. "Stop playing games, boy. It's time to wake up and come home. You're going to finish school and then come work with me at the bakery. Now get up. We're leaving."

XI — The Ball Game

Shel squinted at the apparition. Suddenly, a figure appeared behind his dad. It looked to be a man but he couldn't make out who it was. The figure was blurry as if he were looking through a tank of water. As the image slowly came clearer, Shel sorted out that the man was wearing a military uniform. An instant later, he could see clear as day that it was the man who had stopped him on the sidewalk!

How could this be?!? Shel thought, as he focused on the man's face. Something about him was presently familiar, as if he'd just seen this man earlier that day. But that was impossible. He didn't know the soldier on the street. Yet, he knew *this* man for sure, and the two were unmistakably one and the same. Standing behind his dad, the soldier, with his big, bushy blonde beard was staring at Shel, smiling. Suddenly it struck him: Ingonyama!

With a wink of kindness from the lion-man, Shel instantly felt all the anxiety and fear and insecurity wash off of him like dirt in a rainstorm, and he watched in relief as the residual muck drained to his feet then seeped into the ground at home plate and disappeared. The warmth of sunlight beating down on his back, bare feet against the tan, rocky soil, reminded him of the beach, and of Joy. He looked up to see her running toward him in slow motion and was suddenly reminded of the game still going on, fans waiting for him to snap out of his episode. Feeling rejuvenated and strong, he looked back to the bleachers to see his dad still standing there, arms crossed, glaring. And there behind him was Ingonyama. Instantly, Shel stood up and pointed Shoeless Joe's bat at Patterson. With a resounding "No!" he swiftly spun around and smacked Don's pitch, which had been soaring toward him all the while, straight into

XI — The Ball Game

centerfield, well over the reach of Blackbeard, who didn't even attempt to catch nor chase the ball. The pirate just stood there and watched it sail over his head like a cannonball gone astray. Just like Blackbeard, Shel stood still. He didn't bother running the bases. And because he stayed put, he was tackled by Joy, who was intent on comforting her friend, aggressively. But that was okay. Shel still needed comforting despite his recovery.

Onlookers didn't know what to make of the scene, especially King Longsmiles who was thoroughly perplexed after watching Shel point a bat at him and yell, "No!"

"Good gracious! What did I do?" The king queried, glancing sideways at the queen mother.

Ruth just smiled. "Kids these days. They're so dramatic."

"You okay, Shelby?" Izzy asked as he picked Shel and Joy up off the ground. "You looked like you were having quite a moment there."

"Izzy! ...Hey! Where did you get that red handkerchief?" He pointed to Izzy's neck.

Izzy reached his trunk up to inspect the scarf. "What, this old thing? The Falcon gave it to me when I was a kid. Figured I looked a bit more sporty with it on. Plus, we're playing his game, so, you know, I thought I'd honor him by wearing it."

"Well, it looks pretty smart on you," Shel replied. "But, I swear I've seen it somewhere before. It looks familiar." Izzy

XI — The Ball Game

shrugged. Shel shrugged. "Oh well. You're up to bat, big guy!" Shel handed the bat to Izzy.

"Oh, no. That's okay. I think we'd better call it quits after your little episode. Besides, it's getting late. I'm sure people are tired of watching us play."

"Are you kidding?!" Shel rallied. "We're not ending on *that* note. No way! Besides, I want to see three home runs in a row. Alice's hit was a surprise and mine was a miracle. But you, everyone knows you can hit. Come on, let's see you send it all the way into the pond!"

"I don't know, Shel. Maybe we should just take it easy."

"Izzy, I'm fine. Here." Shel pushed the bat at him. As the elephant lumbered hesitantly toward home plate, Shel added quietly, "Hit one for your dad, like I just did."

Watching Joy and Shel retreat to the bench, arms around one another, Izzy had the urge to follow after but instead dragged himself to home plate, taking a few practice swings as he walked. At the plate, he was greeted with a cheering crowd that made him feel right at home and he confidently faced Don the bear. The crowd was in a frenzy, anticipating something exciting, to be sure. After the back-to-back performances by Alice and Shel, the crowd was so excited they began chanting, "IZ-E, IZ-E!"

Izzy looked at the people standing and clapping and calling his name. He hadn't received such a welcome since his days in the circus. The attention made him forget about Shel. He stepped into the batter's box and with one eyebrow

XI — The Ball Game

poised like a high diver on a cliff, he lowered his head and cocked his father's bat, ready for war.

Don was ready too. He twisted and twirled in his customary wind-up, and then... *ZOOM!*... he let the ball fly. Like Shel, Izzy also forgot about the rule not to swing at the first pitch. He zeroed in on the ball careening toward him, wound his trunk up like a spring, and let 'er rip! *BOOM!* That ball went flying like a rocket... straight UP! The ball flew so high, so fast, that it disappeared completely into the bright blue yonder.

"Where did it go?" asked Skippy. Everyone shrugged. Izzy just stood at home plate, wondering what he should do, until a voice cried out, "Look!" and everyone squinted at the sky. The smallest dot way up in the clouds was slowly getting bigger as it returned from orbit.

"Wait a minute," barked Marcus from behind home plate. "That doesn't look like a—"

"It's a bomb!" another voice yelled as the thing descended. It wasn't a baseball at all. It was far too big. But it wasn't a bomb either. Whatever it was, it was falling fast, heading right toward Izzy.

"Izzy! Look out!" cried Manny from the dugout.

It appeared that Izzy's pop fly had sailed so high it knocked a bird right out of the sky — oh my! — and that bird was now falling, heading straight for Izzy's eye! (Good grief!)

XI — The Ball Game

But Izzy did not move. He was stunned, watching what was heading toward him. In a flash, the bird opened its wings and halted its freefall, pushing down a tremendous gust of wind that stirred up a considerable sandstorm, obscuring the elephant almost completely and forcing everyone to shield their eyes from the encircling dust cloud. Down came the enormous bird right on top of Izzy. The crowd wondered if he'd been crushed. Manny stood up and ran toward home plate. "Izzy!" he cried. "IZZY!"

A few moments later, as Manny — who did not run so fast on account of his short legs and long years — was just getting to his friend, the settling dust revealed a great surprise. Izzy had not been crushed... not his body anyway... perhaps his heart, but in a good way. For there, atop Izzy's back, stood a massive pelican.

"Hello, Charlotte."

Charlotte opened her mouth and dropped the baseball on Izzy's head with a *bonk!* "Lose something, my love?" she said with a dangerous smile, and the two love birds embraced.

"Wow, nonstop excitement!" King Longsmiles commented from the bleachers, stuffing his cheeks with popcorn and peanuts. "I've really been missing out on this baseball thing!"

With Izzy smiling up at Charlotte, Charlotte smiling down at him, and the entire crowd smiling at the two of them, no one noticed that the other two love birds had flown.

Chapter Twelve

Tell Me

Sketch by S. Silvers, teen.

On the sandy shores of Champion Lake, west of Kantytown harbor, Shel and Joy strolled in the late afternoon light of an unforgettable spring day. Their time on that beach, however, was quite different from when they first met on Isla de Sonrisas. The sun on this particular day burned mildly, yawning as it prepared to say goodbye. From the chill in the air, one might think fall was around the corner, but spring wasn't even over yet, let alone summer. Something else, however, was...

XII — Tell Me

Shel didn't know where to begin. He felt he wanted — needed — to say volumes. He'd never met anyone even remotely like this girl before, and no one had ever made him feel the things he'd felt when he was with her. She was stunning to watch; her radiant beauty, her charismatic charm, her passion for life. He felt honored just to be in her presence. *Oh, that sounds stupid!* he thought. He hadn't realized, but all the while he'd been thinking of all of these compliments, the two of them had been walking in silence. Joy's head, as a result, was reeling, wondering what he might be thinking.

"Will you tell me I'm cute?" she wondered aloud, breaking the serenity.

Shel looked at her, surprised. He'd heard what she'd said but wasn't sure she actually said what he thought he heard her say. Oh, his head was full of rocks!

"Sorry!" was his chosen response, regrettably.

"Sorry? For what?"

"What?" he said, obviously distracted and out of sorts.

"Are you feeling okay?" she asked.

"Huh? Yeah! Yeah, I'm okay. Why? You okay?"

"I think so," she replied. "I was just thinking it would be nice to hear a compliment from you."

Shel opened his mouth.

"But be honest!" She added quickly.

XII — Tell Me

He stuttered, "Um… well…" He took a breath to collect his courage while his brows vaulted over his eyes, asking, 'Are we really going to do this?' He was both relieved and frightened to discover his answer was 'Absolutely!' "Um… I think you are very cute." He gulped and then jumped in with both feet. "Adorable in fact."

She smiled on the outside and the inside.

"You're amazing!"

She smiled bigger.

"… But everyone knows that," he added.

Her smile faded.

"No, that's not what I—" He tried to recover. "I just meant it's obvious." This wasn't helping. "I mean, I see more. Way more." He stopped walking and turned to face her. Taking her hand in his, he added, "Joy, you're incredibly beautiful." Her frown melted and she looked down and blushed. "And I don't just mean your pretty face or your fabulous hair…" she pulled her hair back on one side and tucked it behind her ear. "I mean everything: The way you laugh, the way you dance, the way you can cheer up anyone no matter what's going on… You are, without a doubt, the most wonderful thing I have ever known."

His sincerity, although moving, was almost too much. She felt the need to lighten the mood.

"Thing? You think I'm a thing?"

XII — Tell Me

Of course he didn't mean she was a *thing*! He meant it as a compliment! But how can calling someone a *thing* be a compliment?! *Oh, what an idiot!* "No! Of course not! What I meant was—"

"Oh, I'm just kidding! Relax." She reassured him with a sweet smile. "But so long as we're being honest, you may as well know that I think you're moody and sloppy and—"

"What?!" he exclaimed.

"Oh! But it's okay!" she added in a playful, aloof tone. "You just be you. Don't change on my account... 'cause I don't really like you anyway."

Shel's eyes and mouth burst open. He was stunned! *Is she serious?* It took a moment for the obvious to navigate through all the sticks and rocks and mud inside his head. Eventually he sorted out that she was just messing with him. So he decided to play along, maintaining his expression of surprise, playing the part of the offended friend.

"Oh, did I say something wrong?" she giggled.

"Oh, no, no. It's fine!" He dropped her hand and put some distance between them, pretending not to care. She walked slowly behind, grinning silently. He turned back to face her and they resumed their walk together, side-by-side. "Did I say you were beautiful? What I meant was you're hideous!" Joy's face adopted the same expression he'd had only a moment ago, which was his goal. So, he continued. "I mean, you must be part Worst beast I think."

XII — Tell Me

She opened her mouth even wider and then closed it tightly and squinted disapprovingly.

Getting carried away, Shel brought his hands up to his face. "I mean, that smell!"

She gasped! "You did NOT just say that I smell! That is *not* nice!"

Shel couldn't hold back a laugh as Joy punched him in the arm. She turned and walked briskly in front of him as he attempted to recover.

"I'm sorry." He tried to contain a laugh. "Joy! Wait. I'm sorry." He giggled a bit more, which didn't help. "That was too much. I was just kidding!" She knew that, but it still hurt for some reason. It wasn't the ridiculous (and rude) insult. There was something else. She was trying to pretend that everything was fine. But it wasn't. She walked on and he followed. "I actually like your smell."

"Please don't talk about my smell," she retaliated without looking back.

"Okay. I'm sorry. Your scent. Can I say your scent?"

"No!" she replied, again without looking back. Shel was confused. He thought they were having fun, joking around. He didn't mean to insult her. He opened his mouth to say something but decided against it, figuring he'd dug a deep enough hole already. He hurried to catch up and took her hand. She looked at him and grinned then placed her head on his shoulder and they walked on like that, in silence, for what seemed like forever.

XII — Tell Me

oooooo

"That was really fun, playing baseball. Thank you for introducing that game to everyone."

Shel nodded and smiled.

"So, are you feeling okay?" she asked. Shel's brows, like kids raising their hands in class, asked politely for her to clarify. So she did. "It was pretty scary when you collapsed back there."

"Oh. Yeah, I think I'm all right. I think it was just some weird breakdown. For old anxiety, as they say."

"Old Anxiety?" she asked.

"Yeah, you know, that song they sing on New Year's … put the old troubles behind you and move on and stuff."

Joy cocked her head and laughed. "Wait, are you talking about Auld Lang Syne? The song?"

Shel shrugged.

Joy began to sing softly, "We two ha' run a-bout the braes, an' pou'd the gowans fine, we wan'dred mon'a weary fit, sin' auld lang syne."

Shel stopped in his tracks, stunned by her incredible voice. She kept walking.

"Joy," he said.

XII — Tell Me

She looked down and raised her hand to her face but did not stop walking. Shel ran to her and grabbed her arm, gently, very gently, to stop her. Turning her slowly he saw that she was crying. This surprised him and he didn't know what to say, so he just looked at her and she looked back at him with tears in her eyes. Without words he pulled her close and she buried her face in his chest. There he held her a while, as if he were embracing infinity, all the world and everything in the universe, right there in his arms, right there close to his heart.

Without looking up, deep sadness in her voice, she spoke, "That song is about saying farewell." She looked into his eyes and they shared a moment of silent understanding as the sun drowned into the sea, the world of fire and light blending with the world of water, spreading brilliant colors across the sky, extinguishing all time and task. There was nothing left for them to do, nowhere left to be but that very moment.

"This is the last sunset I ever want to see," he whispered. "I just want to hold onto this one — this one right here — never to be replaced by another."

She squeezed him tighter and spoke softly through her tears. "Tell me..."

He wiped his own eyes then wiped the tears from hers, and with a half-smile, said, "You're very cute, Joythea Aquarius Costeros."

And then she kissed him.

XII — Tell Me

oooooo

It was an innocent kiss, unplanned, sincere; an expression of deep caring, gratitude for dear friendship, and of sorrowful farewell. She pulled away slowly and they smiled at each other, remembering the past, trying to see into the future. She touched the side of his face gently and wiped a tear from his cheek.

"You're silly." She smiled softly. "I meant, tell me about your old anxiety."

Shel didn't expect that inquiry and withdrew, his warmth chilling unexpectedly. It was an automatic response. He turned and began walking.

Joy walked alongside, holding his arm. "Talk to me, Shel. Tell me what happened. Please."

Through challenging relationships at home, school, around his neighborhood, Shel had learned to keep to himself, keep his emotions tucked away. He did trust Joy, as much as he could trust anyone really. But maybe that wasn't enough. He wasn't sure the feelings she was asking him to share were even accessible for sharing.

She nodded reassuringly. "It's all right."

Her kindness was thoroughly disarming. He took a calming breath. "Well, um, as I was walking up to the plate, I started thinking of home, back in Chicago." He paused. She nodded to let him know she was listening and that he could proceed. "And I started thinking about school... and my

XII — Tell Me

dad..." Joy put her arm around his waist, pulling herself closer to him. "Anyway, I don't have any friends at school, really... and... my dad, he wants me to be someone I'm not. He wishes I were someone else entirely." Joy looked at him. He stared elsewhere. "Things are just... different back home. Here people accept me for who I am. They like me."

"Yeah," she said. "We do."

He smiled and continued with a sigh and a squint. "It was the weirdest thing. When I was standing there at home plate, I began to see everyone out there on the field as people from my life back in Chicago. Like the witches and Sarah and Sylvia and Don and Alice... even the queen. Everyone started to look like people from my school; people I don't really know that well... and that don't really know me..." He looked at Joy. She looked back with deep concern. "And then, I turned around and saw my dad up there in the bleachers."

"Really?" she asked, pausing.

Shel stopped walking too. "Yeah. The king and everyone else were gone. They just... disappeared. It was just my dad, standing there telling me to wake up. To stop dreaming." Joy looked away and Shel noticed a cloud of discomfort rush over her. "I know it doesn't sound all that terrible, my dad wanting a certain life for me..."

"It's not that," Joy tried to reassure him, but he wasn't finished.

"The reason why it bothers me so much, I guess, if I really think about it, which I try not to honestly, is that...

XII — Tell Me

our parents of all people are supposed to love us, unconditionally, right?"

"Of course!"

"Of course they are, right? Well I'm not sure mine do."

"Wha—?"

"If they do, they have a strange way of showing it."

"Shel, I'm sure they—"

"Because they make it pretty clear they wish I was someone else. At least my dad does. He doesn't like me, Joy. My own dad doesn't even like me."

She wasn't sure what to say. That was a deep sentiment. She knew it likely wasn't true, but what if it was? Shel *must* be exaggerating. Then again, what if he wasn't? She didn't know what his home life was like. Who was she to judge?

Shel knew what her silence meant, knew that last bit was hard to swallow. He'd been trying — unsuccessfully — to digest it all his life. "It's okay. My time here in Arcania has taught me that I'm actually worth liking, that I have something — though I'm not sure exactly what, haha…" He tried a little humor to lighten the mood. "…That I have something to offer; that there are things about me others appreciate… or enjoy… or whatever."

"You have *so* much to offer, Shel! Much more than you know."

XII — Tell Me

He smiled and began walking again, Joy holding tight to his arm.

"But... I don't really care about that," she continued. "I'd like you even if you only had peanuts to offer."

"Oh, Joy, course you would. You *love* peanuts!" He punched her lightly on the arm and they both laughed. "It just feels good to think that I *am* worthy of being someone's friend, of being... loved. I don't know."

Joy stopped walking. "Yes! You are! Of course you are, Shel! I..." she hesitated. "I think you're wonderful."

This time she walked on without him. He watched her walk away for a minute then caught up to her, snatched her hand in his, and they strolled in silence, watching the waves roll in from the sea. The evening sky was growing darker and an early moon was rising in the east.

"It's strange..." Shel said after a while.

"What's that?"

"In the stands behind home plate, behind the image of my dad... I saw... Ingonyama."

Joy smiled. "Ingonyama? Are you sure?"

"Yeah. But, it wasn't him, obviously. I mean I know he's gone. And yet, it *was* him. I saw this man there, dressed just like a man I ran into back in Chicago. I didn't think anything of it at the time, but now, something tells me that Ingo and the man in Chicago are definitely the same person. Don't ask me how that's possible. I just know it. And all the

XII — Tell Me

friends playing the game, reminding me of people back home..." he paused. "I... never told you what happened, but when I passed out in the desert, after the fall from the horse..."

"You mean when Taudello threw you from his horse?"

"Yeah," he laughed slightly. "Anyway, I dreamed that I woke up in a strange house... and there was this guy there. I didn't know who he was, and I woke up before I could see him clearly or find out what house I was in. But in my vision I clearly saw that same red handkerchief that Izzy had around his neck during the baseball game."

Joy remained quiet a moment, then gently challenged, "A red handkerchief is pretty common, Shel..."

"Well, okay, sure. But this one was different. I can't really explain it."

"It's okay," she replied, meandering down to the water's edge, letting the waves crash upon her feet. (Contrary to popular myth, many mermaids do not automatically go from human legs to fish fin at the touch of water, salt or fresh. Many make the transition by intention. Joy was just such a mermaid.) She walked pensively through the waves lapping the beach. "I think I understand."

He sort of skip-ran to catch up with her. Any words that might've been floating around in his head evaporated. He began picking up interesting-looking pebbles in the shore break, turning them over in his fingers and tossing them back into the water. "What do you think that means, Joy?" he asked eventually.

XII — Tell Me

She shrugged. The low, orange moonrise sparkling on the sea was mesmerizing. She felt herself drawn to the water and knew it was time to return home.

"Joy?"

"Hmm?"

"Is... this a dream?" He looked around slowly. The beach was magical: bloodfire moon dancing on a polished, royal blue floor. Anyone would've thought it was a dream. His gaze settled on his bare feet shuffling through the blonde sand. When he looked up, Joy was smiling gently. She took his hand in hers. There were no words for it. "Am I dreaming?" He asked again. "Has this... all of this... Arcania and everything... has it all been just a dream?"

Joy stopped walking.

Without thought, as if under a spell, Shel kept walking ever so slowly, dragging his toes through the wet sand. Their intertwined hands tugged at one another briefly before slipping apart, falling at their sides.

Shel's hand felt more empty, cold, and lonely than it had ever felt. He looked back at her but kept walking forward, compelled by some invisible force. He didn't feel sad. He suddenly couldn't feel anything. It was as if he were watching himself from a distance, detached and indifferent. Of course he wasn't indifferent to anything that was going on, yet some irresistible force was pulling him out of the moment. Even if he could fight it, he sensed it would be folly to try.

XII — Tell Me

Knowing he needed this moment to process things, Joy did not follow but instead stood and watched her love walk away.

His mind was drifting, eyes staring ahead into the coming night, when suddenly he heard a faint splash behind him. He was instantly transported back to the present and a rush of nervousness flooded his heart. He turned quickly to see, staring coldly back at him, the puissant heart-wrenching expanse of nothingness. He was alone.

"Joy?" he spoke to the breeze. "Joy!" he yelled at the sea. He ran back to where she'd been standing but found only emptiness. He stood motionless as a numbing cold took hold of him. The feeling of shock was familiar, the same as when he fell into the lake of boiling water, or when he lost consciousness in the Sonrisa Desert, or when he sank into the sidewalk while in the clutches of the Chicago street cop. The desolation that surrounded him began to seep inside like an eerie song that one hums without realizing. It was heavy, this emptiness; too heavy to stand. And so he sat, weighed down by her absence, watching the earth spin as the deep dark of night fell upon his deserted island.

Chapter Thirteen

No Happy Endings

Shel awoke the next morning to a soft rain through light fog and the sound of small waves collapsing on the shore like shipwrecked survivors…

XIII — No Happy Endings

Somehow he'd fallen asleep despite the cold, despite being utterly despondent over Joy's sudden departure, beyond which he could recall nothing. He couldn't even remember having dreams. That almost never happened. It was as if he were simply placed there, like a freshly wound-up toy set down on the empty beach by some insidious puppet master. He sat up and looked around to see if there were any witches or ghouls nearby who might've been manipulating him, putting him under a spell. Really, he was just looking for Joy. He called out once more, "Joy!" but there was no reply. Still alone.

Drenched from the rain and sea spray, sitting on the wet sand, he began to shiver. He curled into a ball, hugging his shins, head buried between his knee. In that desperate moment, he thought he heard someone call his name.

"Joy?! Is that you?" he lifted his head excitedly.

"Shel! Where are you?"

He stood up to get a better look but the veil of fog obscured the source of the voice. "Hello?"

"Shel?" the voice called out, and from behind a stand of bushes crashed an elephant followed by four dwarves. "Shel! We found you!"

"Izzy!" Shel ran to his friend and they embraced. "Fickles, Pickles, Tickles! Manny! You're here too!"

"Sure 'nough! We're on our way back tuh my place," Manny replied, placing his hand on Pick's shoulder. "Still got a missin' tooth tuh fill fer our friend here."

XIII — No Happy Endings

Shel shot a glance at Izzy, thinking about Manny's house, or what used to be a house but now looked more like the ruins of ancient Rome. Izzy guessed at Shel's thoughts and couldn't hold back a laugh.

"Relax, Shel. I told Manny all about what you did to his house. He's made arrangements to have it repaired by the time he gets back. Put the giants to task on it. Should be no sweat for them!"

"What *I* did?! WHAT I DID?!?" Shel yelled, shocked. They couldn't help it and all burst into laughter.

"He's just messin' with ya, Shelby." Fickles coughed. "Not to worry. It's aaallll good. I mean, it's not good that Manny's house was destroyed. But—"

Manny cut him off. "It's not Izzy's fault, Sheldon. It's mine. I shoulda told y'all where I was goin'... what I was goin' tuh do."

"Bet your buckets you shoulda!" chided Izzy.

"But I didn't really have uh plan," Manny added. "Alls I knew was that I had tuh get Buddha back." There was a moment of looking at one another then Manny quickly changed the subject. "Buhsides, who hasn't ax-uh-dent-ly destroyed a house-r-two b'fer? Lord knows I have!"

The gang looked at Manny with expressions of surprise, confusion, and apprehension. So, Manny continued with a chuckle. "Haha! I wasn't always a dentist, ya know. 'Fore workin' on teeth I worked on bild'ns. Was a forem'n for a prom-y-nint 'struction firm. But, one day, I ordered the demolition uh the wrong house — aaannnd that was the end uh my foreman career — *and* the beginnin' of my life as a dentist!"

"Well, that explains the demolition of that poor brocosmile's mouth," Izzy muttered under his breath.

Shel stared at Manny, or more precisely, at his cat.

"Wuuuuht?! People can change. You yourself uh done changed a fair bit lately, so I hear." Manny smiled at Shel and Shel nodded.

"It's not that. It's just... I thought... Izzy, you told me that Buddha had been eaten by a brocosmile."

Izzy shrugged. "That's what I thought."

"It's what we all thought," admitted Tickles.

"'Cept deep down, I knew that couldn't be right," Manny added. "I mean, y'all saw it! The Gambrine can be mean for certain. And yeah, they can be dangerous..."

"If you mess with their crop," everyone spoke in concert.

Once the laughter died down, Manny continued. "But they're not malicious. Even when y'all attacked 'em with that mess uh food, they barely retaliated. They wouldn't uh just eaten a cat, like a Worst beast... or a Banzakoot, if the cat were a poet... which Buddha is! Huh. I never thought about that..." Manny the rambler was rambling. "Anyway, when that brocosmile came into my office tuh have that abscessed tooth pulled, well I knew right then, *that* was my opportunity to get to the bottom of it!"

Shel looked at Manny and then Izzy. Izzy could see the kid was a bit lost, so he explained. "The Gambrine share everything. There's nothing one brocosmile knows that every other brocosmile doesn't eventually figure out soon enough. It has something to do with chemistry, the scents they give off... or maybe it's their deep guttural growls, tummy vibrations bouncing off the surface of the ground... Who knows? But it's something like that."

"Aaaanyway," Manny snatched his story back. "So me, I strapped that brocosmile down real good like, an' stuck every dental jam I had in that big guy's mouth — keep 'im from chompin' down on me, see? Then, I crawled in that big, stinky mouth uh his and I just started yankin' teeth, one by one, till he told me the truth 'bout Buddha."

Shel's mouth fell open. He couldn't believe his ears. Manny the tooth man sounded more like a hitman!

"It's not as bad as it sounds, kid," interjected Izzy again. "Remember, brocosmiles are polyphyodonts, just like—"

"Ele-fonts! I know! You told me that joke already. It wasn't funny the first time," Shel chided.

"Oh, well, excuuuse me!" retorted Izzy. "Point is, their teeth grow back. Now, does that make it right? Course not. I'm just saying it's not as bad as—"

XIII — No Happy Endings

"Let's just skip to the part about Buddha, okay?" Shel wasn't in the mood to hear any justifications. "That brocosmile must have told you something, Manny, because you just up and disappeared."

"Indeed he did!" replied Manny. "He told me everythin'! Spilled the beans, the broccoli, *and* the bacon, he did! That reptile told me about how he stole a piece of cheese from the grocer when he was nine. He told me about the time he cheated on a math test in eighth grade. He told me—"

"MANNY!" the gang yelled in unison.

"Right. Sorry. Anyway, he told me that the Gambrine had taken Buddha and put him to work in the fields, forcing him to pay off his debt."

"Debt? What debt?" Shel asked.

"Well, apparently Baggs had been hangin' 'round in the broccoli fields for the past few months, makin' friends with the Gambrine, chattin' 'em up on his philosophications, action through nonaction 'n all that. 'Parently he'd inspired quite a followin' and was accident-ly… or maybe on purposefully, I don't know… either way, he was creatin' a culture uh indolence and passivity. Problem was, those partic-ly-er field hands used tuh be a very efficient and productive crew. The Gambrine authoritators calc-uh-lated that Buddha owed a great deal uh service to make up fer lost productivities. So, one day when he was out talkin' with his disciples," — Manny emphasized the word 'disciples' with animated gesticulations — "they arrested him for incitin' laziness. Fer many weeks they just played ignorant, lyin' straight tuh my face! Telling me they hadn't seen 'im, didn't

XIII — No Happy Endings

know where he was..." Manny was starting to relive the traumatic experience, becoming visibly irate and red all over. "But I showed them! I got right down to the truth and I went and found my cat after all! Teeth never lie!"

"And you got captured in the process, Manfred! Some rescue!" Fickles reminded him.

Manny sighed. "Yeah. Lookin' back... I prolly shouldn't uh done it. But I was just so ding-dang-darn tootin' mad!"

Tickles gave him a pat on the shoulder.

Manny took a breath and continued. "What I shoulda did was tell all yous." He looked at the boot crew. "An' we coulda gone together, gathered a small army to get Buddha back like y'alls did in the end. But I wasn't thinkin' straight. I figured that if ya found out what shenanigans I'd got up to, you might try'n stop me, talk me out uh it. Or worse, y'alls might'uh tried to come with."

"You're darned right we woulda!" exclaimed Fickleface. "Together! We shoulda all gone together!"

"Yeah? Then what, eh?! What if somethin' uh happened to one uh yous? I'd never've forgiven myself!" cried Manny. Everyone grew quiet, nodding. "So, I slipped out the back wind-uh quick as an x-ray. Didn't stop tuh think about the broco in my office, or that y'all might uh thought I got eaten. Good heavens! I guess I thought y'all were smarter n' that!" Manny laughed... alone. "Yeah, well, I thought y'all would just figure I went for a walk or somethin', I don't know. Like I said, I didn't think it through. And I regret it, guys. Guys, I'm real sorry. I am!"

XIII — No Happy Endings

The boot crew did not hesitate. The three of them surrounded the dentist with reassuring hugs and murmurs of, "It's okay!" and, "Don't worry about it, old pal."

Shel just stood there shaking his head. Izzy gave him a little nudge and a smile as if to say, 'Pretty crazy, huh?' Then Izzy's gaze drifted and he began looking around at the beach. "Did you stay out here all night, by yourself? It must have been freezing!"

Shel looked back toward the water. "I guess so. I didn't mean to. Guess I just fell asleep." Sensing what might have taken place, Izzy looked at Shel with big, sympathetic eyes and gave his friend a tremendous hug. Shel looked up. "Joy's gone, Izzy." He choked back tears. Izzy nodded as if he already knew.

"I'm sorry, Sheldon," he heard Manny say. "I know she's a close friend. But if I may say, I have a feelin' you two'll be seein' each other again 'fore long." Shel wasn't so sure. "Well guys, it's time we're off too!" continued the dentist. "Put that tooth off far too long. Time tuh git to it!"

Pickles smiled, displaying the gap in his grin.

"What do you mean? You guys are leaving too?" Shel was starting to feel desperate.

Fickleface approached Shel. "We're sure gonna miss you, little man. Turned out to be a pretty great guy, laundry monster and all. Chicago's lucky to have ya."

"Ain't it?!" agreed Pots. "Be sure tuh look us up next time you're in town. Here, I wrote this down for ya. Enjoy it

XIII — No Happy Endings

with some good friends!" Pickles handed Shel a scrap of paper with his broccoli gumbo recipe written on it.

Shel was reeling. He didn't know what was happening. "But—" he started to say but Pickles grabbed him in a fond embrace.

"You're a great friend, Shelby, even if ya did knock my tooth out!" The boot chef smiled. "Take good care uh yerself and don't let no one tell ya who y'are. You know who y'are now."

"Thanks, Pick. Really. But, I'm not so certain. I mean, I've done a lot recently, a lot more than I ever did back home. But as far as who I am..." He shrugged.

"Shel, don't forget, this is *your* story," Tickles offered with a tapping on the side of her head. "Ya got good tales to tell and a gift fer tellin' 'em. Go an' share yer gift with the world. And once ya done that, if ya still haven't figured it out, I'm sure the world will show ya just exactly who y'are."

With one last tickle from Tickletoes, and an embrace from the rest of the crew, they waved goodbye, turned and walked away.

"You're *walking* back to Champion Valley? Why not take Delilah?" Shel called out after them.

"She's in for repairs," the boot captain called back without looking. "Besides, Delilah doesn't belong to us anymore. She's got a new captain!"

"What?! Who??" yelled Shel, the boot crew barely within earshot.

XIII — No Happy Endings

"Ask the big guy!" was the last thing Shel heard before the triplets rounded a boulder and were gone. Curiously, Manfred had stopped walking. He was just standing there on the beach, staring back.

"I think he's got something to say to you, Shelby," remarked Izzy.

Shel looked up at the elephant then back to Manny. The dentist hadn't moved. He was still there, staring at them.

"Go on. I'll wait here for ya," Izzy nudged, and Shel started walking, reluctantly, unsure of what was in store.

"What's up, Manny?" Shel asked cautiously as he approached.

"Well, I got to thinkin' 'bout somethin'... I didn't mention it b'fore because, well, truth be told I didn't even think a lick of it there's just been so much goin' on... Anyhoo, when I first met ya, I didn't know a flea's fart aboutcha. Then when I finally learnt some of who ya'are, just yesterday n' fact, and where yer from..."

Shel quinted.

"Well, anyway," Manny went on, "the Falcon and I usedta be pals. Not super close, mind you, but we usedta get together now and again, blow off steam, shoot the breeze 'n all that jazz... ya know?"

"'Kaaaayyy..." Shel hung in there, waiting for Manny's rambling to go somewhere.

XIII — No Happy Endings

"So anyspit, this one time, he told me this story 'bout a friend uh his who lived nearby, in Chicago. Jewish fella, like you, good guy. I guess the two uh them went way back to when they was kids. Turns out their families were both from Eastern-ish Europe 'n so they had a buncha stuff in common. Anyway, when they got older, this friend of Romanov's had a son who really loved rocks and animals 'n all things related to nature, fossils 'n such... *'specially* fossils."

"Romanov Falconovich... the Falcon," Shel clarified.

"Right!"

"The Falcon had a friend who likes fossils?"

"Had a friend whose *son* liked fossils," Manny corrected.

"Okay. And?"

"I'm gettin' there, kid. Keep your pants on right-side-up. ...Problem was, Romanov's friend was pretty darn strict, stuck in old ways 'n what have ya. *You* know how that goes," Manny prodded Shel's chest.

"Boy don't I," Shel sighed.

"Yeah you do! Well, any-which-way, I guess the family business — butchery or bakery or whatever it was — didn't provide much income. See, Romanov's friend, he wanted his son to do something respectable-like, climb the ol' ladder, become a banker or lawyer or what-have-ya; do somethin' that made good money for the family."

XIII — No Happy Endings

Shel nodded. It wasn't always easy to follow Manny's unique vocabulary but Shel figured he was getting the gist.

"Yeah, so, as you can imagine, the father was in a right frazzled fit about the notion of his son becomin' a naturalist. Said there wasn't no money nor honor in it. Said that if the kid couldn't do somethin' to earn a decent livin', then by golly he'd work the family business, at least then he'd earn *somethin'*, at the very least he'd earn the respect of the family. So, in the end, the son gave up his dream of bein' a rockologist or whatever—"

"Geologist."

"Whatever. As I was sayin', in the end he gave it up. He took over the family business, gave away all his rocks and fossils and began learnin' to bake, just so's he could make his father proud."

"Okay." Shel was starting to recognize some familiar aspects to this story.

"So, a number uh years later, give er take, when Romanov and his friend were gettin' old, this friend got candid, he did, 'n shared that he'd stocked up a good pile uh regret 'bout how he raised his kid, regret about how intolerant he'd been of his son's curiosities, and how he'd forced the kid to follow in his footsteps 'stead uh followin' the kids' dream of bein' a fossiler or what have ya. See, he'd projected his own desires 'n fears onto his son. Said that was his greatest failure in life: failin' to help his son become his own man and achieve his own dreams. And uh course, as fate tends tuh do, by watchin' his son grow up with a

XIII — No Happy Endings

hardened heart, full uh bitterness and regret, the man had manifested his own greatest fear."

Shel stared at Manny, trying to pick out what lesson would be best to take away from the story. "Sooo, I, uh…"

"Can I give ya some advice, kid? When ya get back home, if ya don't have any partic-ly-er plans for that there thing 'round your neck," Manny pointed at Shel's chest, "why not see if yer old man has any interest fer it?"

"Wha?" My pendant?" Shel wasn't sure he wanted to give that away to his not-so-sweet dad.

"I know Ingo gave it uh ya tuh remember yer valiant deeds 'n all. All's I'm sayin' is maybe consider doin' just this one more valiant deed." Seeing that the kid was stuck in his head, Manny clutched Shel's shoulders. "Don't forget, the kid in the story wanted to study *bones*." Manny winked. "You want your dad to accept you, right? Well, sometimes the best way to get somethin' is to give somethin'."

oooooo

Izzy waited patiently as Shel made his way back.

"All good?" the elephant asked.

"I guess so." Shel was still contemplating the story, slowly putting the puzzle pieces together. "Do you think it's possible the Falcon might've known my grandfather?"

XIII — No Happy Endings

"What? Is that what Manny told you?"

"I'm not entirely sure *what* he just told me."

"Huh. Well, that'd be an odd twist, eh?"

Shel nodded.

"But, I suppose anything's possible."

"Yeah, I guess."

"Shel, for real, anything is possible! So long as you keep believing in the magic of the world, the world will be a magical place. Don't ever forget that." Shel smirked, which made Izzy laugh. "Yeah, you'll be all right, kid." The elephant nudged his companion. "Come on, time to be getting back."

"But, I don't know the way back to the castle," Shel sniffled as they began walking.

Izzy smiled. "You'll find your way. Don't worry."

Shel was jolted and stopped walking. "Don't tell me you're not coming back with me either."

"Shel, we're not... going back to Kantytown."

"What? Where are we going? What about the king and Alice and—" he paused, slowly realizing what was taking place. "What about Sandovar?!" he yelled. "What about Taud and the pirates? No, Izzy. Come on! I'm not ready to—" He stopped himself. *Was* he not ready to go home?

Izzy knew that despite his protests, Shel could see what was unfolding and that he knew it was time to say

XIII — No Happy Endings

goodbye. Only, there weren't going to be any more goodbyes. The great goodbye for most had been the incredible baseball game. Shel stared at Izzy while everything sank in like a steel anchor.

Izzy started walking down the path again. "You ever realize that happy endings mostly come from sad times, Shel? And even then the ending isn't really happy... more just relief that it's over. But your time here has been pretty happy, no?"

Shel didn't answer. He wasn't sure that Izzy was entirely right about happy endings, but his time in Arcania *had* been pretty wonderful.

"Happy times often have *sad* endings, Shelby."

Shel figured that seemed about right, but it didn't make him feel any better. As he walked, he thought about King Skippy, about how the king's life was pretty much back to normal — actually, probably much better now that he had been introduced to the magnificent PB&J. He thought about Manny being rescued and Ingonyama being freed. He thought about the triumph of Izzy and Charlotte reuniting and the return of the giants to the Land of Happy. With all these accomplishments, Shel did indeed begin to feel an undeniable impulse to return home to his parents, as if a great many problems had been resolved and stories concluded.

Still, there were a thousand reasons for him to stay in Arcania, and if it weren't for his family back home, he almost certainly would. But a typical twelve-year-old is only *almost* grown and ready to leave the nest. *Almost.* Not quite. And

XIII — No Happy Endings

Shel was no exception. Despite the difficulties back home, whenever he'd thought about his parents and sister, he felt a tremendous weight of grief. He knew that to continue trekking further into the world with such a weight on him would be next to impossible. If anything, he figured he needed to get home, disconnect the anchor, let it fall where it may, then head back out on his next adventure, unencumbered and free.

"Yes, it is time," Izzy said softly.

"Wait, you can read my thoughts?!" exclaimed Shel.

Izzy laughed harder than he had in a long time. "Nah, but I can hear you when you talk!" He smiled.

Shel joined Izzy in the great state of laughter as they walked down a path leading away from the beach toward a grassy field of wildflowers that seemed to go on forever. The coastal fog and morning chill burned away as they walked inland and soon the magical dance of a zillion orbs of insects, dust, pollen, and seeds was in full swing, floating all around them in the hazy sunlight of that warm spring day. The scent of flowers and chirping of songbirds soothed the sorrows of goodbyes and Shel was beginning to feel much better. He was settling in comfortably to the rhythm of being back on the trail, just the two of them. The path cutting through the meadow was well-worn such that little thought had to be given to where one was walking. Thus, the pair meandered in silence for a time, marveling at the surroundings and pondering all that had transpired.

XIII — No Happy Endings

oooooo

"So! I assume you're the big guy Fickleface was referring to?" Shel noted cheerily, picking a dandelion and blowing the bloom into the breeze, watching it float away like miniature paratroopers off to battle.

"Could be," Izzy replied, doing the same with his own dandelion.

"What did he mean by that? Are you really the new captain of Delilah? For real?"

"Could be."

"Wha?! How?!"

"Well, after the Gambrine food fight, the Boot Brigade concluded, sadly, that Delilah was no longer fit for long-distance flights. They made the tough decision to retire her, put her out to pasture as it were. When I got wind of it I offered to restore her, for use as a local touring vessel, something to get me around the Valley, nice and slow like. No big trips, nothing too demanding."

"Woah. So that means..."

"Yup, I get my wings after all," Izzy smiled.

"Woooaaah. Cool! ...Hey! Maybe you and I can go for a ride sometime!?"

"I'd love that, kid," Izzy sighed with a grin.

XIII — No Happy Endings

Shel noticed that Izzy seemed to be drifting a little, not unlike the dandelion tuft — floating in a daydream — because the elephant began straying from the path, slipping haphazardly further and further into the field of wildflowers.

"Izzy, be careful!" Shel warned. "The trail!"

Izzy stopped walking momentarily but didn't look at Shel. Instead, he stared into the distance, lost in thought. "Shel," he said slowly, "there's one more thing to say before..." He paused.

Still standing firmly on the trail, Shel squinted at him, prompting, "Beforrrre...?"

Izzy still didn't make eye contact. He just sighed deeply and bobbed his head uneasily. "You know how everyone in Arcania always says stick to the path?"

Shel's mind leapt, trying to get ahead of the conversation. "Yeeeaaah..."

"Yeah, well... don't," Izzy concluded and walked off through the weeds.

Shel stood motionless, dumbfounded, watching his friend walk away. He had no intention of letting Izzy leave without him... and yet, he'd been scolded enough to make him hesitant to abandon the safety of the worn trail. "Izzy, hold up!" he called after, but the pachyderm didn't stop. Shel was caught in a conundrum. His mind and heart wrestled for a moment until he settled on a simple bit of logic. *Izzy wouldn't leave me behind... He must just be heading into the forest for privacy's sake, to visit the little boy's room. ...Still,*

XIII — No Happy Endings

watching him wander off like that made Shel awfully nervous.

"Izzy! Hey, IZZY!" Shel yelled at the familiar swaying elephant butt, getting smaller with each passing second.

At the edge of the field, where dense forest took over, obscuring anything and everything beyond it, Izzy stopped briefly. Turning his head to the side, he replied, "See ya on the other side, kid." Then he slipped into the understory and disappeared into darkness.

oooooo

It took some time for Izzy's words to register in Shel's brain, like the light of distant stars taking millions of years to reach the eyes. "Izzy?" he spoke softly, figuring the elephant would pop out of the forest any time now. But he didn't. "Izzy?!?" Shel grew more anxious. "IZZYYYY!!!" he yelled and bolted from the path, caution soaring in the wind behind him like a kite cut loose from its tether.

As he ran toward the tree line, desperate to catch up to his friend, something curious happened: He became distracted by the shapes of the trees. Without thinking, he hesitated in his pursuit, marveling at the thick, twisting branches suddenly resembling the trunks of elephants. He squinted in wonder when a moment later shapes of elephant heads appeared in the wood. His gaze lazily drifted up to the green crowns of the trees tangled together like a heap of wrestling crocodiles. "Gambrine," he whispered aloud. A

XIII — No Happy Endings

wind descended, shaking the treetops, making the branches sway and cross, like the clashing swords of pirates. The breeze descended further, running invisible gossamer tendrils through his hair and he felt the dry grass of the meadow brush against his legs. The blades were soft and golden, reminiscent of the mane of a well-groomed lion, or the salty, sun-dried locks of a mermaid... He looked around and turned a half circle. The many colors of the wildflowers appeared as magnificent jewels in the crown of a king. He felt overwhelmed by the beauty surrounding him. It was impossible to feel sad; his heart couldn't possibly feel empty. He looked up at the sky, squinting in the sunlight so bright he could barely see, and he laughed at the sight of a cloud in the shape of a boot. "The Brigade!" he sighed. And there was another cloud in the shape of a pirate ship. ...And there! He squinted harder. His heart raced. ...There was one in the shape of a giant bird... an eagle that appeared to be getting closer, and closer, and closer...

Chapter Fourteen

The Return

XIV — The Return

Sounds of jazz trumpet filled the cool night air, gently rousing Shel from his slumber. When he finally opened his eyes, he found himself staring at a glass of milk and a peanut butter and jam sandwich sitting atop a tray being held out by a large man in faded jean overalls. The man was wearing a large smile and even larger eyes framed behind a pair of spectacles.

"Izzy? Is that you?" Shel asked groggily, slowly waking up, as confused as ever.

"You had quite a trip, young man. The name's Eli... Elijah Isbell. And yes, my friends call me Izzy. You're welcome to call me that, too."

Shel closed his eyes again, reeling from the pain in his head. "What happened? Where am I?"

"You're safe, in my house. I found you lying out on the sidewalk, out front." Eli gestured with a nod. "You were unconscious with a bloody head. Seems you fell trying to run away... after knocking rather loudly on my front door."

"Oh, I'm sorry! I—"

"Oh, psshhh. Don't be silly. I'm just glad you're all right. You had me worried; talkin' a heap while you were out, all sorts uh gibberish. Nearly woke up a couple times but you kept falling back into your slumber. Thought you might be going mad for a spell. I considered tossin' you in my truck and taking you into town to see a doctor, but given the hour, most all doctors'd be closed up for the night. Plus, I wasn't right sure it'd be safe to move you that far. Just getting you

XIV — The Return

inside seemed to cause an awful lot of discomfort. So, here we are."

Shel touched his aching head and encountered the bandage wrapped around his skull. He was pretty sure, given the pain, that the bandage was the only thing keeping his head from falling off.

"Lucky for you, I was a doctor in another life." The man laughed. "No, not really. But out here on the farm I've had to fix a few broken things now and again... tractors, turkeys, gates, goats... I've seen this sort of thing a time or two. You'll be fine, I'm sure."

"How... long have I been asleep?"

"Oh, I reckon you've been out for a good few hours or so. But like I said, you kept waking up now and then so I figured you'd be right in time, just needed to sleep it off. How're you feelin' now?"

"My head hurts. It feels like it's full of spiders..."

"Spiders, eh?"

"Yeah, or webs, catching bits of memories, images here and there."

"Hmm. How about something to drink or something to eat? That might help you feel better." The farmer held out the tray.

Shel was definitely hungry but the pain was squashing his appetite. More than that, he was completely overwhelmed at waking up in a strange place, his friends no

XIV — The Return

longer anywhere to be found, like the light of a candle suddenly blown out.

But a candle can be relit... can't it? How can this be? he thought. "I know it was real," he mumbled and rolled over to face the wall, away from the man in overalls. Eli didn't catch what Shel said but figured it wasn't meant for him anyway. Now that Shel was awake, Eli decided it was high time to get this kid back to his family, assuming he had one.

"Don't suppose you've any recollection of your house whereabouts?" Eli asked. "Figure it's about time we contact your parents. Don't you think?"

"Joy!" Shel called out, thinking only of his lost friends.

When Eli did not reply, Shel thought maybe he'd up and disappeared too, like everyone else. But when he turned over, he saw Eli still sitting there by the bed. Something looked different about him, however. Shel looked into his eyes and instantly recognized the unmistakable likeness of his friend, Izzy the elephant.

"Izzy!"

Eli smiled, and that too looked just like the elephant's smile.

"Joy isn't far, Shelby, of that you can be sure. And I'm right here." Elijah pulled the fateful red handkerchief from his pocket and handed it to Shel. "Here, dry your eyes, kid. You'll be all right."

XIV — The Return

oooooo

The ride in Elijah's royal blue, 1931 Model-A pickup, all the way back into inner city Chicago seemed to take a lifetime, which was just fine with Shel. Mr. Isbell didn't say much, he just listened to Sheldon talk about Arcania and all the friends he'd made along the way.

"Boy, Izzy, I can't believe everything we did. I can't believe you destroyed Manny's house! And that ridiculous raft you made me build! I nearly killed myself on that stupid thing! Hey! Where's Charlotte?" Shel looked at Eli, eager for an answer.

All the man said was, "Charlotte is a long way from here now. But she's in a good place. Don't you worry about that."

"That's nice," Shel smiled, staring out the window at the passing landscape. "I can't believe we saved that stubborn unicorn! A unicorn, Izzy! Can you believe it? I never thought I'd ever see one of those... Oh, my goodness, I don't even want to think about the Worst! That was the worst! I wonder whatever happened to those monsters I ran into. Walter... and... what was his name? Oh yeah. Karl! And that crazy restaurant where you couldn't order anything without offending someone. That was wild!"

Shel went quiet again and looked up at the stars. "I wonder if I'll ever see Fickleface and the Boot Brigade again. I really liked those guys. The pirates too. Tauder the Maurader... What a guy! I feel like Hector might somehow

XIV — The Return

know Sandovar, like they're cousins or something. You think?"

Elijah just nodded slowly.

"He was a good friend, wouldn't you say?" Shel pressed.

"Who's that? Sandovar?"

Shel nodded enthusiastically, which made his head hurt.

"He sure was. Anyone who can swallow a sword is certainly a friend of mine!" Eli laughed and so did Shel.

"Longsmiles! What a nut! Huh?"

More slow nods and soft smiles from Mr. Isbell.

"I'm really going to miss Ingo. Aren't you, Izzy?"

"Mmm."

"Good, ol' Ingonyama. He was really someone I could look up to. A real leader, you know? Of course *you* know! He was kind of like your older brother in a way, both of you being raised by the Falcon and all." Shel paused, realizing the path he was walking down. "Izzy, I'm really sorry about everything that's happened to you; losing your family... and Falconovich..."

Eli sighed, reached behind the bench seat of the pickup, and retrieved a baseball bat with the initials J.J.

XIV — The Return

carved into the stock. "Here. I think this actually belongs to you." He handed Shel the bat.

"Your bat! I can't take this."

Eli smiled, knowing that the kid definitely could take it, and that he would. Sheldon set the bat aside as his eyes grew moist and red. "I'd give anything to see Joy again."

oooooo

"We're here, Sheldon," Elijah said quietly as they pulled up to Shel's apartment.

There was no response. Shel was fast asleep, groggy from his injury. Injury or no, riding in vehicles for any length was a sure way to put the kid to sleep. The ride home took a good hour or so, plus the time needed to stop at a phone booth and ring Shel's folks since Eli did not have a phone at his farmhouse. He wanted to be sure and notify them that their son had been found and that he was on his way home. That, and Eli needed directions, because all Shel knew was that he lived on W. Palmer Street, which was just enough information for the operator to connect the call to the appropriate family.

When the Model-A pulled up outside the Silvers apartment and Elijah gave two light raps on the horn, Patterson and Alanna came rushing out to collect their son and to thank Mr. Isbell for retrieving him, tending to his wounds, and bringing him all the way home.

XIV — The Return

"It's my pleasure, Mr. and Mrs. Silvers. You have a very special boy there. Quite the imagination!"

"Wherever did he get such a dirty face?!" inquired Mrs. Silvers. "He looks as if he's been rooting for truffles and eating berries straight off the vine!"

Mr. Silvers reached into Elijah's pickup and struggled to lift the sleeping youth into his arms. Sheldon felt much heavier than Patty remembered, and Mr. Silvers felt foolish carrying what in the dark looked almost like a grown man. He paused momentarily, attempting to give Mr. Isbell payment for the farmer's time and troubles but Eli refused flat out.

"That won't be necessary. It was no trouble at all. Just doing what any decent person would do. After all, isn't that what community's all about?" He did not, however, refuse Mrs. Silvers' bag of homemade baked goods.

With a firm handshake from Mr. Silvers and a kiss on the cheek from the missus, Elijah turned to leave and make the long drive home.

"Uhp, almost forgot." He turned around. "Your son's journal." He retrieved a small, leather-bound book from his coat pocket and handed it to Mr. Silvers. "I hope he doesn't mind, I took the liberty of writing down some of the things he mumbled while he was out. Couldn't help it, really," he chuckled. "Fascinating stuff! Must've been quite the journey!"

XIV — The Return

"What's this? No. That doesn't belong to Sheldon. I've never seen it before in my life," remarked Patterson gruffly, refusing to accept the book.

Mr. Isbell withdrew, stroking his beard. "Is that so? Hmm. Well, why not let him hold onto it just the same. I'm sure he'll enjoy reading through it when he wakes."

"I'd rather not," barked Patterson. "If you ask me, it's best to leave all the adventure nonsense behind... with you. He's got enough to think about without sticking his head in the clouds!" Shel's father wasn't warming up to Mr. Isbell one bit. He turned and walked away.

Elijah was stunned, unsure of where to go from there. Luckily, Sheldon's mother came to the rescue, gladly receiving the book. "Thank you, Mr. Isbell. That's very kind. We'll make sure it's at his bedside when he wakes up."

Patterson halted upon hearing his wife intervene. He spun back around only to face a stern look from his wife, a look that said, 'Leave it alone,' and he knew immediately that he'd overstepped some boundary. Mrs. Silvers softened her expression to appeal to a more gentle side, if a gentler side to Patterson existed. "What harm could it do? Really," she whispered and started into the house. She stopped just short of the front door and turned back to Patterson. Leaning into her husband's back as if to hug him from behind, she reached around and pressed the book into his chest, right over his heart, and whispered into his ear, "Let the boy dream."

Feeling woefully put in his place, Patterson looked with chagrin at the book now resting atop his son lying

XIV — The Return

heavy in his tiring arms. He felt his ego flare and thought for a half-second about spitting some defensive nonsense at the night, at whoever might listen. But no one wanted to hear his rant and he knew it. Giving way to better judgment, he quietly turned and walked inside the house with his son in his arms. Mrs. Silvers turned to follow.

"Ah, one more thing, Mrs. Silvers, if it's all right with you." Elijah reached back into his truck once more and retrieved the baseball bat, giving Mrs. Silvers a fright, truth be told. "Apparently your son liked the notion of this old bat. He's welcome to it." Elijah handed Mrs. Silvers the bat then quickly jumped in his truck. "Yup, that's one fine kid you've got there. I expect this won't be the last I hear of young mister Sheldon Silversteen."

"Silvers... teen?" Alanna asked with narrowed brow.

"That's what he kept mumbling; assumed it was his surname," Eli replied with a wink. "And what a good name it is!" With that, Eli fired up his old Model-A and puttered off down the road, back to his farmhouse with the light in the attic shining brightly, calling him home.

oooooo

The next morning, Shel woke up in his familiar bed, in his familiar bedroom, in his familiar, noisy apartment, with a splitting headache. A light rain tapped on his window, asking him to come out and play. For a while he stayed in bed, listening to the weather and staring out his window, his

XIV — The Return

mind a rocket, racing through recent events, spinning in circles around his room in search of some place to land. Eventually he sat up, reacquainting himself with his room, feeling considerably out of place at not waking up in a flying boot or in some random cave, on a wandering raft or in a tent in the middle of a desert; not waking up on the back of an elephant...

The rain outside intensified to match his escalating emotions. He sighed and thought about his parents, about how he ought to get up and go see them. He missed them terribly, especially his mother. But he wasn't quite ready to rush back into his old life. Not yet.

Looking around, he noticed the baseball bat leaning against the wall, just next to his bed. He grabbed it and held it a moment, recalling the epic baseball game where Alice hit that incredible home run and the ghost of Ingonyama helped him overcome his fear. He smiled, set the bat down, and immediately something else caught his eye. Atop his desk sat a book he recognized but couldn't quite place. He tossed back his covers and got up to retrieve it, his head throbbing from the sudden movement. As he walked toward the desk, he realized the book looked to be the same journal Joy had given him. He snatched it, hopped back into bed, and began idly thumbing through the pages. Inside were sketches of the characters and scenes he'd encountered in Arcania, alongside scribbled notes chronicling his adventure. The handwriting looked unfamiliar. And yet, Shel sensed it was his. He could almost recall writing the words and sketching the pictures.

XIV — The Return

Noting the foul weather outside and taking advantage of the fact that no one would be bothering him to get up and go to school — not today anyway, what with his injury and all — Sheldon grabbed a nearby pencil and began adding to the stories and sketches.

As the minutes or hours ticked on and his head nodded, succumbing to weariness and fatigue, the words of a certain flying shoe chef drifted through his mind like a biplane dragging a banner. "You have stories to tell. Go and tell them," echoed in his head, sending him into dreams.

oooooo

"Honey? How are you feeling?"

Shel awoke to the sound of his mother's voice. Apparently he'd fallen back to sleep with his journal across his chest. He was now incredibly disoriented as he had just been dreaming about Joy, Izzy, brocosmiles, and all sorts of random things flying (in boots) through his mind.

"Hi Mom," he replied slowly. "My head hurts a little, but I feel okay. I'm just tired."

"Oh, darling, your poor head. The doctor said I should try to keep you awake, if possible. But you've already been sleeping so much... Maybe I ought to get you up to go see Dr. Hook. I'm sure his medicine will—"

XIV — The Return

"No!" Shel exclaimed. He was in no mood to go see a doctor, especially one by the name of Hook! "I mean, no thanks. I'm okay, really."

Mrs. Silvers pulled him close and hugged him tight. "I'm just so thankful you're all right. We were worried sick, calling everyone, driving around everywhere. You know you scared us half to death!"

"I'm sorry, mom. I didn't mean to—"

"What were you thinking, running away like that?!"

The tone in her voice was shifting from consolation to castigation. There was nothing to be done but apologize repeatedly and promise never to do it again. So that's what he did.

"Oh, Shelby, where in the world did you go?" she asked.

I went beyond where the sidewalk ends, to the edge of the world, and over to the other side!

He wanted to say it. He wanted to tell her everything. But he knew she wouldn't believe him. So, he just shrugged and apologized some more.

"Well, all right then. I have to run a few errands. I'll be gone for a little while. Your sister's at school, and of course Patterson's at the bakery. Your father wanted you to go to school today but the doctor suggested you stay calm."

Of course his dad wanted him to go. Never a moment's rest!

XIV — The Return

"Will you be okay here by yourself for a bit?"

Shel nodded and replied that he would likely just lie in bed and read books, which was a satisfactory answer for his mother.

"When I get back I want you to tell me all about what happened. All right?"

Sheldon nodded and, feigning indolence, cracked open an old book from his shelf, lending credence to his charade. As soon as his mom was out the door, however, Sheldon tossed the book and began preparing for the mission. This was no boring rainy afternoon with nothing to do but chase the cat and pour ketchup in one's shoe! No, Shel needed answers, and there was only one place to go for answers like this. He had to go see the Collector.

Yanking off the bandages wrapped around his head, replacing them with a baseball cap — White Sox of course — Sheldon quickly got dressed, grabbed the journal, and headed out the door.

oooooo

The morning rain had finally found someone who wanted to play, someone in Michigan or New York by the looks of the dark clouds to the east. Over Logan Square, the sun had come out to shine for a change, to shine down on him! He hadn't thought about the Gambrine tooth pendant in a while, but passing through his route toward Darwin

XIV — The Return

Elementary he was reminded of it. He stopped and scratched at his neck, suddenly realizing it wasn't there.

"Wha...? Where is it?!" he cried aloud. For a moment he thought it might've fallen off when he was running out the door, as it had during the police chase. But then he recalled not being able to feel it when he changed his shirt a moment ago back at the house. Aha! His mother must have removed it while he slept. She did those sorts of things, as mothers do. It must be hanging on his bedpost or desk chair.

No time to go back for it now, he thought and ran on.

It didn't take long for him to reach Hector's stand. But when he did, he found it completely empty and locked up. In fact, it looked as if Hector hadn't been there in years. All the decorations and trinkets were gone. There wasn't even a residual scent of food.

"No!" Shel repeated over and over. *How could this be?!* He flung his torso over the stand and buried his cracked head in his arms.

"Thought I'd take a little vacation, maybe boogie on down to the desert, someplace warmer and drier."

Shel perked his head up and swung around to see Hector standing there, packed bags in hand.

"Word is, there's loads of people there been eating too many swords; lack of decent food choices, I reckon. Figure they could use some o' them hot dogs with everything on 'em!" Hector laughed his hearty laugh.

XIV — The Return

"Hector!" Shel ran to his friend and gave him a big hug. "I thought maybe I dreamed you up too!"

Hector dropped his bags and returned the young man's embrace. "Funny thing about dreams, Shelby, they're very mysterious. We can never really know where they come from, never know what to expect while we're in 'em, and we're never sure where the dream goes — along with all the characters in it — when we wake."

Shel looked up at the hot dog man, understanding more than ever Hector's signature gibberish. "I need your help, Hector."

"Whatever you need, kid."

oooooo

As they pulled up to the farmhouse, Shel could see the midday sun reflecting in the attic window. Other than that, there appeared to be no lights coming from within the house. That didn't deter him. After all, it was daytime. He jumped out of Hector's truck and ran toward the gate with the latch like a rifle.

"Shel, hang on a sec!" Hector called out but Shel wasn't listening. He wasn't looking either, for as he launched himself onto the farmhouse porch and rapped on the Marley knocker, expecting a reunion with his friend, Izzy, there stood in the yard a sign advertising the house for sale. Hector's heart dropped as a confused and disappointed kid

XIV — The Return

stepped away from the front door and jumped down off the porch. He looked up at the windows to see nothing but emptiness. There was no life in this farmhouse.

"But Mr. Isbell lives here!" Shel yelled at the house as if it were alive. "Elijah Isbell!" Hector didn't say anything. He simply removed his hat and scratched his head. Shel turned and looked at Hector. "But IZZY lives here!" he cried.

Hector exhaled deeply. "Life's full of all sorts of things that don't make sense, Shelby."

Shel slinked his way back to Hector and the two of them sat on the lone sidewalk, feet hidden in tall blonde grass, Shel's mind trying unsuccessfully to pry open the mystery of the farmhouse. After being monumentally disappointed, Shel requested they take a little walk to the end of the sidewalk, just in case, before they headed back to town. But when they got to where the sidewalk stopped and the wild fields began, nothing happened. No one fell up into the sky and no boots zoomed overhead.

Seeing the disparaged look in Sheldon's eyes, Hector put his arm around the kid. "The inexplicable magic and coincidence of life can be fascinating and wonderful. And it can be infuriating and disappointing when we can't figure it out, when we can't unscramble the puzzle to get the answers we seek."

Shel looked at Hector. The Collector was holding out his hand, palm up, displaying a wooden puzzle piece. "Where did you get that?" Shel asked, surprised and confused. Hector just nodded in the direction of the kid's pocket, so Shel retrieved his own puzzle piece — the one with

XIV — The Return

the word imaginæ on it — now quite weathered from all the adventure it'd seen. Though it was warped and worn, it still matched perfectly with the one Hector was holding. Together, the two pieces completed one word: imagination.

"I don't understand, Hector. I found this piece on the sidewalk not far from here. How could you have—"

Hector smiled. "Just because we can't explain how things are possible doesn't mean they're impossible."

Looking at Hector, Shel distinctly recognized the essence of Sandovar of Sandeen and immediately felt a tremendous sense of relief. They both nodded and smiled at one another.

"Come on, kid. It's high time I get going on my journey. And it's time you get back home so you can get goin' on yours. Never a good idea to keep destiny waiting."

Chapter Fifteen

A Dreamer

XV — A Dreamer

When they arrived at Logan Square, Shel asked to be dropped near his father's bakery. He figured he could walk home from there. Plus, it was time, he decided, to confront his dad.

"What are you going to do?" Hector asked.

"Well, Hector, I think you already know... but I'm going to write." Hector's countenance begged for more details. Shel obliged. "I'm going to start by writing down the stories of Arcania, stories of all the folks I met there. I'm going to be a writer, Hector!"

Hector smiled and nodded in approval. As they said their goodbyes, good-lucks, and God-speeds, Shel knew this was the last time he would see Hector the Collector, at least for a good long while.

"One more thing, Shelby. I believe *this* belongs to *you*." Hector pulled from his pocket a rusted chain attached to a crocodile tooth pendant. Shel's jaw dropped as he reached for the necklace. "Some army guy dropped it off at my food stand a while back, said you ran off without it... when you were running from the *cops*!" Hector gave Shel a wide-eyed look of surprise and scrutiny.

"Oh, yeah, that." Shel felt ashamed but also shocked by the turn of events circling him like a hurricane.

"Hmm. Well, best not make a habit of *that*, I'd say."

Shel nodded, lowering the pendant around his neck. "No, definitely not. But Hector, how in the world did he know to give *you* the pendant? That you and I—"

XV — A Dreamer

Hector waved a hand. "Just listen, okay? He told me to tell you that this ought to remind you of the brave things you've done, that you're a man of action now, and that you're ready to stand up to Patterson, or anyone else; show everyone just who Sheldon Silvers is. Although he must've been confused 'cause he kept calling you Silversteen."

"What?! But how did he—?"

Hector just smiled, hopped into his truck, and fired up the motor. Then the Collector winked, adding, "I dunno, I think I might like it better than Silvers. Silversteen... has a nice *ting* to it. Anyway, he said to tell you that Ingo sends his greetings, whatever that means." With that Hector's truck sped off, leaving Shel in a cloud of dust and confusion... and with a great big smile on his face.

oooooo

Patterson was sweeping the floor after a slow day at the bakery when his son walked through the front door.

"We've just closed for the day," said the old man without looking up. "We'll be open first thing tomorrow."

"You're a hard worker," said Sheldon softly.

Recognizing the voice, Patterson stopped sweeping and looked up to see his son standing in the doorway.

XV — A Dreamer

"I don't give you enough credit for what you've done for our family, what you do every day, the sacrifices you make to ensure we're taken care of."

Patterson was silent. He was unaccustomed to hearing such talk from his son, never received such recognition. He resisted the urge to lash out, thinking this could be some kind of a rouge, his son playing a joke. But Patterson had never known his son to be cruel, insincere, or, for that matter, inclined to jest.

"I know I haven't turned out to be the son you hoped for, and I know you think I'm odd, that I waste my time with drawing and writing and things. I know you want me to be more like you, take advantage of my privilege, opportunities that you never had growing up. For that — for all you do for us — I thank you."

"Sheldon," Patterson finally spoke, but he didn't get far.

"With respect, sir, before you respond, I'd like to say one more thing."

"Sheldon," his dad started again, apprehensive and not accustomed to being put in his place by anyone; anyone except Mrs. Silvers, that is. But Shel persisted.

"First of all, I want you to know that I love you, dad. I want you to know that you mean the world to me and that I will never forget what you've done to help me grow up healthy and strong. Next, I want you to know—"

"Sheldon, please. I don't know what you're up to—"

XV — A Dreamer

"Second, I want you to know that I am grateful for the opportunities you've worked so hard to give me; the opportunity to live in a nice neighborhood, attend a good school, and work a good job at your bakery." After that comment, Patterson felt pretty good about where this conversation was headed. His son was finally coming around to accept the plan he'd laid out for him. Thank heavens!

"*Our* bakery, son. It's *our* bakery. I built all of this for you. And when the time's right—"

"And I want you to know..." Shel cut him off again — which at any other time would have sent Patterson into a fit. But, given what was unfolding, Patty let it slide, barely. "...that I intend to take full advantage of my privilege and not waste the opportunities I've been given."

"Great! That's great, son! I—"

"Which is why," Shel pressed his luck and Patterson stifled a frown, "...I will not be working at the bakery." Patterson's broom fell to the floor with a deafening *crack*. Shel forged ahead, nevertheless. "I'm going to use the talents God has given me. I am going to be a writer."

Patterson was stunned, blindsided by the sharp turn in the conversation. He could instantly feel a geyser of fury bubbling up inside, ready to explode. He quickly bent down and picked up the broom, muscle memory telling him it was time to teach the boy a lesson. Yet, standing there, fists tightening around the handle as if wringing a wet towel, eyes burning till he could barely see straight, he felt something else growing inside. It was gratitude. He felt grateful for his son's recognition. And he could scarcely believe it, but he

XV — A Dreamer

was feeling a tinge of pride seeing his son stand up for himself.

Without warning, like a snake bite in the desert, his gratitude turned to empathy, and for the first time he understood his son in a way he never had before. Oh, how confusion washed over him like a baptism, all of these new emotions stirring a storm inside his chest; terribly uncomfortable... and yet refreshing. But before he could act, his son approached, grabbed hold of his hand, and placed the crocodile tooth pendant in his palm. Then, without a word, Shel turned and walked out the door, leaving Patterson utterly beside himself, confused, and exhausted by the emotional rollercoaster, ready to drop to the floor were it not for the broom propping him up like a strawman.

Patterson stood, staring down at a fascinating archeological specimen, head spinning wildly with no way to stop it. This man of impeccable logic couldn't think his way out of this one, couldn't settle on a single word to respond. Since his mind was a muddy mess, he did the only thing he could. He dropped the broom and ran out the front door.

oooooo

"Sheldon!" he yelled. "Wait!"

Shel didn't know what awaited him should he obey. Was his father calling him back for a beating? Did he decide right then and there to enroll his son in boarding school? Or

XV — A Dreamer

worse, military academy? Would he pull him out of school entirely and force him to work at the bakery full-time?

"You think you're a man now, is that it? Gone and had yourself an adventure out in the world and now you know everything, do you?! Well, let me tell you something, you don't know nothin'. You hear me? You hear me, boy?!

Boy? No thanks.

"Don't you bother coming home tonight if you think you're goin' to refuse what I've built for you, all that I have planned for you, the life I've laid out for you!"

It was as he suspected. But this time Shel knew better. He'd learned the sound of empty threats. He recognized it from the bullies on the playground at Darwin. He'd heard it from Mark the Pleaseman, King Longsmiles, and Chancellor Hume: The language of the ego; loud barks from toothless dogs.

He had learned that when people are serious about doing something they'll often not say anything at all. Like when Joy left, or when Izzy left. Now *that* hurt. But his father, making all these threats as he always had — threats that used to terrify him — these hollow words now bounced off him like an echo. The only thing the words made him feel was sympathy. His poor dad, hollow on the inside, plastic on the outside; nothing but a shell of a man.

"A shell of a man," Shel whispered as he stood there watching his father's mouth move but hearing nothing. He shook his head at the pitiful Patterson tossing his arms about in a rage, swinging the broom handle back and forth

XV — A Dreamer

through the air, the threat coming closer and closer and closer—

oooooo

"Sheldon? You okay?"

It had been some time since Shel's mind ran off on him. In Arcania, land of wonder, his imagination had no need to go above and beyond its normal duties. Now back in Chicago, it was back to its old tricks, and he had drifted, indulging in a terrible fantasy induced by Patterson's signature temper.

Shel came back to reality to find himself standing on the sidewalk outside his father's bakery, yet in a place altogether foreign. He found himself in the arms of his father, in a firm embrace not the least threatening but full of gentleness, neither one of them entirely certain how they ended up like that nor where to go from there.

"Thank you, son," Patterson said, eyes watering, 'from the bright sun in my eyes,' it would be said if the story was ever retold. Which it wasn't.

oooooo

It would later come to light that Shel's father had suffered an anxiety attack during his son's disappearance.

XV — A Dreamer

Though he wasn't entirely sure what emotions were coursing through his body, Mr. Silvers was profoundly concerned that he might not see his son again. He didn't admit to it at the time but he'd feared the worst. So, when Mr. Isbell returned Sheldon safe and sound, assuaging Patterson's anxiety, Mr. Silvers had resolved right then and there to be a better father from that moment on. And he was.

oooooo

Along his walk home, Sheldon decided to take a detour to one of his favorite spots, to sit and ruminate in the soft afternoon light. After all, he'd made himself a nice PB&J, which he hadn't had the chance to sample yet. He wanted to take some time and look through his journal, especially since this day had turned out to be so pleasant, with enormous billowing clouds making all sorts of interesting shapes in the sky — just like on the day he departed Arcania. If there wasn't already a sketch of Joy in his book, he intended to draw one now while he could still recall every detail of her lovely face.

He found a cozy spot under his favorite tree, the shade of which was beyond comforting, as if it were tailor-made just for him. The shadow of this magnificent tree was just the right temperature and provided just the right amount of diffuse light by which to sketch. He looked up and said, "Thank you," quietly to the tree for providing this restful spot and realized for the first time that it happened to be an apple tree, not at all unlike the ones in Arcania — except this one didn't have a unicorn stuck in it. That thought made him

XV — A Dreamer

chuckle while he unpacked his satchel, laying out his pencil and sketchbook methodically.

He sat in the generous shade of that apple tree, sketching the various characters he'd met during his adventure, bringing them back to life, one by one. Some of the images made him laugh, some made him cry, and some, like silly old Izzy, made him laugh and cry at the same time. Drawing an image of an elephant with a pelican on top gave him the idea to include a short love poem in honor of his friends. He soon discovered that writing humorous poems about the characters and events of Arcania helped to soothe the trauma he felt over his abrupt departure and the sudden loss of so many wonderful companions. Rhyming came to him with surprising ease, inspiring more and more silly poems, one after the other. (He had a sudden urge to look around and make sure he wasn't being stalked by a Banzakoot!)

He sketched up Fickleface, Picklepots, and Tickletoes, and laughed out loud as he detailed the Boot Brigade in Delilah, their fantastic flying shoe. He described Manny, the ridiculous dentist-with-a-vengeance and his oversized, philosophizing cat. He wrote about the proud Peanut Butter King and his sticky situation. He scribbled about the pirates and the Boogies and the monsters. And he outlined a story about a magnificent lion, uniquely talented with a rifle, who could easily pass as a gentleman.

After taking a break from his journal to munch his delicious peanut butter and jelly sandwich, he decided it was finally time to draw his special friend, Joythea Aquarius. Smiling from ear to ear, he completed a rough

XV — A Dreamer

sketch of a sun-kissed girl with flowing hair, dancing barefoot in the sand. As he did, he suddenly became flushed with an overwhelming sensation that he was most certainly destined to see this girl again.

Looking up, he greeted a friendly ray of sunlight streaking through the branches. Without thinking, he tore the page from his journal, folded it up, and placed it in his pocket, deciding that this picture was not for sharing. This one he was going to keep for himself.

To his astonishment, the torn-out page revealed something in the middle of his journal that he had not previously seen. A short passage written in soft, wispy penmanship read:

Although I'm not there to share your space,
as you sit and write and draw awhile,
somewhere from some far-off place
I think of you, and I smile

He finished reading and closed his eyes tightly to keep the tears at bay. He wanted to feel happy at the memory of his friend, not sorrowful at the prospect of never seeing her again. He took a few long, deep breaths to calm himself and reveled in the late afternoon air filled with the scent of spring.

When he finally opened his eyes, his vision struggling to clear against the bright sunlight, a curious scene slowly came into view. He squinted, half in disbelief, half trying to

XV — A Dreamer

see more clearly. As he realized what it was, his heart raced and his breath floated just out of reach. For a moment he thought he must be dreaming. He pressed the tip of his pencil into his leg to make sure, to be certain this wasn't his imagination playing tricks. The pain didn't bother him. On the contrary, it made him laugh out loud, for it proved this was real. It meant that the day was real, the clouds above him and ground beneath him were real, and what he was seeing, that was real too; and there was nothing he wanted more than to not be dreaming at that moment.

There he sat, under that sturdy, old apple tree, watching in wonder, marveling at the miracle of it all, and laughing from a heart overflowing. For there at the far end of the field was a girl with long, blonde hair, twirling in cartwheels and spinning in endless circles, dancing in the warm sunlight, dancing free to the magical music of the world.

The End.

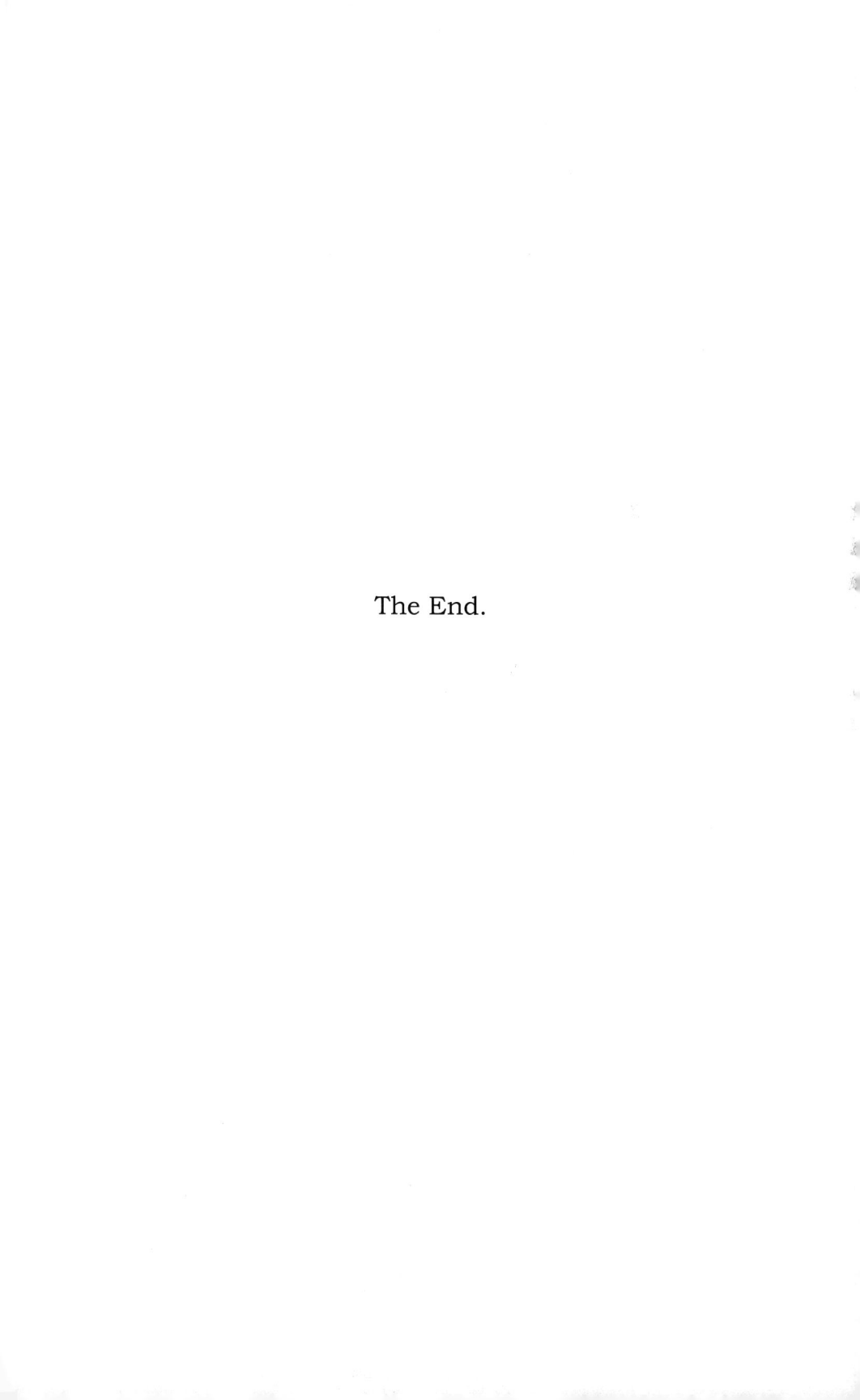

Made in United States
Orlando, FL
12 November 2024